The
Airman's
Girl

BOOKS BY CARLY SCHABOWSKI

CARLY SCHABOWSKI

The
Airman's
Girl

bookouture

Published by Bookouture in 2023

An imprint of Storyfire Ltd.
Carmelite House
50 Victoria Embankment
London EC4Y 0DZ

www.bookouture.com

ISBN: 978-1-83790-373-3
eBook ISBN: 978-1-83790-372-6

To my best friend Rebecca,
the strongest and bravest woman I know.

DECEMBER 1995

ONE

HELENA

Tuesday, 5 December 1995
Wallingford, Oxfordshire, UK

I forgot to remember.

It has happened a few times in my life, this forgetting to remember. Not the little things, like forgetting to buy bread or where I put my glasses; these are not important matters, although they do make me cross. I mean that I forgot to remember the big things, life-changing things – things which perhaps are sometimes best left forgotten. And yet, I can feel time pushing its weight down on top of me, slowly turning me to dust and ash, so it feels right that I tell the things I do remember before they disappear along with me.

So many years have passed that I am sure there are missing parts – much like my jigsaw puzzles that I love to do – there is always one piece missing, refusing to be found no matter how hard I try. But I must scramble about in that rambling mind of mine and search out the missing pieces and try to fit them together.

I sit here now in my office, my old, aching fingers pressing down hard on the typewriter keys, feeling that satisfying *thunk* as each letter hits the paper. Scattered papers, sepia photographs, curling yellow with age, medical files and journals cover most of the desk, and it makes me realise that my thoughts are just as scattered as they are.

Outside, I can barely see Castle Meadows through the early morning fog that rises off the Thames and sweeps towards my house as if it wants to engulf me. Then I see my reflection and for a moment I wonder who is staring back at me. Gone is my chestnut hair, which streaked golden in the summer months; gone are the plump lips, arched into a cupid's bow – now, I am greying, my lips pursed in a thin line.

I shake my head, and try to force out a laugh at my foolishness – time has caught up with me in more ways than one. And it means that trying to start this tale is tricky – where in time am I? Should I begin from when I was a child – a small girl with a father who was a psychiatrist and a mother a nurse? A child who lived in a large apartment in Poznań, alone until she was fifteen, when her parents surprised her with twin siblings? Or should I begin with the thing I am dreading to write?

I feel a light kiss on the top of my head, and I look up to see that my husband has appeared and is now reading over my shoulder.

'Start when it *matters*,' he says to me. Then he adds, 'Biscuit to go with your coffee?'

I look down and realise he has brought me a steaming mug, and I do, in fact, want a biscuit to go with it. I am so English now, so proper.

It is not just my story and that is why I suppose I struggle with where to start, as it is so much more than me, bigger perhaps than I can adequately explain. It is his story too, and yet he never wanted to retell it. He had told me some of it, and I had always prodded him to tell me more – to tell me of other days that had passed about which I knew nothing; about days when he thought of me, or days where he perhaps did not. But his response to my enquiries was always the same: 'That past is the past,' he would say and leave it at that.

But, as I sit here, I wonder: what if the past isn't gone; what if it is still here, rising like the early morning mist, waiting, creeping ever closer, and demanding that we acknowledge it before it envelops us all again?

All of it happened, more or less, within a few months when first the summer sun waned, then the autumnal leaves began to fall, and finally when the icy bite of winter began to nibble at my skin. It happened so fast that even today I wonder if something happened with time itself – did it speed up at this moment, to take us all with it, through the horror as quickly as possible? Perhaps it did. But then conversely, there are moments I remember within those months when time slowed itself to a death crawl – indeed at those moments when death itself hovered over us all, slowly and inevitably coming for us.

Of course, thinking back to when it started, I didn't know that time would do this to me. If I had known, perhaps I would have spent more time in my *ciotka's* – my aunt, Joasia's –garden, feeling the warmth of the sun on my bare arms and legs, the tickle of the grass on my skin as squeals of delight came from my twin siblings Agata and Michal as they hung like monkeys from the gnarled branches of the apple tree. Perhaps I would have taken walks around Poznań, late in the afternoon just as the heat from the day began to wane, when the cobbled pavements had less footfall as weary workers descended on bars and couples sat close together under restaurant awnings. Perhaps I would have walked around Stary Rynek, stopping for an ice cream, watching as children played, running up and down narrow alleyways, chasing each other, hiding and then delighting when they were caught. Above me a woman would shout out for her children to come home, that it was time for dinner, as the scent of roasted pork wafted out to greet me and I would look forward to going home, to seeing my own family.

Perhaps I would have done more.

Perhaps.

AUGUST 1939

TWO

Thursday, 24 August 1939
Świętosławska Street, Poznań, Poland

The heat of this summer is unending. I sit now, in my office at home, the windows open, but there is not a whisper of a breeze, not a hint that the temperature will fall much this evening. I can hear the chatter of people on the street below, the bells of the Basilica, only three doors away, chiming out for the faithful to go to evening Mass – *ding, dong,* they sing.

I should go to church, I think. There is a lot to pray for right now, but I know I won't – I haven't stepped inside a church for years, and I am slightly afraid to now – to me, they remind me of death, of funerals. Those bells are not music to my ears but toll their continuing march to a final end; I hear only *dong, dong.*

The apartment opposite me also has their windows open, and I can smell *kiełbasa* sausages cooking along with fried onions and a hint of sugar and cloves. Normally, the scent would arouse hunger in me, but today I find it cloying, itching at my nostrils.

My macabre thoughts are unusual for me – but I cannot

help them. It was Antoni's fault. He has returned from Warsaw where he works for the government and descended on the house before Helena and the twins returned from their outing to the town square to have ice cream.

His face said it all. Normally, Antoni radiates confidence – his shoulders squared; each word picked carefully, even each movement of his body seemingly pre-planned. And yet, this evening, his face was red and sweating from the heat, his tie askew and his blonde hair mussed. There was a trace of stubble on his jaw, so unlike him, and his blue eyes would not rest and sought out random objects in the office as if he were searching for a hidden clue.

I greeted him warmly and led him to a chair next to the window. A bead of sweat dripped its way down his face so slowly that I had an urge to wipe it away.

'It isn't good, Michal,' he monotoned like he had been practising this one line in his head over and over, and now it had lost all meaning. 'It's going to happen.'

I sat and neither of us spoke for a moment. Those damned bells – *dong, dong* – were emphasising the solemnity of the news.

'How long?' I asked him.

He shrugged. 'We cannot say. But it will happen.'

A war. Our German neighbour marching onto our land, taking it from us.

I didn't want to believe him – the news coming from the government was still saying it probably wouldn't happen. That soon, somehow, Hitler would be appeased, that the British and French would exert so much pressure that he would soon cave in and leave us be. But Antoni knew – he knew everything with his job. He worked ostensibly for the foreign office, but I knew he was working with intelligence, and if Antoni said it was going to happen, then it would.

'You need to send Helena and the twins away,' he told me,

rising from his chair and already making his way to the door.
'Do not delay, Michal.'

After he left, I thought about the brief visit, how his
demeanour said it all and no other words were needed. We all
knew what was happening in Germany, how Jews had been
targeted, how anyone who opposed the new Reich seemingly
disappeared into the night, and I suppose that all of us were in
denial that it could arrive on our own doorsteps.

His suggestion to send Helena and the twins away is something I must consider. I will not allow my children to be put in
danger, even if it hasn't yet appeared. It is there, lurking in the
shadows, waiting.

Although, it is funny, that I call Helena my child – she is
twenty-five – of course still my offspring but certainly not a
child any more. And yet, at times, I see her as one, once more.
The plaits in her hair, the bows tied at the end, how she would
dance and twirl on the street on the way to Mass so that the
neighbours would give disapproving looks – not that she cared.
She would grin at them, then take their hand, and all at once
they would smile – her infectious desire for joy seeping into
them.

I have always wanted her to pursue a career, and she has,
and is a doctor now too. But have I overlooked the fact that
maybe she wishes to have a husband, a family, like so many of
her friends? Antoni, I know, would like to marry her. He is
older, certainly, by ten years, and for that reason I have always
thought it perhaps an inappropriate match, but he could keep
her from danger and make her happy.

My ruminations are folding themselves one on top of the
other. The impending war, the heat, my eldest daughter, those
damned bells, *dong, dong*. And then there is one more worry
that is worming its way into my mind – one that has perhaps put
me in such a bad humour to begin with. A patient of mine,
whom I discharged nine years ago, has become a potential

problem once more. It has pained me that I have had to reopen a file on this patient, for I was sure that the affectations they presented with all those years ago were cured and could be forgotten about. Yet, their family and friends have told me that they are exhibiting the early signs which we all saw for ourselves – headaches, lack of concentration and dreamlike moments where they drift from reality. Further observations have been noted by family and friends of brief, one-sided conversations to a hallucination of sorts.

This is no ordinary patient, but someone I knew in my personal life, and I must endeavour to separate any feelings towards them and act solely as a doctor in this situation. Still, it is hard for me to do, and as I think of them, I am already trying to excuse their behaviour, to find reasons for it to put myself at ease.

There has been no dramatic change in their lives that perhaps could have driven them back into the traumatic state they found themselves in at my hospital nine years prior; yet, when talk of looming war is mentioned, this is when they apparently suffer an attack of sorts and as one family member noted, 'disappear somewhere, as though they were in a dream, and yet they're not.'

Perhaps it is the worry and stresses that we all feel right now that have prompted this, and I am not yet certain that it is a full-blown reversion to their prior mental state. It is, perhaps, as Freud has suggested, a defence mechanism of sorts.

Yet, perhaps it isn't. Perhaps I am excusing them.

I just hope that I am wrong.

The bells have started again, reminding me that I am rarely wrong about things. *Dong, dong*, they sing, on their relentless march towards the end.

THREE

HELENA

Friday, 25 August 1939
Owińska Mental Hospital, Poznań, Poland

I first met Małgorzata in the summer of 1939, in an office that smelled of stale coffee and warm dust. She sat in front of me on an uncomfortable wooden chair that she had chosen instead of sitting on the softened purple couch. Her skeletal fingers worried at an elusive thread of her nightgown – always plucking at it, but never quite managing to hold it steady enough to pull it away.

Małgorzata was in her early thirties and yet her skin had the sallowness of someone much older – each line, each crease marking out the sorrow and hardship she had already endured, and early streaks of grey stood out in her red hair.

She stared at me, as her fingers continued their nervous dance, and her mouth opened and closed as she tried to find the right words to say. We had been sat here now for over an hour, and, normally, I would have given up if a patient wasn't going to talk. But I knew she would. I just had to wait. Mother should be here too, to help; she had a warmth, a kindness that opened patients up; letting them feel as though they were safe and everything would be fine.

I looked behind Małgorzata to the thick metal bars that latticed the window, giving me a small glimpse of the outside. Beyond the driveway and the gates that were always locked, the silvery waters of the Warta River meandered lazily towards Poznań, and the domes and the bell tower of the Abbey seemed to skim the cobalt sky. Suddenly, a shower of skylarks took flight from the bell tower as it rang out that another hour had passed. It was then that she spoke.

'He hit me, you know.'

I turned to look at her. 'I know.'

'I'm not crazy. The police said I was crazy, but I'm not.' She leaned forward, her eyes wide. 'I couldn't help it. They touched me. I couldn't help it,' she added in a conspiratorial whisper.

'I don't think you're crazy,' I said. 'I think you need some help, and I think we can help you.'

'We?' she asked, her eyes suddenly flickering towards the door. 'That man...'

'The one who met you earlier? That man is my father. He's a doctor, and he can help you.'

'No! *No men!*' She stood and began to tear at her hair with such force that burnished red clumps fell to the floor.

I went to her and managed to bring her arms to her sides. 'Breathe, just breathe,' I told her calmly. 'He won't see you today.' *Should I hug her?* I wondered. Mother would, but Father would say it was unprofessional.

'Please,' she whimpered. 'No men...'

I nodded at her. No men. My arm ached to hold her to me, but I didn't do it. Instead, I sat and waited, just like Father had taught me to do. Soon, she settled, and began to talk.

'He always hit me. Morning, afternoon and night. But no one knew. No one. Just me. I knew...'

I went back to my desk and started to take notes as she

spoke, seeing a pattern of behaviour emerge – the more her husband hit her, the more she went inside herself, began talking to herself, and then soon progressed to forgetting to dress herself, turning up in the town square wearing her nightgown without any memory of how she got there, finally ending up in a confrontation with the police.

Soon, Małgorzata tired of talking and went back to playing with the hem of her nightdress. It was enough for now; there was no need to press her for any more. I rang for a nurse to take Małgorzata to her room. When she entered, I began giving her the instructions for the necessary medication, until I noticed that she was barely listening to me.

'Are you quite well?' I asked her.

She nodded, but I could see that worry in her face that so many others were wearing at the moment – she was Jewish, and Hitler was promising to march into Poland and perhaps do what he had done to the Jews already in Germany. I patted her arm as if that would reassure her and let her take Małgorzata away.

Father, I knew, would be waiting for my report, but I took my time with it, every now and then stopping to look out of the window, hoping to see another stream of skylarks coming from the bell tower, trying to ignore a growing pain beneath my scalp.

I dropped the pen on the desk and leaned back in my chair. I was tired. I had been studying for my final certification examinations in October and had been working full-time here too. I was constantly looking out of the window, to the world outside that was within reach, and yet seemed so far away.

But the world outside wasn't the world I had grown up with – it was changing, becoming uglier with each day that passed. The newspapers talked insistently of a looming war, and yet this had been going on for months now and it seemed to me that many people, and even perhaps I myself, had started to think that it would never happen. And yet, it was all around me – the talk of war, the subtle changes in demeanour, even in the most amiable of people.

I thought then, of Mikolaj. Mikolaj, the ice-cream seller was usually a congenial sort of fellow but had recently soured like the cherry-flavoured ice cream he sold. His face, normally open and wide and full of bonhomie, was closed off and as rigid as the green statues that littered the town square, the shining bronze hidden underneath that lime-coloured crust.

Normally, in the evenings, I enjoyed my walk to Mikolaj's with my younger twin siblings, Agata and Michal, enjoying those moments of respite from the heat, sat under the red awning, watching the evening wind itself towards a close. The fountain of Proserpina would bubble away, delighting the children who dipped their hands in and flicked water at each other; the old merchant houses that bordered the square had shops, bars and cafés on the ground floors, which were always a hive of activity.

A few evenings earlier, I had made a joke, commenting on Mikolaj's appearance, and instead of the throaty tobacco laugh I was expecting, I received a grunt and a shake of the head in return.

It was only when the twins had run off in search of their friends and I sat alone under that red awning with a lemon ice cream that was melting quicker than I could eat it that I heard Mikolaj scrape back a chair behind me to sit at a table with a friend.

'You mark my words,' Mikolaj said. 'They'll come for the Jews first, and then us. Do you really think that they won't?'

'I'm not saying they won't. I didn't say that. But what I did say was maybe it won't be as bad as we think,' his friend responded, his voice gentler and calmer than Mikolaj's.

'Then you're stupid,' he spat. 'My cousin was in Berlin that night of thirty-eight. He saw the shops being burned, how people who opposed them were dragged onto the streets and beaten. It frightened him to death. He said that the next day the ground was littered with broken glass and blood. That's what he said. Glass and blood.'

'But that was in thirty-eight,' his friend opined.

'And you think it's got better since then? Ha! Let me tell you what I've heard. They've no businesses now, the Jews, did you know that? Taken from them.'

'But they're the Jews,' his friend interrupted. 'Not Poles.'

'It doesn't matter!' Mikolaj yelled. 'Are you so stupid to think they'll stop there? Have you not read what they're saying about us – that we are animals, that we stole this land that rightly belongs to them, that we are just the same as the Jews.'

His friend said nothing for a moment, then I heard the scratch of a match and then the smell of cigarette smoke. 'You need to stop reading,' his friend said. 'Stop reading it all. It won't happen.'

Sitting here now, safe in my office, the world outside barred from me, I felt a shiver of fear creeping down my spine. If Mikolaj was scared, then shouldn't I be? Shouldn't we all?

FOUR

HELENA

The spicy scent of pipe smoke greeted me as I walked down the corridor to my father's office. I knew he would be taking his break, his feet up on his desk, his lips sucking and puffing at the mouthpiece so that a billow of grey vapour would rise towards the ceiling where it would linger like a cloud until fresh air were allowed to blow into the room and disperse it.

My thoughts of Mikolaj and his talk of war had taken residence in my brain, and a thrum of a headache was now developing at the base of my neck. I rubbed at it as I passed Hanna, a resident of the hospital for the past twenty years, who was sitting on a bench in the corridor across from the matron's office where Debussy's 'Clair de Lune' came from the wireless; the music lifting and bouncing off the vaulted ceilings and bare brick walls.

No one moved her during the day. She needed music as it was the only thing that silenced the voices in her head which had plagued her since she had been a small girl, and now, at almost sixty years old, we had finally found something to help her. As she saw me, she smiled, her open mouth revealing bare, pink gums.

I soon reached my father's office, located at the end of a long, arched hallway, the high ceiling sporting the remnants of spiders' silks in amongst the rusty-coloured bricks. I knocked gently on the large wooden doors, noting a smudge on the highly polished brass nameplate that read, *Dr Rodzynski*, and I reached up and wiped the plate clean with the cuff of my sleeve. Not that it would have bothered my father to have a smudge on his name, but as I did it, I imagined that it was mine, since after my final certification in a few months' time, my name would be there too, another *Dr Rodzynski*.

I pushed one of the heavy doors open with a creak, and as I had predicted, my father was in a half-dream state, his eyes closed as he smoked, his large brown bristly eyebrows relaxed over his eyelids, his salt-and-pepper hair in stark contrast to his brows that had not yet sprouted a single white or grey hair.

'How was she?' he asked now, taking the pipe from his mouth, the two deep creases in his forehead appearing, as if by magic.

'She has a fear of men, and when the police took her from the house, they touched her, which made her react violently.'

He tapped the bowl of the pipe into a stained dish to remove the unsmoked tobacco as I sat across from him and closed my own eyes for a moment, watching the colours and shapes dance under my eyelids. My headache was growing, and I rubbed at my neck once more.

'You need a break, Helena.'

'I'm fine.'

'No. You're not. You're tired. You've been working six days straight and you have your final certification exams after the summer. You should be studying, preparing. You can't afford to fail.'

'I won't,' I muttered, annoyed that he still thought of me as a child. I was about to be a certified psychologist; why did he think I would let myself fail now?

'But you do need a break. Why don't you go with the children to Joasia's house tomorrow?'

'Joasia's?'

'We can't seem to find another nanny for the twins before school starts, and they can't keep getting under everyone's feet here.'

The door swung open and in walked my mother, her cheeks rosy from the heat. Her hair was starting to frizz from the humidity, trying to escape the pins that held it in a tight knot on the nape of her neck.

'The twins are causing havoc!' she exclaimed.

'This morning I caught them in the larder, and then later Michal encouraged Agata to climb a tree, knowing full well she wouldn't be able to get down,' I added.

'Helena,' my mother turned to me, 'You look pale. Are you quite well?' She came to me and placed her palm flat on my forehead.

'You should go to Joasia's. Relax a little,' Father repeated once more.

'You should, Helena. You've got your final certifications coming up—' Mother began.

'Fine.' I told her, cutting her off midstream, my voice mimicking the childish response of my younger sister, Agata, when she was told to go to bed.

It was almost four in the afternoon, and I quickly gave my father Małgorzata's file, including the recommendations for medication and then made my way to the kitchens in the basement, where my younger siblings would be waiting for tea.

My walk to the kitchens took me past the day room, with white columns jutting up to the high ceiling, and large bay windows which gave the patients a view of the gardens – lawns that stretched out, bordered by pink and white rose bushes that the gardener tended to as carefully as he would his own children. It was a calming room, full of light and dust motes that danced in the air, as the more stable patients sat in chairs and played cards or read books.

The keys clanked their metal song on my belt as I walked and alerted the patients. They looked up from their card games or endless games of chess, and I smiled at them, to reassure them that I posed no threat. Yet, to them I suppose I was their jailer, their blockade from the outside world. For a moment, I watched one, Basia, as she carefully knitted another line of pink woollen stitches – the socks she was knitting for her daughter who died at birth. She paused in her knitting, perhaps feeling my stare upon her, so I peeled myself away from them and opened a door that led to a brick staircase down into the base-ment kitchens. As I descended, the throbbing at the base of my skull intensified. I could hear Agata and Michal arguing below me, and I wondered what had happened now.

As I reached the kitchen, a blast of chicken-scented steam billowed towards me as Zosia, the cook, took the lid off a cast-iron pan, thumping it onto the wooden table. Her face was red and sweating and she barely glanced at me as I entered; instead, she focused on stirring the *rosól*, checking the consistency of the soup.

Agata noticed me first, her ten-year-old face screwed up into a furious crease that made her look like an old woman. Her narrowed eyes said it all – Michal had done something, and she was not going to let it go easily.

'Ah, Helena, I'm glad you're here. These two have been under my feet for the past hour.' Zosia wiped her stubby hand across her sweating brow, her grey-brown hair frizzing like my mother's in the humidity.

'What have they done?' I asked, turning my attention to Michal who would not look up from a book he was reading.

'Nothing,' Michal muttered.

'He ate the last one!' Agata exclaimed, reaching across to her brother to pinch him on the arm.

'*Pierogi*,' Zosia explained. 'I gave them two each.'

'And he ate *mine*!' Agata was on the verge of tears.

'I did not.' Michal looked at me. 'She's lying.'

With that, Agata launched herself at him and the two began some sort of wrestle that took me a while to pull them apart. Once separated, they sat at opposite ends of the table, arms folded, glaring at each other.

It was the heat, I decided. Down here in the kitchen it felt as though the air itself were thickened with it, and it had sent the pair into a frenzy.

I sat between them. 'Michal, tell the truth, did you eat Agata's dumpling?'

He did not take his blue eyes off Agata. 'No.'

I turned to Agata. 'Did he?'

'Yes,' she said, her pale blue eyes focused on him.

The headache that had started as a general throb in my neck had now reached my temples and I could feel a bead of sweat tracking its way down my spine. It was too hot for this.

'Just tell each other you are sorry and be done with it!' I shouted.

Perhaps it was the fact I shouted, or perhaps they too had had enough of the heat, but they reluctantly made friends.

Zosia placed a glass of water in front of me, then squeezed my shoulder. 'The pair of them will make you a patient here, I'm sure of it,' she said.

Agata was quiet for a minute before she felt the need to fill the silence. 'Do you think that when we go back to school in two weeks, there will be more new people? Last term there were lots – all from Germany and Ela said that they were running away because they're Jewish. Why are they running away, Helena? Why does no one like Jews?' she rambled.

'You're so stupid,' Michal said. 'It's because there's going to be a *war*.'

I snapped my eyes open. 'No, there isn't.'

'There is. Everyone says it. Even Father said there will be. Germany will come here, and we'll all be German,' Michal responded.

'So people *do* like Jews then?' Agata asked.

'We do, yes. We like everybody, Agata,' I told her.

'So why did they have to leave then? Will Germany really come here? Will we have to learn to speak German? Because I don't think I will like that very much. I don't think I want Germany to come here, Helena—'

'Would you look at the time?' Zosia exclaimed, her hands on her hips, finally interrupting Agata's anxious chattering. 'I think it's time for you to go upstairs and play with the other children, but only if matron agrees.'

The pair did not need to be told twice and raced out of the steaming kitchen headed to the staircase at the rear of the kitchen, which would lead them outside, and eventually to the children's wing.

'Thank you,' I said to Zosia.

'They're too young to have all this worry,' Zosia replied. 'They shouldn't have to listen to it all.'

First Mikolaj and now Zosia, I thought.

'I got a postcard the other day.' Zosia had not picked up on my reluctance to talk and much like Agata, felt the need to fill the silence. 'My cousin. She's finally leaving Berlin and going west. I told her years ago to leave, but did she listen? No. And now look. Her business is gone, her house. I told her to leave sooner. We should all leave, all of us. Jews, Poles, it doesn't matter to them.'

Whether it was the humidity in the kitchen or Zosia's continuing chatter, I suddenly felt claustrophobic. I got up and raced to the door that led to the garden and there I stood, under a weeping willow, taking grateful gulps of air, all the while a worrying voice in my head that insisted that Zosia was right – that we all should be leaving.

But perhaps it was already too late.

FIVE

MAKSYMILIAN

Saturday, 26 August 1939
The Skies over Poland

In the summer, the sky forgets to darken completely. It forgets whether it is day or night and hums a dark blue, where clouds that seem lit up from inside streak like plumes of feathers. It was the time of year when I loved to fly the most – to be a part of a world that never really slept, that was constantly changing, renewing itself.

The moon was a waxing crescent and lit up the inside of our cockpit with a sliver of brightness that created strange shadows on Karl's face as he concentrated on keeping the plane level.

I looked to him for a moment, watching as he scanned the sky, and wondered if he was still in awe of the scene in front of him as I was. He must have felt my eyes on him. 'You all right?' he asked.

I nodded instead of replying. My voice was still missing since three hours ago when I had received the news that my father had died, leaving me alone in the world.

'Almost ready to turn back,' Karl's voice came through my headphones once more, and I checked the maps to make sure we had covered as far as we were supposed to.

Looking down, I could just about make out the patchwork of the ground below me as the dawn was beginning to break over the land. I could see tilled fields and tiny rooftops of rural houses and imagined the occupants asleep, still dreaming.

'You get a look at it at least,' Karl's voice came through my headset once more. 'You know, for your father. He would be glad that you got to see his country again.'

'It was mine too,' my voice crackled back to him.

I fingered the release button of my harness, almost ready but not quite. I told myself to breathe – in, out, in out, trying to calm the hammering of my heart.

'We need to drop further,' I told Karl. 'We have to check near the river.'

There was no instruction to fly low over the Warta River, but Karl was not to know that – he trusted me, even if this time, it was entirely misplaced.

He confirmed and began a descent in the direction of a streak of silver in the moonlight, ready to circle the area to see if any Polish military were either watching or had grouped troops together.

As soon as I saw the water, I was taken back to my childhood. The same river that was below me flowed through Wroclaw where my grandparents had lived, and I remembered the days when I was sure of who I was – a Polish boy who would visit his grandparents in the summer, on their farm, where his grandmother corralled sheep with his grandfather, who always seemed to chew on a piece of dried grass, no matter the season.

I was a Polish boy once, who lived in Gdańsk, who would run down cobbled pavements to reach the sea. And I would stand on the promenade and look out at the waves, which in winter were grey, and in summer lightened to the same blue that I saw in my picture books. On windy days, I would stand there, my parents either side of me, and we would wait until a wave crashed against the rocky shoreline, sending up a spray of cold salt into our faces and each of us would laugh, delighting in being so close to something so dangerous, but knowing all the while that we were safe.

But then things changed.

I stopped being a Polish boy and became a German boy, who developed a stutter when he joined a school in the city of Berlin with boys he did not know, and who would tease him for his accent.

Mother and Father never became German. They were too old. They were still Polish. But I didn't have a choice. My memories of Poland faded with each turn of the leaf, and I was soon in this half-world, this half-breed with two languages competing constantly for attention in my brain.

Then I became a German man, and I soon found it was not what I wanted to be. I needed to go home – I needed to find myself again. I could not be the German man who perpetrated crimes against his own, I could not be a German man who believed the lies about Polish people. I was Polish. I was. And yet, there was a voice in my head that always murmured to me that it was too late, that that part of me was lost.

But Mother was dead. And now Father – he had died just three hours before, at the moment when I was preparing for this flight. With his illness, we could not return to Poland, and I had stayed in the air force to care for him. There was nothing left in Germany now for me to return home to – indeed, it was no longer *home*.

This was never clearer to me than a few hours ago when I arrived at the base for the flight. I had felt uncomfortable – as though I was in the wrong skin, the wrong uniform. I had seen Karl talking to the gunner, Peter, outside the mess hall with the hum of the radio playing Zarah Leander breezing through the open windows to catch at our ears.

Suddenly, the music from inside stopped and a news announcement began, for which someone inside turned up the volume. Both Karl and Peter looked at the open window as the announcer began: *'More reports of Polish atrocities against our own countrymen are coming to the fore. Three hardworking German men on a business trip to the city of Warsaw were brutally attacked and murdered last night...'*

As the news continued, I could feel both Peter and Karl shift and angle their bodies towards me. They did this every time there was news of more Polish atrocities, and I knew they didn't even know that they were doing it.

I looked to Peter and smiled. 'Not me, I was here all last night,' I joked.

Karl let out a barking laugh, then slung his arm over my shoulder. 'We would never think that of you, Max. You've been German since you were what, nine or ten? All the Polish has been replaced by now, I'm sure.'

Peter was not smiling, and I knew in his mind he was turning over what he had just heard on the radio and trying to decide whether I should actually be recategorised as one of the Poles who had committed such acts.

'Polish atrocities,' the radio announcer reasserted, then went into another supposed incident. I didn't believe the news any more. I had, I suppose, at first listened and been drawn into it, wondering why Poland wanted to be so aggressive towards Germany. But my father had seen it for what it was – lies and propaganda. 'Hitler wants Poland,' he had told me time and time again. 'Listen to the BBC Overseas Service. You'll soon learn the truth.'

And now I knew the truth, just like my father had. But now, Father was gone, and I was alone with no home.

Looking down at the Warta River, I felt such longing to go

back to my childhood, to being that Polish boy once more who would make little boats with his father and sit on the riverbank, setting them sail on their adventures. The longing was strong – deep inside my gut – and the more I stared at the river, the harder it got to ignore it.

As Karl levelled the plane, I quickly undid my harness, removed my flying helmet and with a quick motion unlatched the canopy, letting air cut razor sharp into the cockpit with a heavy *woosh*. Before he could even ask what I was doing, never mind stop me, I turned to look at him and smiled my goodbye.

I was going home.

SIX

HELENA

Saturday, 26 August 1939
Żerków, Poland

'Dinner, Helena!' Aunt Joasia's voice rang out across the garden as I dozed on the grass, the late afternoon sun warming my bare legs and feet.

I didn't respond, enjoying that relaxed threshold between full sleep and wakefulness, where my mind swam with snippets of dreams, and yet I was still aware of the trill of birds as they flew overhead and the rustle of leaves that danced in the breeze. In the half dream, I was in our family apartment in Poznań, and the twins were playing in the sitting room. I was a strange entity that could be in each room at the same time and could see my father listening to the radio in the kitchen, my mother chopping vegetables next to the sink. I went to Mother, to wrap my arms around her waist, to smell the scent of her and hear her laugh at my sudden wish for connection.

I felt such comfort at the scene, at being able to see my family together; then I suddenly wondered why I was focusing on it – my family were fine, I would see this scene in real life again. Just as Mother disappeared in my arms, a nudge at my side woke me from this half sleep.

I felt the tickle of hair on my face as Agata lay down next to me, her sweet voice whispering a secret in my ear: 'We've started to build a fort, Helena. We started it yesterday afternoon. Don't tell Ciotka. We've taken a blanket from the house and some things from the kitchen. You won't tell, will you, Helena?'

I opened my eyes and turned a fraction to see her eagerly waiting for my response; her thick black lashes making her look like a living doll. 'I won't say a word,' I whispered back, receiving a huge grin in return. I loved that they still called Joasia the word for aunty, *ciotka*, and wondered at what age I had started calling her by her real name.

'Good.' Agata sat up now her mission was complete. 'Michal says that you can see it tomorrow when it's finished as long as you promise not to tell Ciotka.'

'Helena!' Joasia's voice sang out once more, with a little more impatience in it that meant she would soon stride across the lawn, then stand above me, hands on hips as if I were still a child.

'Go get Michal,' I told Agata. 'Ciotka's getting angry.'

Agata ran towards the thicket of trees that acted as a border between Joasia's home and the fields beyond, soon disappearing into the wooded darkness. I noticed that she had something in her arms and thought it must be from her pilfering in Joasia's house. As I stood, I wondered what they had taken and chuckled to myself as I thought of Joasia searching the kitchen for a missing spoon or bowl.

I walked towards the cottage. Ivy grew over the white-washed walls and pots of pink and red geraniums grew in between marigolds. I loved this house and much preferred being here than in Poznań; at one time I had thought of living with Joasia, but the trip to the hospital each day would take an hour or more, and my father soon talked me out of it.

'Helena, *finally*,' Joasia's voice snapped me out of my thoughts.

I looked to my aunt who could easily pass as my sister. She was tall like Father, with high cheekbones and pouty lips that had earned her the childhood nickname of *mój cherubinku*, my cherub. It was an apt nickname for her, although her cheeks no longer had the chubbiness of youth that people had loved to pinch until they turned pink, and friends and family would call her by it, much to her annoyance, or perhaps because of it. Her dark brown hair was only showing the tiniest slivers of grey, and her skin was as youthful as mine – not a line, nor any crow's feet in sight.

'Where are the twins?' she asked, as she walked back into the house, her bare feet slapping on the tiles of the kitchen floor, her trousers – that were clearly a man's – rolled up to show shapely calves.

'On their way,' I replied.

'They've been out there for the past two hours.' She rummaged in a drawer, then shaking her head, looked at me. 'What are they up to?'

A smile escaped my lips as I realised that whatever she had been searching for in the drawer had no doubt been purloined by the twins. I shrugged, then noticing the slices of cucumber and fresh tomatoes, helped myself to them, popping the tiny tomatoes in my mouth, letting my teeth pop the skin to release the earthy and yet sweet flavour.

Joasia slapped my hand playfully. 'They're for dinner. Bring them through.'

I stole another tomato whilst her back was turned, then placed the plate on the dining room table that was filled with a baked ham, fresh bread, sweet cabbage salad, boiled potatoes and breaded *kotlet schabowy*.

In the dining room, a guest had arrived: Olek, the local bar- and inn-keeper, who sat at the head of the table, his hands already holding his knife and fork. He was a bear of a man with a full black beard and thick chest hairs escaping from the top of his collar. Even his beefy hands sprouted black hair, and I had heard Agata and Michal making up stories about him at night – that he was in fact the bear from one of their favourite stories who lived in a hut in a forest and rescued children who were lost.

'Helena,' he grunted softly at me, his lips obscured by hair.

'You're early.' I went to him to place a kiss on his wiry cheek.

'Been here for an hour,' he said importantly, 'I brought the tomatoes.'

I liked the way he spoke – always short, gruff sentences without any hint of emotion, but he did enjoy telling the occasional joke which most of the time I didn't find amusing. I liked to tease him at times, and would ask personal questions to see if I could find out some snippet of information about his life. But he always gave me very little.

Yet, despite his reticent nature, I had noticed that he was at Joasia's more often than not lately, and that her demeanour towards him had changed. Whenever I tried to tease him, she would tell me to leave him alone – that he was tired or busy.

'How's the bar?' I asked, plopping down next to him.

'Busy,' he replied, his eyes firmly locked on the battered pork.

'Have you been enjoying the summer? Been anywhere?' I probed.

'It's hot.' His eyes shifted to Joasia briefly as she skirted past him with a bowl of salad in her hands. 'And I've been busy working. Not sure where I would go anyway.'

'You could go into the city,' I suggested.

'And what would I find there? A bar?' He laughed at his own joke.

'He's hungry, Helena,' Joasia came to his defence. 'Leave him be.'

There it was again! I grinned at her and noted that she blushed a little. I would get to the bottom of this – was Olek a new suitor of hers?

The twins suddenly came careering in from the garden, their hands smeared with dirt, their clothes holding on to the remnants of twigs and leaves.

'Did you wash?' I asked them.

'Yes,' they both chimed.

'I don't believe you.'

'We did.' Michal already had filled his mouth with bread and spattered crumbs on the white tablecloth.

'A bit of dirt never hurt anyone,' Olek added.

I shrugged and waited for Joasia to sit, batting Michal's and Agata's hands away from the food as they tried to pick at it. Finally, she settled herself, and steepled her fingers in prayer. All of us followed suit, listening as Joasia asked that, whatever happened in the coming months, we would all remain safe and together.

It was a deviation from her usual prayer at dinner, and I knew she was thinking about a possible war, but she had not yet spoken with me about it or given a hint that she was fearful. It made my stomach do a funny leap at the thought that Joasia, too, was feeling nervous – she was simply not the nervous type.

'Eat, Helena,' Joasia's voice pulled me away from my thoughts. 'You disappeared for a minute there.'

I took a napkin and laid it on my lap, filling my plate with pork, salad and tangy lemon cabbage.

'It's good,' Olek mumbled between mouthfuls, his plate piled high.

'Helena,' Joasia started, 'do you remember I told you that I have a friend in England? He worked with me on one of my books a few years ago.'

I nodded. 'You went to see him, didn't you?'

'I did, yes. In Oxford of all places. A wonderful city, simply beautiful.'

I noticed Olek's eyebrows rise as she spoke, and he gave her an odd look, then gently shook his head.

'It was nice,' she added.

Then, turning to the twins, she asked them about their afternoon. She talked so much about nothing that I could not ask her why she had abruptly mentioned Oxford, of all places. It was a strange dinner, and with every mouthful, every look between Olek and Joasia, I felt myself getting more and more uncomfortable. I was glad when the clock on Joasia's mantle-piece chimed seven tiny bells, and I could order the children to bed.

'Did Agata tell you about the fort we made?' Michal asked me, as he climbed under the sheets, dirt still under his fingernails.

'She did,' I replied, as I tucked the covers tight under Agata's chin, just how she liked it. 'Did you wash before bed?'

He ignored my question and said, 'We wanted to ask you something, but we didn't want Ciotka to hear. In the fort we took some bread and some honey, and we thought that maybe in the morning, before you all wake, we can go and have breakfast there.'

I was surprised that Michal had asked me, as usually he would have done as he pleased and worried later about the consequences. 'Is that all right, Helena? Can we?'

I looked to Agata who did not return my stare, and I could feel that the pair of them were up to something much more than an early outdoor breakfast. 'Yes, yes, that's fine,' I said, leaning over to kiss the top of Michal's head. 'I'll come and find you when I wake.'

'No, don't!' Michal suddenly yelled at me.

'Why not? Agata said I could come and see it as long as I didn't tell Ciotka.'

Michal eyed Agata, something silent passing between them. Then he smiled at me. 'You can. We're just not ready yet. We're making it into a house and then we will invite you for tea. You just have to wait.'

I watched him for a beat, trying to decide whether I believed him or not, when Olek's voice boomed from downstairs, and I distractedly nodded my agreement to Michal and closed the door.

Downstairs, I found that Olek and Joasia were not alone. Filip, a distant cousin of sorts, was sitting on the couch next to Olek. He stood as soon as he saw me, clipped his heels together and made his usual theatrical bow by way of greeting – something he had learned from his father and could not shake.

'Helena, are you well?' he asked, with such formality that it made me laugh.

'I am, Filip, and you?'

He ignored my laughter, and pushing his black wire-rimmed spectacles back up the bridge of his nose, he sat down again and shook his head, his raven-black hair catching the light.

'Not well, Helena. It has all come upon us, hasn't it? But I suppose, using the laws of physics, life appears and replicates and we must too...'

I had no idea what he was talking about – but then I never did. He was an academic in physics and much of what he said I could never get my head around. I liked to simply watch him as he talked, nodding along with him, letting him think I understood. He was a strange fellow, that was for certain. We had grown up together and were of a similar age, and yet you would not think so when looking at him. He had pale skin, long elongated features – even his legs and arms seemed impossibly thin and stretched – and he always wore an air of gravity about him as if the weight of the world were upon his shoulders.

'...so that is that,' he finished what he was saying, reaching up with his finger to push the glasses up his nose. 'There is little more to be said about it really.'

'I haven't the first clue what you are talking about, lad,' Olek said. His face was now a little ruddy, and I could see in his hand a glass of vodka. 'You need to speak to us like you would a child.'

'I did!' Filip exclaimed, raising his eyebrows in surprise. 'Shall I begin again?'

'Oh for the love of all that is holy, *no!*' Olek roared. He took a swig of his vodka, then chuckled.

'I think,' Joasia began, 'that what Filip is trying to say is that the war is going to happen whether we like it or not, and that we should, I think, be prepared.'

I wasn't sure Joasia had it right, and I was certain that wasn't what Filip had been saying. Or had he?

The front door swung open, stopping Joasia from continuing, and Antoni, my father's friend, walked in.

'Antoni!' I greeted him with a kiss on each cheek, noting a smattering of stubble along his jawline. 'You're back?'

'I am,' he said, nodding his greetings, then moving to sit next to Joasia. He had barely looked at me, barely given an explanation for his sudden appearance, and yet it seemed as though no one was surprised by his visit.

'Have you seen Father?' I asked.

'I have,' he replied, 'and that is why I am here.'

The solemnity with which he spoke made me think that something awful had happened. 'What is it, Antoni? Is he all right?'

'He is well, Helena. Please, just sit.' He pointed to the rocking chair that had once belonged to my grandfather. It was uncomfortable, and no one ever sat on it, and yet it seemed appropriate given the tone.

'Then what is going on? Why the tense greeting? Do you not wish to ask how I am? How the twins are?'

Antoni looked at me then, properly. His pale blue eyes focused on mine, and for a moment, I thought he was going to ask me, there and then to marry him. It had been suggested a few times over the years, and I knew of his affection for me – but to me, Antoni was my father's friend, not quite as old, but still, older than me and at times a little boring. Now, I suddenly had a vision of the two of us together, married, sitting next to the fireplace, me telling him a joke, him creasing up his brow with annoyance; then we would go back to sitting in silence. The thought of it terrified me.

'Helena!' Joasia's voice sliced through like cut glass. 'You disappeared again. What's wrong with you?'

I looked about at the expectant faces. Had he asked me, and I had ignored it? What had he said?

'Oxford,' Antoni said, slowly now, as though I was one of the twins. 'It's in England.'

'Why are you talking about Oxford? Joasia mentioned it earlier too.'

'Take this.' Olek handed me his glass. 'Take a sip. Do it.'

I did as he suggested, enjoying the warmth of the vodka as it caressed the back of my throat.

'We were saying,' Joasia said calmly, 'that Antoni has spoken with your father, and we all think that it might be best for you and the twins to go to England.'

'Why?' I asked, already knowing the answer to the question.

'The war,' Filip said, once again sliding the glasses up the bridge of his nose.

'It's not happened yet,' I informed him.

'No, it hasn't. But if you remember what I was saying earlier about inevitability and chance, then—'

'Stop!' Olek boomed. 'I've told you, lad, no more of that talk. Do not repeat all that nonsense again.'

Filip, suitably chided, leaned back against the sofa cushions.

'It *will* happen, Helena,' Antoni's voice had taken on his usual business tone. It was how he spoke in the government, I supposed – perhaps they all did. 'The indications are that it will happen soon – very soon, and I think taking this measure now will ensure the best outcome for you and the twins.'

The way he delivered the news was as if he were speaking to a patient in a hospital. 'The best outcome?' I spluttered. Then I started to laugh. I couldn't help it.

Joasia stood and wrenched the glass away from me. 'That's enough for you.'

'It's not a laughing matter,' Filip began.

'It is!' I replied. 'Leaving here, going to Oxford? Are you all quite well? Nothing has happened yet – not a single thing.'

'But it will,' Antoni impressed. 'It *will*.'

'And when it does... *If* it does, I will take my own measures, Antoni. I am an adult, after all.'

I stood and stalked from the room and busied myself in the kitchen, drying pots and pans and slapping them down on the worktops so they were all aware of my annoyance. Soon, I heard goodbyes, and the front door open and close.

Joasia came into the kitchen and stood by my side. 'Do you think they are dry enough?' she took the towel from my hands that had been circling the inside of a pan for far too long.

'You ambushed me.' I turned to look at her, noticing how she suddenly seemed older to me, her face creased in a frown.

'I know. It was executed poorly. Your father asked me to speak to you, and I thought if there were others here who agreed, you would feel better about it.'

'I'm not going.'

She nodded. 'I know you're not. But it was an option.'

The pair of us began to put the plates and pots away properly, neither of us speaking for a while.

'It won't happen, will it?' I asked quietly.

'I don't know.'

'Why is Antoni here?'

'Because he thinks it will happen. And we are close to Germany, so they would get here first. We cannot be naïve about it, Helena.' Joasia approached the window and rubbed at the back of her neck.

I went to her and placed my head on her shoulder. 'I'm not a hysterical old woman,' she said in a whisper. 'I just have to take care of you. I always promised that I would.'

'I know.'

'I can see them, you know, each night, up there in the sky, steel bird silhouettes as they fly low, their engines humming and whirring. I sit here each night and watch. It will happen, Helena, and I fear it will be worse than anything we could ever imagine.'

I did not respond, and she fell silent. The both of us stood together, with my head and the weighted pain it contained on her shoulder, watching the sky for planes from Germany that Joasia was sure would come.

SEVEN

MAKSYMILIAN

Saturday, 26 August 1939
Żerków, Poland

I woke in a crumpled heap and could feel the trickle of warm blood coming from my scalp. I stretched out my fingers and felt thick soil and tiny pebbles. I tried to push myself up to sitting, but, as I did so, my leg screamed with pain and the ribs on my left side followed suit. I rolled over instead and lay flat on my back, looking up at the sky as dawn broke above me, letting my breathing become normal again.

I could not see a plane, nor hear one, and I was glad of it. My biggest fear was that Karl would have been able to land the Storch on the fields and find me. I licked my lips and tasted the copper of blood, then bit by bit moved my body, starting with my toes, to assess the possible damage. The toes worked fine, although restricted within my tight-laced boots. My right leg could bend; the left could too, but fire seemed to shoot from the ankle to the knee as it moved. I felt my ribs on both sides and then reached down to my thighs to see if there was any blood.

Finally, I raised my arms one at a time, and each did as they were told without giving too much discomfort.

After counting to ten, I eased myself up from sitting, feeling the weight of the parachute still attached to me. With shaking hands, I unbuckled the straps and let the silk billow.

It must have taken me ten minutes or more to finally get to my feet, and as soon as I was upright, a throbbing in my head took over and I became cold and shaky. I sat down again, breathing deeply, feeling the cut on my head that had split the skin and hair from close to my ear up to the middle of my scalp.

I needed to move. The sun had broken through the murkiness of night, and now the sky was filled with the morning swoop and flight of birds as they searched for their breakfast. For a moment, I placed my hands on the soil once more, feeling the clods of dirt, the earth of Poland, my home and suddenly a sweep of happiness rushed over me, and I began to laugh.

'Look, Tata,' I said to the sky, 'I'm home. I made it. I did it!'

Whether it was the adrenaline or the fear that I could be found, I managed to stand and dragged my parachute behind me towards a thicket of pines and old oak trees where I would not be visible. To say that I had thought out the plan in its entirety would be lying. And now that I was here, hiding in amongst the trees, I realised that perhaps I had been foolhardy.

My father had been a member of the Social Democratic Party in Germany, opposing Hitler's rise to power and had fought against it as much as he could, until his illness took his ability to walk, even to speak sometimes, away from him. We had discussed at length returning to Poland and I had been eager to leave, yet Father had decided that he must fight. *'Fight from the belly of the beast,'* he would tell me. *'What can we do if we go back? Very little. We have to fight it here, where it starts and hope that it does not spread like a disease.'*

He fought – hard. Against the cancer that riddled his body,

against the tide of oppression, and I stayed by his side, working in the air force, wondering what I could do to help.

It was only when I heard that Father had died that I knew what I could do – what I had to do. I would return to Poland, and find a way to become Polish again, someone who knew where he belonged, and would help those who needed it.

The pounding in my head was getting worse with each step I took, and I stopped my thoughts from running away with me: the priority now was to keep moving – one step in front of the other, to get to the trees, and to rest.

The tilled earth was hampering my progress; the soil falling away with each tread, and my left leg seemed to drag itself rather than bend and step. Although the trees were perhaps only half a mile away, it took me almost an hour to reach the cool earthiness of the small woodland copse.

Using the tree trunks to hold myself up, I went deeper and deeper inside, the twigs and leaves crunching underfoot, the flutter of birds above me and the scurrying of woodland creatures escaping the noise that each of my footsteps made.

Sweat dripped from my brow and I started to feel nauseated. I was far enough inside, I decided, far enough for no one to see me whilst I rested and tended to the wound on my head.

Just as I was about to sit, I saw planks of wood that had been arranged around a large pine, creating a sort of wooden tent. I moved closer and saw that whoever had made it had left behind a blanket and oddly, a saucepan, a wooden spoon and two egg cups.

Suddenly, the world began to spin above me and a buzzing in my ears made the sounds of the birds seem far away and then, there was nothing.

When I woke up, I wasn't alone.

Two faces, so alike with blue eyes and rusty blond hair peered down at me. One of the faces had hair in pigtails, the other had hair short and floppy that almost obscured their features. I realised it was a boy and a girl, yet they looked almost interchangeable to me.

The boy nudged me with his foot and then turned to the girl. 'He's not dead.'

'Are you sure?' the girl asked, then began to bite her lip.

'You can't open your eyes when you're dead.'

'Why's he in our garden?' the girl asked.

The boy shrugged.

'Water,' I managed to say, my mouth like sandpaper. 'Please. Water.'

Neither of them moved; instead, they looked to each other as if they were speaking silently, then the boy nodded his head, and the girl ran out of the strange hut, leaving me alone with the boy.

'I'm Michal,' the boy introduced himself. 'And that's my sister, Agata.'

'Max,' I replied, my tongue sticking to the roof of my mouth as I spoke.

'Why are you wearing that?' He pointed at my uniform.

'I was in the air force,' I said wearily. I needed water. Where was the girl?

Suddenly, she appeared, a glass in her hand, half-filled with water, and I wondered whether she had spilled the other half of it running back to this place.

I took the glass from her and drank it back quickly, feeling the coolness of it sliding down my throat and some of it dribbling down my chin as I lay on the ground. Finding some strength, I pushed myself up to sit and winced as the pain in my lower leg blistered upwards to my thigh.

'Why are you in our fort?' Agata asked me. 'And why do you have blood on your head? And why—'

The boy, Michal gave her a shove. 'He's in the air force,' he said with authority. 'He fell out of his plane.'

'I didn't tell you that,' I said.

Michal pointed at the parachute, then raised his eyebrows at me as if I were the child instead of him.

The girl crouched down and very gently traced the cut on my head with her finger. 'Ouch,' she said. 'I'll get some help. My ciotka can help and then there's Helena too—'

'No! Don't, please,' I said, my voice coming out a shade too loud and making the pair of them jump with fear. If an adult saw me in this uniform, I would be arrested and possibly sent back. I couldn't let that happen.

Agata edged away from me, and Michal held his hand out to her for her to take, ready to run away at any moment.

'Please,' I said, lowering my voice now. 'If you can just get me some gauze or a bandage perhaps, and then I'll leave.'

'Where will you go?' Michal asked.

'I'm not sure. You see,' I said, suddenly realising what would calm them and perhaps encourage them to help me, 'I'm playing this game.'

'A game?' they asked in unison.

'Yes. A game. You see it's like hide and seek, but I got hurt. And I just need to rest a little and then I'll leave so I don't get found.'

I could see that the girl was beginning to smile – she liked the idea of a game, but Michal was not so easily swayed. 'Adults don't play games. And even we don't play hide and seek any more.'

'It's not really hide and seek,' I blustered. 'It's all secret. You see, I had to come here, but no one can know, just yet, that I'm here. It's a surprise.'

'A surprise for who?' the girl asked.

'My family,' I said, hitting on an idea. My aunt was still alive in Wroclaw. 'I'm surprising my aunt for her birthday, and she can't know yet.' I knew that my story was thin at best, and I had very little chance of them believing me.

Yet, the girl let go of her brother's hand and sat by me once more. 'I'm Agata,' she said, formally introducing herself, even though her brother had already done it for her.

'Max.'

'Michal doesn't like games or surprises,' she said, gesturing towards her brother. 'He says they're for babies. But I do. I play games all the time. Do you like cards? I do.'

'That's wonderful,' I said, cutting her off midstream, getting the feeling that she would not be able to stop on her own.

'Michal,' she turned to her brother, 'go and get something to clean Max's head. And maybe get Helena. You'll like Helena, Max. She's nice.'

'No, please,' I started once more, and I tried to stand – I had to leave. But the dizziness overcame me again and I had to sit back down.

'We won't get Helena,' Michal said, his arms crossed, eyeing me with suspicion; and yet I could see flickering looks from me to the parachute, and I knew that despite himself, he was intrigued by me.

'But if she sees us taking things from the house, she's going to ask,' Agata argued.

'Tell her that we built the fort, tell her that we don't want Ciotka to be mad for taking things, and if she promises not to tell, we'll show her the fort tomorrow, and maybe Max will be gone by then, so it won't matter.'

The way in which he spoke so authoritatively made Agata stand up and leave, ready for her mission.

'You're German,' he stated, having made sure that his sister had actually gone. 'Your uniform is German. I know it is. I saw it in a magazine that a boy had at school. He's from Germany too and I know it. You're German. This isn't a surprise for your aunt, is it?'

'I'm Polish like you.'

'Well, I know that, you speak Polish,' he mocked. 'But you're German too.'

'I *was* German,' I said wearily. 'But I was born here. My parents were Polish. We just lived in Germany, and now I've come back.'

'But why would you jump out of a plane to come back?'

I let the question linger for a few moments, unsure how to tell a child how disillusioned I had become with Germany, how my father and I had wanted to return to Poland after my mother's death, how I felt I had to be here, how I had to be where I was supposed to be.

'I just don't want to be German any more,' I simply said.

'Because of Hitler,' the boy nodded as if he understood.

I tried to shuffle myself backwards so that I could lean on one of the planks of wood that held up the makeshift house they had built. Noticing my discomfort, Michal came to me and took my arm, helping me.

'You don't look well,' he observed.

'I don't feel very good,' I admitted.

'My ciotka, she has a telephone. There's only her and Olek who have one. She hates it and never uses it, but maybe I could ask her to use it. I could telephone someone for you?' he suggested.

'I don't have anyone you could contact.'

'What about your parents? Or your aunt?'

'My parents are dead, my aunt – I don't even know if she has a telephone.'

Suddenly, a voice rang out, calling for the children by name, and Michal moved to the opening to look out towards the seeker. Then Agata returned with her arms full. She dropped the bundle on the floor, revealing a blanket, a first-aid kit, a slice of bread, honey, a bottle of milk and, oddly, a book.

She saw me look at the book. 'I thought in case you get bored, you can read. I like to read.'

I reached for the first-aid kit, a small tin that I knew would hold only what a family would need, some shreds of gauze, cotton wool, and, if I was lucky, some iodine. It was, in fact, more amply stocked than I had hoped, and someone had added two small brown glass bottles with tiny yellow pills inside, a pair of scissors, some sticking plaster and some form of paste in a small jar.

'These are Ciotka's,' Agata told me, as she held the two bottles of pills up. 'She says we can't take these. She has them for her headaches, but Father says she shouldn't take them. I had a headache once and I wanted to take one, but then Michal told Ciotka and she shouted at me. So maybe don't take one because if she finds out, she might shout at you too.'

With a grunt of irritation at his sister, Michal began to unravel the bandage whilst Agata very gently put a few drops of iodine on my cut, then pressed a piece of gauze against it whilst Michal bandaged my head.

I was impressed with their abilities and told them so. 'Scouts,' Michal said. 'We both go.'

'Last time, we had to build a fort to live in overnight and ours fell down so that's why we've built this one because Michal says we have to learn to survive in the wild,' Agata said.

'In the wild?' I asked.

'Yes.' Agata carefully undid a safety pin to secure the bandage in place. 'There's this book about Africa. And in Africa there are wild animals, and when we were little, Michal and I used to say we would be explorers and we would go and see the wild animals, but we had to be able to live in the wild too, do you see?'

'We're not really going,' Michal clarified.

'I'm still going. I'll go without you,' Agata affirmed, then sat back and smiled, admiring her handiwork. 'All done.'

'Thank you.'

I nodded, wishing they would both leave me now. The pain had hit me full force and that small bottle of pills that their aunt took for her headaches was calling to me.

'We have to go now.' Agata got to her feet. 'Helena, that's our sister, says it's dinner, so we'll be back tomorrow.'

Dinner? I looked at my watch, the glass scratched and smudged and yet I could see the time and realised I had slept most of the day.

Agata ran off, although Michal stood a moment with a look that made me sure he was going to tell his aunt about me, but then he waved and said, 'See you in the morning,' and disappeared into the trees.

As soon as they left, I grabbed the bottle of milk and the glass bottle of pills. Shaking them into my hand, I counted three and figured that would be all right. I took them, drank half the milk and lay down, pulling the blanket Agata had brought over me, smelling the scent of home cooking mixed with someone's perfume.

As I closed my eyes, I inhaled the scent of someone else's home, of someone else's body, feeling comforted by it, as if I weren't completely alone in the world, and drifted into a thick, warm sleep.

EIGHT

HELENA

Sunday, 27 August 1939
Żerków, Poland

I slept badly, if at all. The sheets twisted around my legs as I tossed and turned, as if they were trying to anchor me to the bed to force me to endure the insomnia. Each time I closed my eyes, my brain focused on the conversations from that evening.

There was no getting away from it any more. I had tried to ignore the chatter, and I had closed my eyes and mind to the possibility of war because it felt so impossible. Each day when I took either the bus to work or drove with Father, I would look out of the window, at people scurrying about, cars, trams – *life* – and feel how incredible it was that a war could come here, to these streets that I had known since I was a child.

Antoni's presence that evening had solidified it all for me. He worked for the government and if he said it was going to happen, it would. But when would it happen? Would bombs rain from the sky? Would armies march into the town square and round up Jews and Poles alike like Mikolaj had said?

I wished I could escape my mind that buzzed with those

incessant bees of random thoughts, bumping up against one
another so that I could not firmly grasp one thought in its
entirety. Why was my brain doing this to me? *Focus, Helena.
Always focus*, I heard a voice in my head and knew it to be
Father's and wondered when he had said this to me, letting my
brain once more fumble about, trying to find the memory of him
saying that, and yet I couldn't.

Around 4 a.m. I decided that sleep was not going to come,
and I wrapped a blanket around my shoulders and sat on a chair
next to the window, watching the sky lighten. As I did so, I
chided myself for refusing to face what was right in front of me
– to focus on the facts, on the reality of the situation. I thought
back to two weeks ago when I had gone out for a rare evening to
the theatre with my friend Anna and her husband Rolf. Afterwards, we had stopped by a bar, and at first had discussed
Anna's new home in the city and how she might decorate it. Yet
soon, the conversation had turned to politics, and Rolf, whose
parents were both German, had surprised me with his views.

'It's understandable,' he had said, leaning back in his chair
and knocking back a large glass of red. 'I mean, you look at what
they all have – the money they have, so you can see how unfair
it all is.'

'They?' I asked.

'The Jews, silly,' Anna had half laughed at my ignorance.

'So you think they deserve to be punished?' I exclaimed,
half joking.

'Not punished, Helena.' Rolf leaned forward now. 'Just, you
know, put in their place. I mean, think about it. Say they weren't
here any more, think about what we all could have. You should
read these books I have and some pamphlets my cousin sent me.
They're dangerous, the Jews. You have no idea.'

I looked to Anna, whom I had known since school and
waited for her to chide her husband, to tell him to be quiet, that
he was drunk and had no idea what he was talking about.

Instead, she was nodding along with him. 'You should read the pamphlets, Helena. Honestly, I had no idea how bad they are. You should see them, with their squinty eyes, their large noses. I know they don't all look like they do in the pamphlets, not really, but it shows you, doesn't it, what they're like – how they're taking everything away from us. They have the money, and we don't. Have you ever wondered why, Helena?'

If my father had been there, he would have been able to argue with them. He would have pointed out how Polish people and not just Jews were considered undesirable too. He would have pointed out that Anna was Polish, and technically so was Rolf. And yet, I wasn't my father; I was too weak, too stupid to argue with them, so instead I asked Anna how many children she wanted.

Thinking about it now, I felt a wave of shame. I was an educated woman, and I knew of the danger of Germany and what threat we were all facing, and yet I had sat there like a mute, like one of my patients and laughed along with them as they told me about a problem they had had, to do with acquiring the correct sofa from Italy.

Was Joasia right? Should we really be thinking about leaving?

Before I could answer myself, I saw a shadow on the lawn. I stood and squinted out into the half-light, seeing yet another shadow, this one running to join the other, then both disappeared into the treeline. Agata and Michal. What on earth were they thinking at this time of the morning? Yes, they had said they would get up early for breakfast, but this was ridiculous.

Tired and annoyed I left my bedroom and padded down the stairs and out into the garden, only realising I was barefoot once I stood on a twig.

Although the sun was beginning to rise, the stand of trees had yet to let in any light, and shadows of trunks appeared suddenly in front of me as I carefully picked my way across the leaf-strewn ground, calling out for Agata and Michal, yet receiving no reply.

I was about to turn back, to find a torch and some shoes, when I heard Agata scream. My heart pounding, I followed the sound and found myself face to face with a tepee of wooden slats – their fort.

I ventured inside to see Michal standing over a pile of blankets on the floor and Agata next to it, weeping.

On hearing me enter, they both looked up.

'He's dead!' Agata cried.

It was then I realised that there was someone underneath the blankets, and although Agata was screaming that whoever it was, was dead, first a leg twitched, then a howl of agony escaped their mouth.

'No, he's alive!' Michal shouted.

I stepped forward to see a man whose brown hair was half-obscured by a bloody bandage. His eyes were closed, but his mouth was moving, yet no sound came out.

A wave of *déjà vu* overcame me. I had seen this before; I was sure of it. A body crumpled, bleeding.

'He's alive!' Michal shouted again.

'Who is he?' I asked, crouching down to unpeel the blanket from him, seeing a uniform that I knew was not Polish.

'He's Max,' she said simply, as if I should already know. 'He fell out of his plane, and Michal said he's Polish, but he's German too, and he said that Max told him he fell out of the sky because he wanted to come home.'

'What should we do?' Michal asked.

'I... I don't know.' My mind was racing – a German airman, *here*, injured. Had the war started, and we hadn't realised?

'Should I get Ciotka?' Michal was already edging his way out of the fort.

'I – yes. Get Joasia,' I told him.

'He just fell out of the plane, and he said it was a surprise for his aunt and he was going to go and see her, and he said—'

Agata's description of events made little sense, and I knew that Michal would be able to give me a more accurate picture of how this man, this man dressed in a German uniform, came to be in a children's fort in my aunt's back garden.

The man, who Agata assured me was called Max, continued to open and close his mouth, reminding me of the fish we used to catch as children, watching as they gasped before throwing them back into the river.

'I'm Helena,' I told him, watching as he tried to open his eyes to look at me, yet he could not keep them open and soon seemed to fall into a fitful sleep.

Beside him I saw Joasia's first-aid kit, and a bottle of pills spilled onto the floor. Agata saw what I was looking at. 'I told him not to take any of those,' she said, as if that explained everything.

'What in God's name?' Joasia's voice rang out.

'He's German, but he's Polish too,' Agata started her tale of events once more, but Joasia cut her off.

'A pilot?'

'I don't know – maybe. What should we do, Joasia?' I whispered.

For a moment that seemed to stretch on far too long, Joasia said nothing and did not move. Then she bent down and began to fuss at Max's head, lifting his eyelids, then leaning down so that she could press her ear to his chest.

'He's not doing well,' she said.

'Should we fetch the police?'

She leaned away from him and crouched on the ground. 'We should. We probably should.'

'But if you get the police, will he get in trouble?' Agata started crying again. 'Michal said that because he's German, we're supposed to hate him. He told me before we went to sleep last night that if someone finds him, they'll kill him because he's the enemy and that's what happens...'

I shot a look at Michal, and he had the decency to look contrite. He was forever scaring Agata at night with tales and stories, but this time, I suppose, Michal was right – it was the truth; the man would be arrested and possibly worse.

'What do you think, Joasia?' I looked to her, willing her to come up with an answer.

'I think Michal needs to use the telephone,' she said, standing now. 'Go and telephone Olek. We need to move him inside, and we can't do it on our own. We can still fetch the police, but either way he needs to be moved, and he needs medical care. We can't leave him here.'

I felt a wave of relief that Joasia had taken charge, yet I could see the fear in her eyes, how they darted about and how her hands were shaking.

'Michal told me some garbled story about him being German and Polish and wanting to come home?' Joasia declared, trying to force confidence into her tone with this statement.

I nodded. That's what Agata had said too.

'How long has he been here?' she directed this to Agata.

'Since yesterday afternoon. We found him when we came back from town, and we said we would get adults to help, but he said not to. He said that he was working, and it was a secret, so we got him the first-aid kit and some food and—'

Joasia held up her hand to silence Agata, then gave me a look and shook her head gently as if she had been expecting this for months as she watched the planes fly overhead each night.

Michal soon appeared. 'Olek is coming.'

'Good,' Joasia told him.

Whilst we waited, Michal told us what Max had told him; that he was Polish and he no longer wanted to be German, that he had wanted to come home.

'What does that even mean?' I asked.

'He said he was playing a game – like hide and seek. He didn't want to be found, but then he said he wanted to surprise his aunt,' Agata added, making the mystery of this man even more strange.

Olek was not long in arriving, and by his side was Filip who clicked his heels and gave a little bow even though the situation was not one of greeting. I wondered if it were some sort of affectation that he could not shake – I had seen patients at the hospital who had rituals that they had to complete. Then I realised my mind was once again wandering and not focusing properly.

'What have we got here then?' Olek asked, and despite his size, very slowly and gently bent down to inspect Max.

'An airman,' he muttered. 'German,' nodding at his uniform.

'But he's Polish too!' Agata said. 'He said he didn't want to be German any more.'

'Michal, take your sister inside,' Joasia commanded, not wanting to hear Agata's laments again.

'But—' he started, obviously wanting to be a part of whatever was going to happen next.

'Go!' Joasia was not to be argued with right now.

'Polish and German, eh?' Olek said. 'Not sure I buy that one.'

'What are we going to do with him?' Filip squeaked from the doorway, pushing up his glasses with a nervous finger.

'Take him inside, obviously,' Joasia said.

Olek took charge and decided he would lift Max from beneath his arms, Filip and I were to take a leg each and Joasia would try and hold him underneath his torso.

As we lifted him, another agonising groan escaped from his lips; quieter this time as if he was losing energy. Awkwardly, we made our way out of the hut, and through the trees. Thankfully, the sun had now peeped over the horizon, and we could see where we were going.

Although Filip, Joasia and I were holding him, he felt light, and I realised that Olek was bearing the majority of the weight, his face turning red with exertion.

We lugged him into the sitting room and placed him on the largest of Joasia's sofas; pink and stuffed with horsehair, with a slight dip in the middle from years of use.

'What now?' Olek asked, sitting across from the airman. 'I say we fetch the police.'

'We could,' Joasia replied. 'But what will happen to him?'

Olek shrugged. 'It's the right thing to do.'

I looked at Max, his head lolling to the side, a swipe of dark brown hair across his forehead, the blood from his wound trickling down to his ear, and there was something deep down inside that was telling me we should help him, despite the fact that he was German – it was what Mother would do.

'Mother would tell us to help him,' I said almost to myself.

'What?' Joasia asked.

'Mother,' I repeated, gaining confidence now. 'She would tell us to help him. He's injured, and we know what could happen to him if we call the police. Even more, we could get in trouble too – maybe they would think we knew him or were already trying to help him. Do you not remember when Mother took in that stray cat that hissed and scratched everyone? She said then it was the right thing to do. And she helped it, and made it tame.'

'That was a *cat*, Helena,' Joasia remarked drily. 'This is a bit different.'

'It's not, though, is it? I mean, he's injured and needs help. I say we help him get better; the children said he was Polish, and what if he is? What if he did want to come home and then we just send him away?'

'I have an idea.' Filip stood next to Joasia, and clicked his heels.

'I hope it's one that we can all understand in the first instance,' Olek muttered.

Ignoring him, Filip continued. 'I say he stays here. We get him well enough to talk and then we get Antoni. He'll know what to do. I mean, this man, he could know something important that we could pass on to the government. But if we call the police, Helena is right, we all know what will happen.'

He finished his speech and gave a gentle cough, then fussed with his glasses again, even though they hadn't budged an inch.

Joasia and Olek began to discuss the pros and cons, Filip weighing in with theories, and it was then I saw that Max's eyes were open, and his lips were moving.

'Hush! He's awake. What did you say?' I asked him.

He spoke again, yet I still could not hear him. I crouched down and placed my ear close to his mouth. He grabbed my hand, and I felt a strange warmth spread through me.

'Help me, please. Don't send me back,' he managed to say. 'I want to come home.'

His eyes closed once more, and his breathing became a little ragged; his hand went limp and let go of mine. I stood, oddly feeling a lump in my throat from his plea, which sounded child-like and reminded me of the patients at the hospital when they cried to return to their homes.

'He stays,' I said, looking at the trio. 'He stays until he is well enough, and then we will decide.'

My tone said it all, and thankfully everyone bobbed their heads in agreement.

'Come, Helena, we need to clean that wound of his.' Joasia beckoned me to follow her out of the room. As I did so, I turned and glanced at Max, the stranger who had fallen out of the sky, all because he had wanted to come home.

NINE

Tuesday, 29 August 1939
Owińska Mental Hospital, Poznań, Poland

Time is a strange beast, is it not? In just a day, our lives have changed once more.

I arrived at my sister Joasia's house late on Sunday afternoon after a two-hour drive south of the hospital. I was exhausted and looking forward to some respite, however little duration it may be. Indeed, as I drove, I let the windows down and enjoyed the warm breeze that wafted in and felt a little bit lighter. Antoni had telephoned to say he had spoken with Helena, and although it had not gone well, I was sure that I could convince her that leaving to go to Oxford was the best thing for her and the twins.

As I turned left into the town, I passed the nondescript houses, so common in such small villages, and wondered, as I often did when I came to visit, why Joasia preferred living here rather than in the city.

Olek's inn was closed, as it should be on a Sunday, yet I

knew that by five o'clock, he would open the door to a few friends and allow them to partake of a drink or two.

Within a minute I was out of the town and turned a sharp right that led down a rutted track towards Joasia's house. Limes and oaks lined the edges of the road, the branches almost touching to create a leafy tunnel. The smell of the lime trees was sharp in my nostrils, once more lifting my mood and making me excited to see my children, relax in the garden and look out onto the green and brown patchwork of the country-side that spread out for miles outside of Joasia's garden.

I pulled up to the house, noting that the purple clematis that Joasia had planted a few years ago was doing well and had crept up over the whitewashed bricks and over the door. Humming a tune to myself, with an agile step I went into Joasia's house, ready to relax, laugh and be with my family.

But it was not to be.

As soon as I entered, I heard voices raised in argument in the kitchen, noting Olek's gruffness and Filip's dulcet tones. What were they doing here?

Michal and Agata leapt up from the sitting-room couch to greet me, wrapping themselves around my legs so that I could not move.

'Tata! Tata! So much has happened. Just wait until you meet Max! You'll love him. He's nice. At least I think he is, and we saved him,' Agata rambled at me.

Michal's hug was briefer than hers, and he stepped back, perhaps suddenly realising he might be too old to greet his father in such a way. I certainly hoped that was not the case – I was not ready for him to grow up just yet.

'Do you want to see him, Tata?' Agata asked.

'See who?'

'Max, of course.' She giggled.

'Maybe later,' I told them both, extricating myself from her grasp and making my way to the kitchen at the rear of the house. Max? Was this a bear, a doll that someone had bought her?

Olek and Filip were sitting at the kitchen table, Olek furiously smoking whilst Joasia fussed at the stove. I could smell sauerkraut and pork and knew she was making *bigos* – my favourite.

'I'm here,' I announced.

Olek and Filip looked at me, then at each other, Filip fussing with his glasses as he always did.

'Filip, I haven't seen you in months.' I went to him and shook his hand, then slapped Olek on the back. 'I thought you would be readying yourself for your secret customers this afternoon.' I directed this at Olek.

'Not today,' he replied.

'Michal, we weren't expecting you.' Joasia barely glanced at me before she went back to the cooker.

'You were. I told you I was coming.'

'Did you?'

'I did.' I sat down and realised I had walked into something – a disagreement perhaps? It was only when Helena walked into the room, a first-aid kit under her arm that I knew something was very seriously awry.

'Father!' she exclaimed, quickly placing the first-aid box on a side table.

'What's going on?' I looked to each of them, but no one would meet my gaze.

Before I could ask again, there was an almighty scream from upstairs – like an animal in pain. I looked up at the ceiling. 'What is happening?' I demanded.

'Don't worry,' Agata's voice came from behind me. 'It's only Max.'

'And *who* is Max?'

There was a moment of silence before everyone began talking at once, and I had to take charge, asking them to speak one at a time. It was Joasia who explained it all – a German airman, injured, upstairs and they had decided to nurse him back to health.

'We agreed that you would talk to Helena about going to England, and instead you take in a German? Are you going *crazy*, Joasia? Do I need to admit you to the hospital?'

'Don't talk to me like you own me!' she yelled in return. 'I make my own decisions and so does Helena.' She pointed at Helena as she spoke, trying to draw her into the argument.

'And you both thought that this was best? Keeping a German upstairs and nursing him back to health? For what, Joasia? Tell me!'

'It's my house, my rules,' she announced. 'Besides, he's Polish,' she added.

'Ah, so a traitor then? That's so much better, Joasia!'

I cannot remember all of the choice phrases that we threw at each other, although they were cruel and childish, until I announced that I was contacting Antoni to come immediately and sort this out. If anyone knew what to do, it would be him.

Yet, Antoni was not as useful as I had thought he would be. When he arrived, I saw that the whites of his eyes were shot through with red, and there was a lingering smell of whisky on his breath. He had not shaved either, letting the stubble grow thicker so that soon he would be sporting a beard to rival Olek's.

'Are you well?' I asked him.

'Of course,' he replied, and tried to smile to reassure me, but it lasted less than a second.

'I'm sorry to trouble you about this,' I told him, ushering him into the kitchen and motioning for Joasia to bring him a cup of coffee.

He listened as Olek, Filip and I explained, with Joasia and the twins chiming in with their own version of events. I felt keenly that Joasia was only opposing my fears and worries about this man because I was going against her. She was contrary, I knew that, and I also knew she too was scared of the impending war and what it could mean.

Antoni offered little in way of advice and left fairly soon after arriving, promising me in the doorway that he would think and get back to me. I wondered as I closed the door, how much he did know about what was going to happen, and how much was weighing on his mind?

I left Joasia's, defeated, early on Monday morning. The arguments with Joasia had continued well into the night, but as she said – her house, her rules. I reminded her that the twins were staying with her, and she was putting them in danger, to which Helena told me she could look after herself and she would stay a few more days before returning to work to make sure that the twins were fine.

'Besides, Olek can stay if we need him to,' Joasia said by way of compromise.

I was so tired that I conceded, and talked with Olek about checking in with them each day, to which he readily agreed.

This exhaustion that is plaguing me has an obvious cause, or rather, causes. War, Max, Helena, the twins, work, my patients.

Ah, my patients.

They take every drop of me, every bit of my knowledge, of my time, and the patient I was worried about earlier now occupies my thoughts once more. I have finally seen them, and my fears are perhaps not without merit. They are indeed exhibiting the same behaviours that I witnessed in them nine years ago, a psychosis of sorts that was brought on by grief and trauma. A recurrence is not completely unheard of; and yet, I did not expect one after this length of time.

I blame myself, of course. If I had read more, consulted more, perhaps I would have seen that there was always a chance for this to reappear. And for that, I am utterly cross with myself.

I am a learned man, and yet I feel so despondent that I have let this patient down, let them suffer, when I should have been more vigilant. I let the business of the hospital, of my children, of life, overshadow the continual learning that I must always do – what do I always tell Helena? *Keep learning, keep reading, keep trying to understand.* And yet I had not heeded my own advice and had not fully realised the possibilities of a relapse.

Perhaps I have not realised a lot lately. Perhaps I am not the learned man I think I am. I feel myself losing control and I am not sure how to rein it back. I should talk, I know. I encourage my patients to do this – to expound upon their fears and worries. And yet, I do not. But then, who do I have to talk to? Who would want to listen to me?

Perhaps this man called Max?

I am laughing at the suggestion and realise I am more tired than I thought I was. I must go. I must sleep and *hope* that tomorrow I will know what to do and what to say.

Hope. That's all I have.

SEPTEMBER 1939

TEN

HELENA

Friday, 1 September 1939
Owińska Mental Hospital, Poznań, Poland

'This means war. From now on, all other matters and issues become of secondary importance. We set our public and private lives on a special track. We have entered war. The entire effort of the nation must go in one direction. We're all soldiers now. We need to think about only one thing: fighting until we win.'

Mother, Father and I huddled around the radio in Father's office, each of us hearing this message for the fifth time that morning and it was not yet 10 a.m.

I looked to Mother who smiled reassuringly at me – she would not show her fear.

The announcer continued to outline what had happened early that morning – the battleship *Schleswig-Holstein* had fired shells at the Polish military depot on the Westerplatte peninsula in Gdańsk in retaliation for a supposed Polish attack on a German radio station.

'I can't believe it,' my mother protested.

'You should go to Joasia's,' my father declared, finally stopping his incessant smoking, only to pack the pipe with more tobacco.

'What will happen?' I asked, sounding more and more like a scared child.

'We'll fight, but we won't win,' Father answered.

'We might,' I said.

'I agree with Helena. We might win,' Mother agreed.

He shook his head and looked out of the window as if expecting to see German troops marching down the driveway.

'You should go to Joasia's,' he repeated. 'Go and check on the children, and that *man...*' his voice trailed off and I wanted to tell him that that 'man', had a name, and yet I knew now was not the time to begin this same argument.

There had been arguments aplenty when father arrived on Sunday, and I had crept away to the spare bedroom that Olek and Filip had managed to get Max into.

He was still asleep, and I could see beads of sweat on his brow. I took a cool cloth from the basin and laid it on his head, wishing he would wake up.

As Joasia and I had undressed him earlier that day, and tended to his wounds, he had groaned and then shouted out for his father and mother, and at times had opened his eyes and stared at nothing, then spoke as if a ghost were standing in front of him. 'Tata. I'm here. I made it home. I did it...'

His pleadings to the ghost of his tata made me sure that he posed no threat – for whatever reason, he had made it back home, and yet, I wondered why it had been so drastic – why had he jumped out of a plane to do so?

Now though, Max was still, his breathing a little ragged, his eyes rapidly moving under his eyelids, the veins blue and purple highlighted against the paleness of his skin. I watched his chest carefully for each rise and fall. I wondered whether to insist upon calling a doctor again, sure that he needed one, but Joasia and Olek had been adamant that no one should know.

Suddenly, he opened his eyes and stared at me. 'Tata?' he asked.

His fever had obviously not yet broken, and his delusions were continuing.

'Yes,' I said, playing along, noting how green his eyes were, the pupils small, allowing the full force of the colour to burst forth.

'I stayed in the belly of the beast for so long. But I had to leave. You said to stay, but I couldn't. Do you understand? I couldn't.'

'The belly of the beast?' I couldn't stop myself from asking.

He nodded gently. 'As long as I could. As long as I could. I stayed. We saw, didn't we, what was happening around us and you said to stay. I did. But you died, Tata, you died and left me, and I saw our country, our home. I had to come home, Tata. Do you forgive me?'

'I forgive you,' I told him, and as soon as the words left my mouth, his body relaxed and a thin smile appeared on his lips. He quickly fell back to sleep, but now he did not whimper like a small child enveloped in a nightmare; he was quiet, at peace, his breathing calmer.

'Is he awake?' A childish whisper came from behind me, and I saw Agata at the doorway, half in, half out of the room.

'Not really.'

She chewed at her bottom lip and stared at her bare feet for a moment as the argumentative voices from below billowed up towards us.

'It will be all right,' I pacified her.

'Father's angry,' she worriedly told me.

'I know.'

'And Ciotka says we must help him. Michal and I were

sitting on the stairs, and we heard her. She told Father not to be so cruel and Father said he wasn't cruel, then Antoni said—'

'Antoni?'

She nodded once more. 'He's here.'

I stood and ushered her out of the room. If Antoni had been summoned, I knew he would be on Father's side and would try and convince the others to follow whatever Father said.

Antoni was sitting at the kitchen table alongside Filip, Olek and Father, a fug of cigarette and pipe smoke hanging ominously above them whilst Mother and Joasia busied them-selves making dinner.

No one spoke and I could see that the men wore similar expressions – ones I had seen on the twins when they had been scolded and knew they were not going to get their own way.

Joasia slammed a plate of sliced bread down in the middle of the table, then went to the kitchen door and held it open, her eyes on the smoke hanging from the ceiling. 'You want to smoke, you do it outside,' she remonstrated.

All of the men, apart from my father, extinguished their cigarettes whilst Father stubbornly sat with the pipe clenched between his teeth.

'Look what I found.' Michal pushed Joasia, as he entered from the garden.

'How long have you been out there?' Joasia asked.

'Look!' He held up a backpack.

Antoni was the first to get to it and opened it with such force that I expected the material to tear.

He produced a gun, a small tin and a handful of photographs. He scowled at the findings, seemingly disap-pointed.

'Photographs.' Joasia already had her hands on them and was looking intently at each one. 'How very odd,' she said, as she surveyed them.

'Why odd?' I asked.

'Look for yourself.' She splayed the photographs on the table, and we all leaned in to look. One was of a couple, newly married, their smiles reaching their eyes. Another was of the same couple, this time with a small child outside the famous Basilica of the Assumption of the Blessed Virgin Mary in Gdańsk. Then another of the same child, older now, holding a model aeroplane and laughing as he held it up in the air.

'Not what you'd expect to see in a serviceman's bag, I'll give you that,' Antoni said.

'See. I *told* you so. He's not dangerous. There's a reason he's here, I'm sure of it,' Joasia said.

'You're a fickle woman, do you know that?' Father started. 'One minute you're wanting to get to England, fearing the Germans and then the next, you're defending a man from the very same country you hate, whom we know nothing about, and who could be dangerous.'

I thought this would start a new argument, but Joasia smiled at him. 'I reserve the right to change my mind, as and when it suits *me*,' she said, delighting in annoying her brother.

'I say I should stay here with you all, just in case,' Olek gently coaxed.

'Just in case *what*?' Joasia looked upwards. 'In case he suddenly drops through the ceiling and murders us all? Don't be so ridiculous.'

I knew that this was all bluster. Joasia was scared, but she would be damned if she was going to show it to her brother and the other men. She would say the opposite just to infuriate them and somehow take some strange confidence and comfort from doing so. Oddly, I was now completely unafraid. I knew I probably should be, but Max's pleadings to his dead father were still ringing in my ears, his emerald eyes that stared at me had made me feel close to him – made me feel as though in a strange way I knew him.

Olek's face reddened, but he knew better than to insist, as

did Filip, and it seemed Antoni, who was preoccupied with the small tin that had come out of the knapsack.

'What is it?' I asked.

He had opened the lid to reveal a small paper aeroplane, dirty with age.

'Can I have it?' Michal asked, already holding out his hand to take it.

'I don't see why not,' Antoni said.

Before the exchange could happen, I whipped the tin out of Antoni's hand. 'It's not yours to give away. You can't do anything you want, and you can't always have what you want,' I said, directing this to both Michal and Antoni. It was Max's. They were his treasures – the only things he had brought with him, and I would keep them with me, keep them safe until he was well.

Suddenly, the headache that had plagued me all day livened up and I put my hand on the top of my head, pushing down, hoping that it would somehow release the pressure.

'Are you all right, Helena?' Mother asked me, placing her hand on my shoulder.

I nodded, and then said, 'I'm fine.'

Antoni gave me a strange look, then his eyes darted to my father who was staring at me too.

'I'm fine,' I told them. 'It's just a headache.'

'I need to go,' Antoni announced abruptly, and made his way to the front door, my father trailing after him, a quick hushed discussion ensued and then Father was back in the room.

'Helena? Helena?' my father's voice interrupted the memory of the past week and I saw that he and my mother were both staring at me.

'It's fine to admit you're scared,' Father said, coming out

from behind his desk to perch on it instead. 'You'll go to Joasia's to check on the children. And I think you should stay there for a few days until we know more.'

'But what about the patients?'

'I'll stay here for now. I can manage.' His voice was calm, gentle even.

'But what if—' I started the sentence, not really knowing what I was going to say – what if what? What if there were bombs? What if soldiers came? What if something happened at Joasia's or what if something happened to my parents here? And what about the patients? Who would take care of them if something happened – *if, if, what, what* – the constant questions flooded my brain.

Suddenly, and unexpectedly, I was in my father's arms. And it was then that I realised I was weeping.

ELEVEN

MAKSYMILIAN

Sunday, 3 September 1939
Żerków, Poland

I woke in a bed that was not my own, and, I was sure, clothes that were also not mine. The room felt all at once familiar and yet alien to me. I knew the smell of the room – a fresh scent of air that came through the propped-open window, mixed with talcum powder that was on my skin. The yellow curtains I knew, too, and yet I had never looked at them before.

'Hello,' a gentle voice was beside me. 'You're awake.'

Turning, I saw it was the girl from the garden. Who was she again? I searched my brain for her name, but it seemed to have vanished.

'You've been awake a bit,' she continued, 'but now you're properly awake. Before you just looked about and moaned and things, but you're not doing that now, are you?'

'I suppose not,' I said, my tongue furry and dry.

'Do you want some water?' She half ran to a side table that held a white and blue wash basin and jug. Fetching the jug in her small hands, she spilled water into a glass on the bedside table, much of the water soaking into a linen doily.

'There.' She held the glass out to me to take and waited until I had taken a few sips before taking it back. 'Much better, yes?'

I nodded my thanks.

'I'm not supposed to be in here, you know.' She sat gently on the bed. 'So if you see Helena, Ciotka or Michal, don't tell them, all right?'

'I won't say a word.'

'Good. Because Michal always tells on me. He always runs to Father and says, "Agata took extra bread, or Agata took more honey",' she mimicked his deeper voice. 'It's always food that I take too much of according to Michal. But then, I like food.'

Agata. Her name was Agata. I remembered now and I also remembered opening my eyes as she had said I'd done, seeing the room, but again, not really seeing.

'Do you like food, Max? What's your favourite? Mine is chocolate, but Michal says that's not really food even though you eat it. He says that it's a special thing and you can't call it food.'

'I don't know anyone who doesn't like food,' I said, cutting off her ramblings. 'My favourite is my mother's *bigos*. I like it with extra vinegar.'

At the mention of the meaty stew, her eyes opened wide. 'I love *bigos* too! Oh Max, shall I ask Ciotka to make it for you? I will! She made it last week, but I'll tell her to make it again!' She leaned forward and patted the top of my head gently and ran from the room, screaming for her aunt to make *bigos* and to do it right away.

I managed to inch myself into a sitting position and took stock of my injuries. Holding my hand against my head, I could feel blunt thick stitches – who had done this? Then I moved my legs, my toes and my hands and arms. Although my left leg was throbbing, it was not as bad as I remembered it to be. How long had I been here?

'I need to go,' I said aloud.

'Not yet, surely?' another voice responded.

I turned to see a woman entering the room, wearing men's trousers with a blue shirt tucked into them, spattered with paint.

'I must look a fright,' she said, taking a seat next to the bed. 'But I was painting this morning for my new book, and I have to admit I'm a little messy at times.'

She spoke to me as if we had known each other for years, and although I knew I should be wary of her, I couldn't help but instantly like her.

She crossed one leg over the other, and leaned back in the chair, ready for our conversation to continue.

'I'm Max,' I said dumbly, unsure of what else to say.

'Oh, I know that.' She waved my name away like she was swatting a fly. 'Old news. Don't you want to know who I am?'

I nodded.

'Joasia, Joasia Rodzynska. You may have heard of me? Or maybe not. It depends on what you read I suppose. But in some circles, I am a little famous, you know. So, you had the very good fortune of finding yourself in my garden, I must say.'

'Well, I think I owe you a debt of thanks. You have taken very good care of me.'

'Very good, especially considering the circumstances,' she said slowly, and I saw her quickly look towards the window as if expecting someone to be there.

'Circumstances?' I asked.

'The war. Of course, you slept through the start of it – it has started, you know? More of your damned planes in the sky, air-raid sirens going off day and night. But you, you slept through it. So tell me, Max, did you come back to Poland to begin the war a few days early? Are there more of you that seemingly fell out of the sky just a few days before the armies marched in?' Her tone had taken on a sudden edge, and I raised my hand to my head to finger the stitches.

'Does it hurt?'

'A little,' I told her.

She stood, suddenly irritated, her mouth pursed into a thin line. 'I'll get you something for it,' she said, and stalked from the room.

Her personality unnerved me, and I wondered whether she was playing some sort of game with me – a game whereby I obviously knew none of the rules.

War? Was she right, had it happened? Of course, I knew it would, we all did, but had it started?

I reached out to take the glass of water that the chatty Agata had left for me, and as I did so, my fingers brushed across a glossy surface. I looked to see photographs – my photographs of my parents that I had stuffed into my knapsack on my last flight.

'I hope I'm not disturbing you?' Another voice was now in my room. I looked to the doorway and saw a woman. She was tall like the other woman, but carried a little more weight and was younger. Her brown hair was coming loose from its moorings, wafts of it framing a heart-shaped face and cupid's-bow lips. I felt that I knew her and yet, I couldn't, could I?

She smiled at me, a wide smile that reached her eyes and made them crinkle. 'It's good that you're awake. I've been worried.'

She bustled into the room and tucked in the blankets around my legs, even though the room was suffocatingly warm. Then she stood, unsure of herself, clasping her hands in front of her as if waiting for me to tell her what to do next.

'I'm Max,' I told her, feeling foolish once more – she of course knew who I was, but who was *she*?

'Helena,' she replied, holding out her hand for a formal

handshake. I took it in mine and stared at my hand as it shook hers.

'We've met,' she said, her eyes roving about the room but not landing on anything in particular. 'A few times when you opened your eyes, I told you who I was, and you spoke to me.'

'I did?'

'About your tata.'

'What did I say?' I asked, nervous now about what I had possibly said in my delirium.

'You talked about "the belly of the beast",' she said, then dragged a chair close to my bed. 'What did you mean by that?'

Her eyes were on me now, her face close. I could see that her eyes were hazel and as the light hit them, a streak of orange appeared too. She was so earnest, so close, that I began to sweat.

'I – I don't know,' I stammered.

'Am I making you nervous? It's all right if I am. Just say so. Some of my patients say I am too intense – too much. Just say.' She grinned at me.

'I – I,' my childhood stammer was back, and I had to swallow three times to get it to go away. 'I'm fine,' I managed to get out.

'So. I know you're called Max, and I know your tata died – tell me – what else do I need to know?'

Her hand was resting on the bed, an inch from my own, and I felt like taking it in mine. She was warm, open, and I felt instantly at ease with her and yet filled with childish nerves all at the same time.

'He died, yes,' I said, trying to say something, anything that would keep her interested and sitting here with me.

'I found you, you know? Well, the twins did, in their little makeshift fort. You were in a bad way.'

The change in subject was swift, and I let her tell me about how they had brought me inside and tended to my wounds.

'The stitches, that's Joasia's workmanship. I'm sorry about

that. I told her it wasn't neat and the thread too thick, but she didn't listen to me.'

She smiled again at me, and I grinned back stupidly.

'Tell me about your tata,' she demanded now. 'It will help you, I think.'

Her words to me were like magic – as though I wasn't in my right mind. As soon as she told me to speak about my father, I did so, there was no hesitation. It was as though she had hypnotised me in some way, and I desperately wanted to please her.

TWELVE

MAKSYMILIAN

'My tata died on the night before my flight – before you found me here. I saw him before he died and for that I am grateful – I saw him one last time.

On that final night in Berlin, the birds trilled their evensong as I walked along Friedrich Strasse in the direction of my father's home.

Reaching the polished black door of Number 7, I noticed that Ingrid, my father's nurse, had been busying about again, the brass knocker now polished to a garish gleam, the front steps swept and even the iron railings had not been spared her hard work, with dust and cobwebs banished.

I had barely knocked when the door swung open to reveal Ingrid, her wiry greying hair tied roughly at the base of her neck, her round face red and beaming at me.

"Max!" She enveloped me in a meaty embrace, one which had become a custom of hers these past few months. "You're wasting away. I can feel your bones."

She let me go and eyed me from head to toe and tutted. "They're not feeding you well. I can see it. You tell them that you need more food."

"I will, Ingrid," I said with a smile. "I'm sure the Generalleutnant will give me a little more."

"You joke, but you never know until you ask. You're there, protecting us in the skies and when you get on the ground, they should feed you more. It's only right."

Her logic amused me, and I wondered what the officers at the airbase would make of Ingrid if she were to tell them how to run their units. No doubt they would be scared of her, as Father and I were – whatever Ingrid said went in this house, and it would be the same anywhere, I wagered.

"How is he?" I asked, as I followed her into the hallway.

She shook her head and almost immediately her eyes began to swim. "Not good. Not good. It won't be long now."

I swallowed deeply, feeling the lump of sadness in my throat. "Where is he?" my voice was low and threatened to break.

"He's in the sitting room, napping. Give him a few more minutes."

I selfishly wanted to wake him – to savour every moment I had left with him, but Ingrid had said to wait and there was to be no arguing with her.

"Come with me to the kitchen," she beckoned. "I'll make you some supper."

I wasn't in the mood to chatter with Ingrid about her grandchildren and her lazy husband, whom she would no doubt lament about, so instead I told her I needed something from my old bedroom and climbed the staircase, noting that she was watching every step I took.

Opening my childhood bedroom door, I felt the ghosts of the past confront me. The room had not changed since I had left home, and I half expected to see a shadow of my childhood self, sat at the desk, wrapped in an old brown dressing gown, carefully building a small wooden plane. I walked to the desk that still housed my schoolbooks and placed in the centre was a small paper aeroplane. I had forgotten about this and believed it to have been lost, destroyed or thrown away, but there it sat as if it had been waiting for my return.

I picked it up, then sat on my single bed that was still made up with a blue eiderdown and lay down, twisting and turning the plane, smiling at the memory that it brought of the day Father had returned home with it, and we had spent the next half hour building it and watching it fly and flutter about the room. That began the obsession with model planes – ones which took hours and even days to build, both of us huddled in concentration at the dining-room table whilst my mother would scold us for making such a mess.

I looked up to the ceiling, where fifteen model planes all dangled from pieces of string, the light air in the room making them circle slowly – it was the scene I had fallen asleep to as a child, with dreams of one day flying amongst the stars, seeing a patchwork world below me.

And now, here I was, not a pilot, but a navigator and observer after not quite making the cut in the then restricted number of pilots allowed. Of course, since Hitler came to power the air force had grown and many a time people had asked if I would now re-train, but it no longer bothered me – as a navigator, I was in the air, I saw the world from above, and that was all I had ever wanted.

I heard coughing from downstairs; a distinct painful rattle that made me hold my own hand to my chest as if to ease the burden.

Swinging my legs off the bed, I picked up the little paper aeroplane, placing it in an empty tobacco tin that it had once lived in, and took another look at my bedroom with some intuition that I would never see it again.

The sitting room was dark – the heavy red curtains already closed against the dying light, the windows underneath open, letting in the warm breeze, making the material flutter and sway like ghosts.

My father was sitting in his pale green armchair that seemed to swallow him whole. I remembered how when I was young, he had seemed like a bear of a man who had never stopped caring for Mother when she was dying, who fought against the rising Nazi party with his role in the SDP and took being imprisoned three times as if it were nothing.

Now though, he was like a baby bird that had not yet grown its feathers. His head seemed too large as his body shrank, the hair on his head diminishing day by day to reveal shiny bare skin. The irony that he looked somewhat like a baby now he was leaving this life was not lost on me, and I wondered if everyone looked like tiny newborns when it was our time to go.

The light from the table lamp cast a murky orange glow over him and made the rest of the furniture into shadows that seemed oddly ominous to me. I wanted to switch on each light, and bring some warmth, some sense of life into the room, but I knew that he wouldn't allow it – he liked the dark, it somehow comforted him.

"Ah, Max!" He noticed me and raised his head too quickly so that his glasses slipped off his nose onto his lap.

I went to him and picked up the glasses, placing them back on his face, then took a moment to stroke his head and place a kiss on its crown.

"They're always falling off, always. I need some new ones. But then, I suppose I won't need them where I'm going!" He tried to let out a laugh that soon turned into a coughing fit, shaking his whole body so that the blanket on his lap slid to the floor and his glasses once more escaped his face.

I gave him a glass of water to sip as the coughing became a splutter, then quietened to wheezy breath. Even though the day's heat was still lingering in the room, I felt the ice cold of his hand and wrapped the blanket around his legs once more, tucking it tightly in case another coughing fit overcame him.

As I placed the glasses back on his face once again, he reached up and this time stroked my face, starting on my cheek, then running his fingers over my nose and gently along my brow.

"I'm taking one last look," he told me. "One last feel. I can take your face with me now."

I choked back the lump that had once more appeared in my throat and sat beside him, taking his gangly fingers in mine.

"You'll see me again," I told him.

"Maybe. Maybe not..." Then he eagerly sat forward. "Now tell me, what news of the outside world? How goes our plan?" His eyes suddenly lit up, and for a moment, it was as though his illness had disappeared.

"It is much the same," I said, not wanting to douse his spirit with more news of impending war against our homeland of Poland.

"I wonder, Max, if anything I did has had any impact at all? Did I make a mistake? Should I have just taken us both back to Poland and be done with it?"

Over the past few months, we had had this conversation many a time over, discussing his regret at taking his young family away from their homeland of Poland to take a job as an art curator. At the time it was a dream come true for him – he could finally work in larger museums and galleries – and for some time, our lives in Berlin were picture perfect. Father's work sent him around the country and then as far away as France, Italy and England, where he always delighted in bringing back souvenirs for me and Mother. I think the word Mother used to use was *prosper*. We had prospered here in Germany and even become naturalised citizens, happy to be a part of a country that was rebuilding after the war and once again taking its place on the world stage.

But then, as happens with life, things changed. I was two years into my training with the air force to become a navigator, when Mother fell ill. Her sickness consumed my father, who never left her side. And as she weakened, in the world outside, Hitler was gaining strength and my father, along with many others, was getting nervous.

He tried to get us back to Poland in time for Mother to see her siblings, but on a cold Saturday morning in February, she turned her head one last time to look out of the window at the snow-laden trees, and was gone.

It was then, I think, that my father had started to get sick too. Of course, the doctors assured us that cancer did not grow from grief, but I was sure that the shock and loss of his wife had stirred up something in his body.

He fought bravely for years and engaged with local politics as much as he could, seeing that his purpose in life was now to stop the Nazi regime. "If I can leave this earth with the knowledge that I have done all I can, then I will be a happy man," he would say. In those days, there was no talk of me and him returning to Poland. "You must fight from inside the belly of the beast," he told me each day. "Fight it from the inside. Stay in their air force, and one day you will fight your way out for the good of others."

I had never known what he had meant by it – how could I fight from inside? Would it not be better to leave, to disappear and have nothing more to do with it. But Father had insisted I stay where I was, and that my opportunity would come soon – and I was eagerly waiting.

It was only in the past few months as his health declined further that he had spoken of Poland and his regret at not going home. I think he had come to realise that his political endeavours had led nowhere, and nothing could stop whatever was going to happen next.

"Max, I think I made a mistake," he told me on that last

evening together, drawing me out of my memories of the years gone by.

"You didn't," I said. "If we had left, it wouldn't have changed much."

He nodded his balding head. "You can still fight from the inside, can't you?" He looked at me, his eyes dull and pleading. "You can find a way. You know how they work now, what they want. You can help people, I know you can." His hand was suddenly like a vice gripping onto my own.

"I will," I promised him, "I can."

It seemed to work, and he loosened his grip. "Tell me, where will you go next?"

Of course I wasn't meant to tell my father anything about our operations, but I couldn't see how it mattered any more. "This evening I have a reconnaissance flight. Guess where?"

"Poland?" he asked excitedly.

I nodded.

"You'll look out and see it all, won't you? Look at it for me. I wonder what it looks like all the way up there. Like a little patchwork maybe? Or toy houses. All of Poland there beneath your feet." He closed his eyes, and I knew he was imagining being up there among the stars, looking down on his homeland, remembering the smells and sounds from his earlier life, finally free from his regrets and pain.

I left Father in the capable hands of Ingrid who, by 7 p.m., insisted I leave. "It's time for his medication and bed," she had said.

My father had rolled his eyes at her behind her back, and I saw then a glimpse of his old self, the man who would tell jokes and delight in having a proper belly laugh. I kissed the top of his head before I left and allowed Ingrid to bustle about him, not quite catching his eye as I left the room.'

. . .

'Are you quite well?' Helena asked, then placed her hand over my own.

I felt moisture on my face and wiped away the tears that had escaped without my noticing.

'That was the last time you saw him,' she murmured.

I nodded.

'Do you want to tell me more? I can sit here for as long as you like,' she said.

I shook my head, but I didn't want her to leave, and it seemed, neither did she. She held my hand in hers, and we sat in a comfortable silence for a few minutes, listening to the birds trill outside and the chatter of children wafting up from downstairs.

THIRTEEN

HELENA

The silence was becoming uncomfortable, and I was very aware of my hand in his. Did he want me to hold his hand? Was this wrong? Should I have pulled it away by now?

I felt utterly foolish – I had come in here and acted like a doctor, as though he was one of my patients – and now I was holding his hand. What was I thinking?

The truth of it was that I hadn't been thinking. When I saw him there, lying in this bed, I had suddenly remembered how a week ago I had helped Joasia undress him, and now that was all I could see when I looked at him. I had seen male patients naked before, but this had been different. He didn't look like any patient I had ever seen, with a flat stomach, muscular thighs and arms. I had tried to tend to him swiftly, not looking at his underwear, which seemed to draw my eyes.

Even Joasia had noticed my awkwardness and had said, 'Not all men look like this, Helena, trust me!' Then she had laughed, and instead of breaking the tension, it had made me feel embarrassed.

So, when I had come to talk to him today, that was all I could see in my mind – him in his underwear, and all that skin, so I had tried to act professionally. But I had made him cry and now I sat holding his hand – what on *earth* was I thinking?

He didn't seem to mind me being with him, and now and then his fingers squeezed my skin gently, so gently that I thought I had imagined it. But it was there, I was sure of it and, oddly, I was happy about it.

'Helena!' Joasia marched into the room, her eyes on our hands clasped together and as if by magic we both let go of each other at the same time.

'Come, time for you to get up,' she told Max, barely looking at me.

'You can't move him just yet, Joasia,' I warned. 'He's been in and out of consciousness for a week and is injured. He needs to rest.'

She placed her hands on her hips and raised her eyebrows at me. 'Rest, indeed.'

'He does,' I repeated.

'Well, there's no time to rest – what is it Olek says – *no rest for the wicked?*'

'I – I'm not—' Max started, that stammer in his voice once more.

'Well, we'll decide that, shall we?' Joasia busied about, then pulled the blankets off his legs.

The left leg was a purple, blue and red kaleidoscope, although his right seemed fine next to this foreign one, and I watched as he wiggled the toes on each foot.

'They work.' He grinned at me, then upon seeing Joasia's sour face, he dropped his smile immediately.

'It's not broken,' Joasia told him, nodding to the left. 'Just badly bruised. And your head, well, I sorted that of course.'

He ran his fingers over the coarse stitches, checking Joasia's work, I was sure.

'Come on, up you get,' she demanded, holding out her arms

for him to take her hands and rise. 'You have to make it down-stairs somehow.'

I stood and helped, holding on to his waist as Joasia walked him towards the door.

'Keep going!' she shouted now. 'I've seen a one-legged chicken move faster. I've told you it's just bruised.'

'Joasia!' I chastised. 'He's trying his best.'

'*Is* he?'

'Why the rush?'

'Because we have a German airman in our house whilst air-raid sirens call out that more of his like are on their way!'

'So he's leaving?' I asked.

'We'll decide. All of us. That is, if we can get him downstairs.'

Max did not speak, and I could see that his jaw was set and tense, the little muscle underneath jumping as he walked. He was in pain, and talking was obviously too much for him.

Bit by bit, he made it across the landing and then inched his way down the stairs. Once at the bottom, Joasia guided him into the sitting room where Antoni, Filip and Olek sat.

'Sit, sit,' she instructed as if he were stupid, pointing at the rocking chair close to a cold fireplace.

I let go of him and watched as he shuffled his way across the room, the eyes of the audience on him. His face flamed with embarrassment, and I could see why – there he was, injured, wearing one of Joasia's old nightdresses, shuffling in front of people he did not know, waiting to be judged. It was humili-ating and sad and a sudden wave of empathy washed over me – I knew his story of his tata, I believed him, and all I could see was a broken man, one in deep grief and I wanted to protect him.

As soon as he made it to the chair, I went to him, wrapped a red and white woollen blanket around his legs, then pulled a seat close to him.

'Helena,' Antoni said, nodding at the empty space on the couch for me to sit on.

'I'm fine here,' I told him, then patted Max's hand.

'This is everyone,' Joasia said, finally settling herself next to Olek, who placed his meaty hand for the briefest of moments on her knee, then swiftly removed it as if forgetting himself.

There was a creak on the floorboards coming from the parlour, then a giggle – Michal and Agata.

'I told you two to go upstairs.' Joasia frowned at them, as their faces appeared in the doorway.

'We wanted to listen,' Michal said. 'We found him!' He pointed at Max.

'He doesn't belong to you,' Joasia retorted. 'Now go!'

Michal and Agata reluctantly left the room and climbed the stairs with such leisure that I knew they would reach halfway, and then perch themselves on a step to listen anyway.

'We've got a decision to make,' Joasia started, looking at each face in the room apart from Max's. 'He's awake, he can walk, he can talk. So, I've decided that first we hear him out – hear what he has to say, then we make our decision.'

I shifted in my seat, feeling as though we were in a court-room, deciding the fate of Max on the stand – but for what crime? *Should I speak up now on his behalf?* I wondered. His hand dropped off the armrest and I could feel his arm against me. I didn't move away.

'You may begin.' She waved her hand towards Max.

He looked at me, his eyes wide, reminding me of so many patients I had seen – the fear, the worry.

'It's all right,' I told him and managed a smile. 'They look scary, but they're not,' I joked.

He nodded, then relaxing as best he could, his green eyes scanned each one of us, finally resting on me once more, and he began to talk as if there were no one else in the room but us two.

'I am uncertain where I should begin, or what I should say.

But I'll start with first saying... thank you. I have already said my thanks to Joasia, but with you all sitting here, I assume that each one of you had a role in my being here, so, I thank you for that.'

His words were measured, educated and I knew Mother would love the way he spoke – polite and careful. She would say that he obviously came from a good family.

'I understand that you are wondering why I am here, or rather, why I was in your garden.' He nodded at Joasia. 'It's not a particularly easy thing to describe and the simplest thing is to say that I wanted to come home.'

'Home?' Olek asked. 'But you're German. This isn't your home.'

Max suddenly looked angry at this suggestion but took a deep breath and continued. 'My parents and I, we are all Polish. I was born and raised here, and we left for Germany when I was ten years old. At that time, none of us could have known what was going to happen – how quickly the tides would change.'

He continued to tell us of his life in Germany, how his mother had died, how his father had been in the Social Democratic Party and fought hard against the rise of Hitler, and had then become ill. How he had encouraged Max to stay in the air force and not to leave, persuading him that being in the 'belly of the beast', as he put it, would give him a greater opportunity to help others.

'He was, of course, mistaken,' Max said. 'My father had got this idea in his head from a friend who had seemingly joined the Nazi party, but under the guise that he was doing so to gain information – which he did. He rose in the ranks of the party and was able to let many neighbours know what was going to happen to them – how their businesses and homes would be attacked, how they should leave and never look back. But for me, my role afforded me no information I could pass on, no help I could offer to those who were suffering or perhaps going to suffer. But I had promised my father.'

'So what made you change your mind?' Joasia was leaning forward now, fully engrossed in his story.

'My father died,' Max said. 'That same night I was to fly reconnaissance over Poland, he died just as I was sorting my knapsack out before the flight. My friend and fellow pilot, Karl, came to give me the news that he had passed.'

Max suddenly stopped, fatigue making him pale and drawn and I was going to tell Joasia that we should stop – he was clearly still unwell. Suddenly, his hand sought mine, and I took it, giving him the comfort he needed to tell the rest of his tale. I ignored the looks from both Antoni and Joasia who seemed as though they were both going to demand I let go of him, giving them both a quick smile to reassure them that all was fine.

He started again, a little stammer here and there as he spoke. 'As I – I checked our route for the evening, I saw that it would take us over the Oder River, then low across small towns of Świebodzin and Nowy Tomyśl, then close to the city of Poznań before returning to base. We had not been on this route before, which was considered fairly innocuous as no one thought that the Poles would be watching the skies in these areas, which I supposed was the point.

'"Max," Karl's voice was behind me. I turned to him to tell him that the route was a strange one, but with clear skies ahead I would, in fact, be able to see much of Poland, and perhaps relay the image to Father when I saw him next.

'But Karl's face was taut, his eyebrows knotted together.

'"What's wrong?" I asked.

'"Your father. I'm so sorry, Max." He placed a hand on my shoulder, and I looked at it as though it were a foreign object and he quickly removed it.

'He told me more – the telephone call from Ingrid, how someone was going to fill in for me that night, and that I could go home and grieve.

'"No," I said. "I want to go. I want to do it for Father."

'Karl tried to talk me out of the flight, but a nugget of an idea was already forming in my mind, and as soon as he left me, I emptied out my knapsack, adding in only what I needed – the tin that held a small paper aeroplane I had first made with Father, some photographs that I had in my footlocker and a pistol. There was no need for anything else. I knew I had all I needed.

'When we had taxied off the runway, I took one last look at Germany, a place that held nothing for me any more. Then I focused my eyes on the skies in front, on the knowledge that we would soon be flying low over Poland, and that finally, finally, I could leave.'

Max stopped talking and leaned back in the rocking chair that began to swing back and forth with the shift in weight. No one spoke, each of us perhaps waiting for someone else to break the silence. As always, it was Joasia.

'So, you just decided to come home – and by coming home, you thought you'd defect by jumping out of an *aeroplane*?'

I saw a smile appear on Max's face. 'I admit it wasn't well thought through. I can't really describe to you how I felt – how knowing that my father was gone meant I was all alone now in the world, and there was this urge – this *need* to come home. It was stupid. A stupid idea and yet I don't regret it.'

'And what were you going to do when you got here?' Antoni was leaning forward now, and I saw that he still looked dishevelled – his face still spotted with stubble, his eyes bloodshot and tired. 'I mean you have to admit it all sounds a bit fantastical, doesn't it? Especially now we find ourselves at war. Maybe I should have said convenient – maybe it's all a little too *convenient* for me to believe.'

'You don't have to believe me,' Max's voice was strong, assertive. 'But you also have to realise that, for me, in that moment, I had no other choice. I had heard on the radio how Poles were being targeted; I could see what was happening around me – I wasn't blind to it, but I had to take care of my father – I couldn't leave.'

Another silence permeated the room whilst each person thought about what Max had said. I believed him – I had spoken to enough patients over the years who had tried to lie to get out of the hospital quicker and Max was not lying.

'He could be a spy,' Filip broke the quiet. But I could tell by his tone that he did not believe it himself.

'I'm not asking for anything from you,' Max reassured them. 'I'll leave as soon as I can. Tonight even.'

'But where would you go?' Joasia asked.

Max was stumped for an answer.

'I say he stays,' Olek declared. 'He's one of us. No one would jump out of a plane and risk their life like that. I say he stays.'

'I agree,' I said, and felt Max squeeze my hand.

Antoni was staring at Max holding my hand and did not hear Joasia when she asked him his opinion.

'Antoni!' she prompted him loudly.

As if waking from a dream, he finally looked away and shook his head gently. 'If he is telling the truth, he could be useful,' he admitted. His voice carried an air of defeat rather than enthusiasm.

'I'll help any way I can. I can—' Max leaned forward, but Antoni stood and held up his hand to silence him.

'Let's not get ahead of ourselves. Let me think. Get better – you can't help with your leg like that. I need to speak to a few people.'

'Resistance,' Olek said, nodding.

Antoni shot him a look.

'We're all talking about it – setting up a home army. You're not the only one who knows things, Antoni.' Olek was smug.

'I'll be in touch.' Antoni turned from us all and left quickly without saying a proper goodbye.

'I suppose you're staying then.' Joasia stood and motioned for Olek to do the same. 'Help him back upstairs, would you? I need a drink.'

Olek and I manhandled Max to his room, the pain once more etched on his face. I went to pull the blankets over him, but Olek ushered me out of the room and told me he would see to him.

The last thing I saw before Olek closed the door in my face was Max, lying in bed, smiling at me, and I felt a little flip of something in my stomach.

FOURTEEN

MAKSYMILIAN

Tuesday, 5 September 1939
Żerków, Poland

I had not seen Helena for almost two days. I knew she was still in the house, as I could hear her talking and laughing with the children, but she did not come into my room. Instead, Joasia busied about me, cleaning my wounds, making me get up and walk about, telling me to ignore the pain.

I did ask her where Helena was, and she told me she was 'busy', with a curt nod of the head.

Was it because I had held her hand? I wondered. Was she not allowed to see the 'dangerous' man upstairs? I hoped that wasn't the case and wanted to find the right words to explain to Joasia that although perhaps inappropriate, I was in pain, tired, scared, and Helena, I felt, was my only ally in that room.

But every time I tried to explain myself, Joasia would stop me mid-flow, and announce that I was being lazy, and needed to move more, try more.

I did as she told me. I was a little frightened of her, I admit, and would walk slowly up and down, up and down the tiny bedroom, the floorboards squeaking as I moved. I would grit my teeth and try to ignore the searing pain in my leg – oddly wanting Joasia to smile and say she was proud of me for doing better.

Hearing them all downstairs made me feel all at once lonely and almost part of a family. Lonely because I was shut away from it yet comforted by the noise of everyday life – the chatter, the laughter, the bangs and bumps that came with the twins tearing about the house.

The twins visited me often – almost every two hours and in such a short amount of time I had come to like them, and looked forward to the little knock on the door and their footsteps padding into my room.

Michal brought me newspapers and told me what he had heard on the radio, and I soon learned that bombing raids were occurring all over the country and troops were already nearing Poznań.

In the quieter moments, I would study the newspapers, reading how there was little hope that the Polish army could defeat the Germans. I knew, from my own experience, that it was probably true. Air-raid sirens echoed at least five times a day in the summer skies, the wail of them coming from far off in the distance, and now and then I would hear a plane flying low. I imagined Karl up there and realised that I was supposed to be by his side, watching the ground, giving instructions for where to go, where next to drop a bomb. And when I thought that way, it made me sweat with nerves and fear of what could have been.

The children seemed to find the air raids fun. They told me how Olek was building a shelter for them in the woods, right where their fort had sat and that soon, when the sirens wailed, they would be allowed to run out into the garden and into the bunker, taking with them food, toys and books. It was a game for them, I supposed, and when they talked of it, I made sure that I kept my voice light and in agreement that, yes, it was fun.

At 11 p.m., I hobbled around the room, trying to be quiet as possible, leaving only one candle lit on the bedside table that cast wobbly shadows of myself around the walls. As I turned from the door back to track my way to the bed, I heard a creak behind me.

Assuming it was Michal or Agata, I gave a little chuckle and told them to come in, but to be quiet.

'I'll try,' Helena's voice came as a whisper behind me.

I sat on the bed and looked at her. She held a candle under her face and came into the room, sitting on a chair next to the bed.

'I thought it was the twins,' I told her.

'They're fast asleep, so is Joasia. I wanted to come and see how you were.'

I suddenly felt happy, at ease and wanted to tell her I was glad to see her, but I couldn't.

'I'm doing well,' I said instead.

'I'm sorry about Sunday – you know, all those people in the room. It wasn't nice of them to do that to you.'

'It's fine. They had a right to.'

'Maybe.' She shrugged. She placed the candle down on the table next to the other, then began plumping my pillows. 'Lean back,' she instructed. Then she pulled the blankets over my legs.

'I – I...' Stammering, I tried to find the words to tell her I was sorry for taking her hand, that it was wrong of me, but she beat me to it.

'Joasia's a bit wary of you. The hand-holding did it, I think.' She laughed a little after she spoke, and there was a hint of nerves hidden in there.

'I'm sorry. I shouldn't have.'

'Yes, you should. I'm not sorry. Not one bit.' She found the chair and slumped back into it, seemingly exhausted and irritated all at once. 'You needed someone, and I was there for you. I am a doctor, you know. I take care of people.'

'I know you are. Agata told me.'

Suddenly, she shook her head quickly and looked at me wide-eyed. 'I'm sorry! Oh gosh, that was so rude, so pompous of me to say that. Please, I didn't mean it like that. I just get annoyed sometimes that Joasia and the others still treat me like a child.'

'It's because they love you,' I told her. 'My mother was the same, as was my father. They never stopped worrying about me, and I think that made them treat me like I was small again. My father told me on my twenty-sixth birthday that when he looked at me, he still saw me as a little boy, wearing shorts and a shirt, running barefoot around the garden, pretending to be a lion!'

She giggled, and I decided I liked the sound and would try and make her laugh more.

'Really – I mean I was twenty-six! But no. He saw me as a child. He couldn't help it.'

'That's how they see me – I mean not as a child pretending to be a lion! Just someone who needs to be protected somehow. Joasia told me not to come up and see you, you know. She said it was inappropriate. Which I thought was funny considering that she is not married and there's Olek—'

She suddenly stopped.

'I'm sorry,' she said again. 'I don't know why I'm saying these things. I don't know you and you don't know me. It is wrong.'

'So let us remedy that.' I turned onto my side so I could look at her properly. She returned my gaze and gave a little shake of the head, a little smile on her lips.

'How?' she asked.

'Tell me about yourself. Tell me why you became a doctor.'

'That's a long story, and I don't know if I have time to tell you. If Joasia finds me in here at this time of night, she will not be happy.'

'But I'm happy.' I grinned at her, and she gave a little laugh.

'All right, but if I get into trouble, I'm taking you with me!'
She raised her hands in the air in defeat.

'So tell me,' I prompted her. 'Tell me why you became a doctor.'

'All right. Well,' she began. 'When I was seven or eight, my father became the head of the hospital and decided upon sweeping reforms of how to treat patients, inviting the local newspaper, academics and other doctors to come to an afternoon tea on the grounds, to see his work.

Of course, as a child, I had no idea of what to expect, and yet was excited as I knew that children lived at the hospital, for whom my mother cared as a nurse, and thought of all the games that I might get to play in the large grounds.

Perhaps we would play hide and seek, perhaps they would have toys that I did not have, and we would sit whilst the adults talked and make-believe stories. But I was not prepared for what awaited me.

The children's wing was one of the first that was shown on the tour of the hospital. As Father opened the locked door, the scent of carbolic soap, cooked food and a sweet, sickly smell that I could not place greeted me. It made me want to turn around and leave, but I was swept along in the tide of adults that surrounded me, each talking about the large room we entered, each commenting on the cleanliness and the quiet. I realised that I had let go of my mother's hand, who was now by Father's side, introducing pale-faced children who sat rigidly on chairs, with smiling nurses by their sides.

I nudged my way forward to finally get a look at the other children and saw that they were not like the children I knew from school. Their eyes were wide and glassy; some stared at the floor, others at the wall even though there was nothing there. One small girl had bandaged hands and she rocked gently forward and backwards, as a nurse stroked her head as if she were a dog.

I felt terrified. As though before me was some sort of nightmare and this could not possibly be a place that my parents came to work each day. I wanted to run away, run back to the gardens outside, then find Father's car, climb in and drive myself back home.

My father was busy talking to the guests and I saw Mother walk over to one of the children who stared into nothingness. The child was one with no hair, just a small stubble like a baby bird and I could not tell if it was a boy or a girl. She knelt in front of the child and gently placed her hand under their chin and raised their head so that they had to look at her. I could see her mouth moving, but I could not hear what she was saying, then the child smiled, and Mother kissed the top of the child's head.

In that moment, a young boy, this one a bit different from the others as he was not dressed in a white hospital gown, but normal clothes, was led to my father by another nurse.

"This is Piotr," my father told the group. "He came to us almost one year ago and today, when you all leave, he will be going home, cured of his nightmares that plagued him since birth. He no longer sees things that are not there, and I believe that little by little, we can, no, we will, help many more like Piotr."

Piotr looked to my father with a grin on his face, and within a second, took his hand. My father took it back and the guests moved further forward to congratulate my father and Piotr.

It was then that I realised I was not scared any more. Instead, something had unfurled in my belly and made me pull at the buttons of my dress with such force that one popped free and rolled across the floor. I was jealous. Mother and Father never treated me like that. Every time I had wanted to take Father's hand, he had told me I was a big girl, and did not need him. Every time I had tried to hug or kiss Mother, she had patted my head absentmindedly, then turned to Father to discuss a patient she was concerned about.

They were my parents. My mother, my father, and I was furious with my parents and the children that were so easily able to win their affection. I walked to my father and took his other hand, then looked at Piotr as if to say – *he was mine*.

Father chuckled, then shook my hand free and then led the visitors away. I was left standing with Piotr, who looked as lost as I felt and I don't know why I did it – still now, I think about that moment and wonder if it shaped who I was to become – but I took his hand in mine, and the two of us stood there for some time, not speaking, just feeling the clammy warmth of each other's skin.

That evening, I was still angry with my parents and refused to eat and would not talk to them. I carried this game on to the next day, and the next, soon feeling quite delighted when both of them started to worry.

"You must eat, *maleńka*." My mother sat on the edge of my bed, a bowl of steaming *rosół* in her hands. *Maleńka*, my little one. She had not called me that in my entire life, at least not that I remembered, and because of it, I allowed her to spoon-feed me the chicken noodle soup, the noodles slipping from my mouth.

"You look like a baby bird, trying to eat a worm," she joked.

I smiled back and sucked the noodle into my mouth, and that was when I thought of the child with no hair that Mother had been so kind to, the one with the stubbled crown, just like a baby bird too.

I clamped my mouth shut once again and saw the worry in her eyes. "Tell me, *maleńka,* what is wrong? Are you sick? Has someone been cruel to you at school?"

It was then I started to cry confused tears. I was mad at my parents, I was glad of their affection, but I was not happy at the way it had happened. And a new uneasy feeling of guilt had appeared too – my parents took care of those children like that because they were sick. Because their parents were not there. Because they sat in that room with glassy eyes and bandaged hands. I knew then that my parents loved me, and although I would perhaps feel jealous at times, I could not be selfish. I was not sick; I had a home and parents.

My mother took me in her arms and rocked me until I stopped crying, and through choked sobs and a snotted nose, I told her, as best I could how I felt.

"Helena," she soothed. "The fact that you have understood why your father and I treat those children with such care, shows to me just how alike we are. You are a clever, intuitive child, and whilst perhaps you feel left out at times, you must know how much your father and I care for you. We love you with all our hearts and that will never change."

This was the most emotion my mother had ever shown to me, and from that day forward she always made sure to offer me words of comfort and advice – always checking how I felt, what I thought and would give me little hugs throughout the day to remind me that she loved me and I had no need to feel left out. And even now, when I think of Mother, I remember that she and Father love me, that I was their *maleńka*. Indeed, that speech did make me become more like Mother and even Father in every way. I went to the hospital as much as I could, I learned about the ailments that afflicted the patients, and was determined to show my parents that I would be just like them – I would care for others just as they did.'

She finished her tale, and her hands were on my bed, one next to the other. She stared at them. I placed mine on top of each of hers, and we sat there whilst a distant scream of a siren told us that more planes were flying overhead, neither of us moving, at last neither of us scared.

FIFTEEN

HELENA

Thursday, 7 September 1939
Żerków, Poland

Joasia was not happy. She had heard Max and me talking on Tuesday evening, and she made her displeasure known by giving me cross looks and thumping about the house, constantly tidying and rearranging.

'I think it's clean,' I told her, as she wiped the kitchen table down once more.

'I suppose there's no point any way – we're going to be bombed to bits, so why does anything matter!' she screeched, then turned and started to scrub at an already clean pot.

'Joasia.' I approached her calmly, like I would one of my patients. 'It won't come to that. No bombs have fallen here.'

'Not yet!'

I tried to place my hand on her arm, but she brushed me away crossly.

'And then there's you – and him!' She pointed at the ceiling.

'I was simply talking to him,' I repeated again what I had already told her, yet I knew there was something more – something that made me want to talk to him, to make him laugh, to just be near him. But I couldn't admit that to Joasia.

'*Ha*! Talking. I know what happens after talking.'

I sat down at the table and stared at the coffee in my cup as she bustled about. I liked talking to him too – about myself, about things that were nothing to do with what was happening outside these walls. Olek had come by, three times a day, Filip too, who had now moved into the inn after a few academic friends of his had been arrested and had simply disappeared.

There was much to fear outside. A lot, and each time anyone spoke about it, I tried to ignore it – going into my own head, thinking of Max, thinking of work, of anything but the reality that we all found ourselves in. I was glad that I had not been in Poznań to see the tanks roll down the streets; I was glad that I had not seen the soldiers with guns. By not seeing it, I could pretend that it hadn't happened, and oddly, I thought that my way of thinking was best for everyone.

Joasia was a whirlwind of fear and anger, the children noisier than ever, playing up to these strange times we found ourselves in. Olek was morose and cut his sentences shorter and shorter each time he spoke, and Filip had stopped talking about science. Instead, he barely uttered a word and had stopped pushing his glasses up his nose. It was good that I was not giving in to it – someone had to stay calm, someone had to be level-headed.

'Your father needs you back tomorrow.' Joasia sat across from me. 'I'm sorry,' she muttered. 'Really I am. I have been hard on you, but I just don't know what to think – what to feel.'

'I know,' I reached across the void of the table to take her hand in mine. 'It's all right.'

She wiped a stray tear from her eye. 'I'm a silly old woman, I suppose.'

'You're not. And I'll go to the hospital tomorrow and come back in a few days,' I reassured her.

She nodded, comforted by this, I think. 'The twins will drive me crazy,' she asserted.

'They will.' I laughed. 'But maybe that's what you need, some distraction.'

She nodded again. 'I wanted to go into town, but Olek said not to. He says that a few German soldiers have already been there, paid to stay for a few days whilst they are on leave!' She half laughed. 'Isn't that madness, Helena? They're making themselves comfortable already! Yesterday we fell to them – we are now under their control and within that time they're already filling the towns, making it seem all normal!'

'But isn't it better that they have come here and are not causing trouble,' I tried to soothe her concerns. 'Isn't it better that they're paying and just eating and drinking?'

'I just want to get out of this damned house—' she started.

'And you will. Soon. I'll talk to Father. We'll sort something out.'

She didn't answer – probably not believing me – and pushed herself up from the table. 'Your father is sending a driver. He'll be here at seven a.m. tomorrow.' She picked up a broom and began to sweep. 'So, you'd better say your goodbyes.' Her eyes lifting up for the briefest of seconds to the ceiling.

With her blessing, of sorts, I made my way to Max's room, chiding the children who were playing with marbles on the landing.

'You'll kill someone with those things. Move them and play in your room.'

Michal put out his tongue at me and Agata laughed. I should have shouted at them for their behaviour, but we were all out of sorts right now, and I doubted anything I said would be able to change that.

Max was standing at the window when I entered the room, and turned to look at me, offering me a wide grin.

'It's not night-time,' he joked.

'It seems I have a reprieve. Joasia told me to come and see you.'

'She did?' he asked, his eyes wide with surprise. He shuffled towards the bed and sat down and nodded at the chair for me to sit beside him.

'She did. She said I could say goodbye.'

'Goodbye?'

I nodded. 'I have to go back to work tomorrow. Father needs me. But I'll be back.'

'When?' he asked, a note of desperation in his voice.

'As soon as I can.'

'I... the twins will miss you.'

'They will,' I agreed, waiting to see if he would say he would miss me too.

'And Joasia.'

'She will.'

'My leg is getting better,' he said, instead of saying what I wanted him to.

'I noticed. You're moving much more easily already.'

He nodded and wouldn't catch my eye. The break in conversation was unnerving, and I could hear my heart thumping against my chest and wondered if he could hear it too. In the corridor, Agata and Michal argued about whose marble had travelled the furthest, and downstairs Joasia could be heard talking to Olek who must have arrived. *Should I leave?* I wondered.

'Mine went the furthest!' Agata screamed in the hallway, and Max gave a little laugh.

'What were you like as a child?' I suddenly asked him, desperate to fill the silence, desperate to get him talking again. 'I bet you weren't like those two!'

'It's a pretty sad picture if I'm honest.' He smiled at me.

'Well, that makes me want to know even more!'

'You like sad stories, do you?' he teased, and I could see he was warming up to the conversation now, the tension seemingly disappearing.

'Well, I hear them often enough from my patients. So I don't think it can be sadder than the tales I get from them.'

'Only if you're sure. I don't want you crying tears over me.' He grabbed my hand with a serious frown on his face, then he laughed.

I laughed along with him. 'Go on,' I told him. 'Tell,' and I did not let go of his hand.

'All right. Well, when I was a child, my father was my best friend. I wanted friends my own age, of course I did, but nature had not been kind to me in my youth and I soon found that my lack of athleticism, my small stutter that I had worked so hard with Mother to get rid of, and the extra weight I carried around my middle made me a target during my school years. So I never really had any friends. I was a sad little thing who looked to his father for company.'

'That is sad,' I said. 'But you did mention you had a friend – I remember you did say that—'

'Karl,' he finished for me. 'Yes, Karl was, *is*, my friend, I suppose. But I didn't really find him until I was in my second year in the air force.'

'What was he like?'

He shrugged. 'Karl was everything I was not. He came from a rich and influential family, he was tall and muscular, and chatted easily with those around him – especially women. I envied him and yet was entranced by him at the same time.

'When Karl first approached me in the mess hall and told me that I was to be his navigator that day, I was taken back to my awkward childish years and my tiny stutter made an appearance.

'Whether he noticed the stutter or not, he never said, and within a few minutes I had become easy and relaxed in his company and that very evening accompanied him to a bar.

'"Now Max," he told me as we ordered drinks. 'You just need a bit of confidence. Look at you – you're tall, and have those green eyes, I tell you, you say the right thing to a woman and she will melt like butter."

'I didn't believe him at first, but then over the coming months, I soon started to see myself as Karl did – I was intelligent and excellent at my job, I told witty jokes, I was tall and handsome – basically I was no longer the stuttering, fat child that I had still hung onto all these years.'

Suddenly, he stopped. 'I'm sorry,' he said. 'Why did I just tell you that?'

'Because that's how you see yourself – you are intelligent and good at your job.'

'Do I tell witty jokes?' He laughed.

'You do!'

'And am I handsome?' he quipped.

It was as if all the air had been sucked out of the room in that moment and both of us looked at each other with surprised expressions. I willed my brain to say something – a witty comeback, to agree with him – just something – but nothing came out of my mouth.

'Helena!' Agata ran into the room, then stopped dead in her tracks at the sight of us both. She crinkled up her nose. 'Ciotka wants you and Max to come downstairs. She says you have to come *now*.'

I stood and smoothed down my skirt and could feel Max looking at me. I held out my arm for him to take.

'It's all right. I think I can manage on my own,' he mumbled.

'Yes. Yes, of course you can.' I walked away from him and placed my hands on my cheeks, feeling the warmth underneath my fingertips and told myself to calm down and stop blushing before Joasia got a look at me.

.   .   .

In the sitting room we were greeted by Antoni who had finally shaved and seemed to be back to his business-like self. Although, he now wore plain trousers and a shirt, his suit seemingly banished and no longer needed.

He kissed me gently on the cheek and shook Max's hand – all very polite, all very strange.

Max sat directly opposite me on the other couch, free from the uncomfortable rocking chair that remained empty. I wished that he was sitting next to me, so that I could brush my arm against his, or perhaps our knees would knock together, then suddenly I was hot and red with embarrassment again – what if I had misjudged this? Did he feel something for me too?

'Helena?' Antoni elbowed me in the ribs gently to pull me out of my own mind as he got comfortable next to me.

I realised that they had been speaking about something – something which I had drifted away from. 'What?'

'Do you think it's a good idea?' Max asked gently.

'She wasn't listening,' Joasia observed.

'I was,' I insisted.

'Antoni suggested that I can help in some way – I can still do something. I can become a translator for the Germans,' Max filled me in.

I nodded along as if I had heard it already.

'The Gestapo in particular,' Antoni added. 'I'll be able to get you some new papers, Max, changing your surname to one which is German, and through Olek and those officers at his inn, we think we can get you a role with them. Offer to translate, to help their cause, and then, of course, you do the opposite – you give them false information and any information you do gain – round ups, movements, you pass on to me.'

Max nodded his agreement.

'Can you do it?' I asked. 'I mean, you'd have to pretend to be one of them – to agree with what they are doing.'

Max smiled. 'I've had a lot of practice doing that already.'

I had a funny feeling in my stomach. I didn't like the thought of Max leaving, I didn't want him to put himself in harm's way.

As if reading my mind, he turned to me and said, 'I'll be fine. Trust me. This is what I came home for.'

That night I sat on top of the covers in bed, a candle by my side and tried to read notes that I had made for my final certification exams. Not that they would happen now, and yet I acted as though they would – I wanted to remain in the past before everything had changed. I heard a gentle knock at the door as I re-read the same sentence over and over again.

'Come in,' I said, welcoming the distraction of perhaps Agata or Michal.

The door creaked open to reveal Max, dressed now in clothes given to him by Antoni. He walked to me, limping slightly.

He sat on a chair next to my bed, smiling at me with that way of his that made me feel excited and stupidly childish all at the same time.

'I have barely had a chance to talk to you since Antoni left,' he said. 'It's as though you're here but not here at the same time. Everyone is always talking over each other.'

'I've been wanting to speak to you too,' I told him. 'Your story, of your father and what happened.' I raised my arms in disbelief. 'It was brave of you. I don't think I've told you that. And it's brave of you to help Antoni. Really brave.'

He laughed and shook his head, and I could see the black stitches peeping out amongst his hair. 'Brave or stupid, you could say both, I think.'

I blushed.

'You're nervous,' he said. 'Why?'

His question, so direct, so unexpected, made me stutter and

bluster some response that I was fine. I was just busy, but both of us were aware of the unanswered question from earlier – did I think him handsome?

He gave a little laugh again.

Neither of us spoke for a moment; then he looked directly into my eyes, and once more, candidly asked, 'Tell me about yourself, Helena. I still know very little. And yet you know so much about me.'

In my nervous state, I told him more about the hospital, and then about taking care of the twins. He nodded as I spoke, seemingly interested, until I ran out of words.

'You're not married,' he simply stated.

I shook my head.

'Why not?'

'The hospital has been very busy,' I said. 'And I'll run it alongside my father someday.'

'So you have no room in your life for love?' he asked, his face so serious that I wasn't sure whether he was mocking me.

'There is, I suppose. I just haven't met anyone.'

'No one?' he asked.

'Not yet...' I replied slowly, my eyes never leaving his.

He shrugged and stood. 'I'll leave you to your studying,' he concluded, then turned and left the room.

As soon as he was gone, I was all wrong. My face was hot, my legs restless, my mind wondering what all that meant. I had wanted to tell him to stay, to talk more, and yet at the same time, I had wanted him to leave me alone. What was happening?

I stood and walked around the room for a moment, before flopping onto the bed, face first, and screamed into a pillow, so intense were the feelings I had that I couldn't put words to.

As I lay there, I thought back over the years, of how boys and men had shown interest in me, and I had rebuffed each one. My friend, Anna, had once set me up on a date with a man,

Wojciech, her then fiancé Rolf's best friend, and the four of us had gone to a picture show, followed by a meal.

Wojciech was tall, slim with a crop of unusual red hair. His eyes were lime-green and he barely spoke to me at the start of the meal. But once he and Rolf had had a few drinks, he would not be quiet and thought of himself as some great raconteur, although for me, the stories were told were boring – talk of sport, of how well he and Rolf had done at school, of how he was the best lawyer that ever was. Each story he told about himself highlighted his greatest achievements and added in a joke or two, keeping Anna and Rolf laughing along with him.

As we walked home, Anna peeled herself away from Rolf, and came to walk alongside me.

'He's wonderful, isn't he?' she had asked, her face aglow with Wojciech and his red hair.

'You should leave Rolf and marry him then,' I said, tired and annoyed with her that she would think I would enjoy the company of a man like that.

'Don't be silly, Helena. He likes *you*.'

'Does he?' I asked, surprised. All he had done was talk about himself – how did she know if he liked me?

'Of course he does! All he did tonight was try to impress you, and you barely gave him a smile in return.'

'That was for me? All that talk and nonsense?'

Anna laughed, making Rolf and Wojciech turn their heads to look at us as they walked in front.

Once she had calmed herself, she said, 'That's what they do, Helena. They strut about like peacocks so that we will be amazed by them. And it works, you know. I mean, when I met Rolf, he went to so much effort to try to get me to laugh at his jokes, or see how wonderful he was – and it worked. I saw him with all his achievements and saw how he would make a wonderful husband.'

'But it's not real,' I told Anna. 'It's all bluster.'

'Oh, Helena.' She linked her arm through mine and rested her head on my shoulder. 'What on earth will become of you?'

Now, lying on my bed, face down in a pile of pillows, I wanted to laugh. *This is what has become of me!*

I turned over and faced the ceiling. Max was not like Wojciech. He hadn't strutted and preened like a peacock. He was earnest when he spoke, he looked at me, willing me to join in and give him my thoughts. He asked me about myself. He told me, and others, with complete honesty about his family, his life and his worries. He was not afraid to share how broken he had been when his father died, he was not ashamed to show who he really was.

I liked him. Of course I did.

But, did he like me? I needed Anna now, more than ever, to tell me if Max felt the same way. But I had not spoken to Anna after that evening with her and Rolf and talk of Jews. Then I realised that seeking Anna's counsel on this was silly in itself – she liked the peacock men, she did what they told her, she believed what they believed in – she was not one to see the uniqueness in Max.

Instead, I would have to trust my own judgement, but I was so inexperienced, so naïve, I wasn't sure that I could.

OCTOBER 1939

SIXTEEN

PRIVATE JOURNALS OF DR M. RODZYNSKI

Sunday, 15 October 1939
Owińska Mental Hospital, Poznań, Poland

I need to begin by stating that as I write this, the hospital is no longer under my control.

Since mid-September the hospital has been overrun with soldiers, and is now under the authority of the Gau-Selbstver-waltung of Poznań. The new chief commissioner, whom I have met just once – a thin, wiry man who sniffed constantly as he spoke and yet never reached for a handkerchief. He demanded a list of all the patients and instructed me to take on no more, as technically, from his perspective, the hospital was now closed.

'They'll be taken to different hospitals,' he said, sniffed, then looked at the notes that he held, and I wondered whether he had scripted what he had to say. 'You will stay on, for now.' He sniffed again. 'Then we will discuss later.'

'Where will they go? Some cannot be transferred. Their families are close, and they would not do well with moving so far away from where they feel safe.'

He sniffed, checked his notes, then repeated, 'The patients

will be transferred, Doctor. Just give me the list of who is currently here, and we will make the necessary arrangements. This is no longer a concern of yours.' Sniff.

He left quickly, seemingly uninterested in the welfare of the patients and left behind a few uniformed men who stood guard at the front and rear exits as if we would all flock out of there.

There is, too, a constant growl of aeroplane engines flying low in the skies above me and some days I can hear the pop of gunfire, yet I never see where it comes from, nor who it is aimed at. It has rattled me, and has of course, affected my focus these past few weeks.

I worry for all my patients at the moment. They, too, can hear the engines; they can see the fear in the nurses' eyes, and they have been either unusually quiet or unusually loud and affected by their diseases. Each day in the hospital is now a new challenge, and Helena, whilst working hard, cannot quieten the likes of Małgorzata, or Basia, who scream, terrified at the sight of all these extra men and the only resort we have is to sedate them, yet we have had orders of late, not to use so much and I wonder why they want us to stockpile it, or perhaps, they know that no more medication is coming this way.

Both Helena and I now live at the hospital. We moved in prior to the arrival of our German occupiers, thinking that perhaps it offered more safety than being in the city, and departed our apartment with a few clothes and books, entrusting the rest to fate and now we have been told by the soldiers that we are not allowed to leave. Yet, we still hear the rumble of the tanks in the distance, the *pop pop* of gunfire that comes out of nowhere and disappears just as quickly. It is a reminder that we should not feel too safe – the war rages just outside and feels closer each day.

Helena arrived here on 8 September and neither of us thought that we would be barricaded in this long. She and I of course worry for the twins, for Joasia and we make attempts to telephone them or send a letter, a telegram as much as we can, sometimes receiving a reply, but more often than not, there is silence.

I can see the worry in her face, yet she never voices it to me – she works hard, too hard, and talks constantly of the patients, yet one night, I walked past her office and could hear her talking out loud about Max. I stood there for the briefest of moments as she wondered how he was, and, if he liked her too and then she gave a silly laugh and went silent.

Embarrassed at eavesdropping on her, I went back to my office in a hurry. She liked Max? When had this happened? She had barely been at Joasia's before coming here and staying here – could she fall in love so quickly?

It was then that I laughed to myself, and remembered the day I had met my wife at a dinner held by her father – also a doctor of psychiatry. It had been a moment, less than a minute I was sure of it, but I knew just from seeing her, her blonde hair piled high, her face open, smiling at something another guest had said, that I loved her.

It's a strange thing – love. It is an emotional response to something, a person, an animal even, yet it is one that lasts throughout time and does not diminish like our other emotions do. Perhaps I have been foolish in thinking that it would not happen for Helena, and perhaps I should be happy that it has. But, although he is working with Antoni, my reservations about Max remain. He was in the German air force, he lived in Berlin, and maybe one day soon, if this war ends, I will be able to get to know him for myself, and perhaps those reservations about him can be assuaged.

But for now, I am full of fear. Fear for Helena and her feelings for Max. Fear for the twins and my sister. Fear for my patients, for everyone. It consumes me and makes me want to vomit. It makes it hard for me to concentrate and even sleep. It makes me want to scream as loud as my patients.

I am not sure that fear is the only thing I feel, and I am not sure that there is a word that describes exactly this feeling – perhaps hopelessness is the closest. I cannot do anything. I cannot stop my patients from being taken, I cannot stop my home from having a new family or soldiers living in it, I cannot now even leave to go and see the twins. I am stuck here; a puppet being used to keep everyone entertained until something happens. I think, it is the *something* that scares me the most. The unknown. What will happen? Where will we go?

I have managed to get word to Joasia to tell her to get the papers together, passports and such things, to get as many of us to England as she can. Helena and the twins should have gone before all of this, and I will always blame myself for not insisting upon it.

And then, to compound of all of this, I cannot shake the concern I have over that one patient who has relapsed into their psychosis. You would think that at a time like this, that this should not perhaps worry and consume me as much as it does. And yet, because I have witnessed them talking to their hallucination, I cannot now in good conscience ignore it – I must do something, I must. I cannot let it progress to the way it was when they were first admitted.

I think back now to that time, when they came to me.

They were not scared; of that I remember clearly. Not like so many other patients who scream and tear at their hair and clothing, fearing what might lurk behind the walls and bars on the windows. Instead, the patient sat quietly on their bed, simply talking to someone who was not there. Their psychosis had come upon them after losing a loved one, and I had seen for myself what grief could do to a person. And, as I had said at the time, if the patient had been a small child, and not an almost adult, I would have perhaps let the imagined world continue for them – they simply had an imaginary friend, and it was their way of dealing with it.

Yet, this had gone on now for six months or more, and was beginning to frighten those around the patient. They had conversations with their invisible friend for hours at a time, laughing, arguing and ignoring the pleas of those around them when they tried to tell them that what they thought they saw, was simply not there.

I have to admit that I, too, was scared. After two weeks I had made little progress with them, and each time I tried to get them to talk about the trauma they had suffered, they would disappear inside themselves and then begin a new conversation with their imagined friend.

It was only when they began to engage with the other patients that I saw a change in them. They talked less and less to their hallucination, and more and more to the patients themselves; their curiosity of why they were there, who they were and their stories, began to overcome the desire to talk to someone who was not there.

After a month or so, I realised that their progress lay in their desire not only for knowledge, but for caring for others, and I saw all at once, that they felt the need to save others, and perhaps in doing so, assuaged some hidden guilt that they could not save their loved one.

Perhaps this is where I made an error in judgement. I let them care for others, I let them indulge in their saviour attitude, so glad I was that they were no longer talking to invisible people, I encouraged their new obsession. And when, finally the day came, that they returned to reality and could accept that their loved one had in fact died, they did not cry, they were not scared about what had happened to their mind. Instead, they had wanted to understand their illness more and had asked for material to read so that they could educate themselves.

They went a step further too, and began to discuss ways of

coping with grief, that even I had not thought of and were just as active as I in their diagnosis and subsequent recovery. Perhaps this obsession, this need to control, to understand and to save people had now triggered a relapse – the thought of war, of impending death, perhaps led them to believe that they could not save everyone, they were not in control of everything, and they turned inward once more, finding comfort in their lost loved one.

This is all conjecture. I must read more, learn more. I must get them to reveal something to me – to open up. But the planes – those damned planes, those uniforms, those reports of death already are clouding my mind, and my time seems to be continually spent wrapped up in trying to allay the fears of my patients before I collapse onto my makeshift bed and feel my own fears of what may be, of what may happen and the certainty that there is nothing I can do to stop the inevitable.

SEVENTEEN

HELENA

Thursday, 26 October 1939
Owińska Mental Hospital, Poznań, Poland

They came for Father first. For him and the male patients.

The day began like any other. I woke on my makeshift bed in my office, taking my time to rise. I wanted to take a moment to savour the dream I had just had, where Max and I were in a dance hall, him holding me close, the band playing some tune, whilst I span around in his arms.

I felt like a foolish child when I thought of him. Did he like me? How stupid did that sound? I wanted to talk to Mother about it, but I was too embarrassed to admit that finally I had some romantic notions towards a man, and I was acting like all those silly girls I had once heaped scorn upon. Turning onto my side, I saw how doubly foolish I was being – the hospital had been taken over, the streets in Poznań teeming with soldiers, Nazi flags hung from buildings, people disappearing, and yet here I was thinking lovesick thoughts about a man.

Chiding myself, I got up and stretched out my back that was becoming stiffer day by day, as the thin mattress I had found for my bed was lumpy and made me feel as though I were sleeping on rocks.

I dressed quickly and scraped my hair back into a rough bun at the nape of my neck, patting down the few strands that refused to comply.

Skipping breakfast, I went straight to my father's office to see what was to be done that day and whether perhaps there was any chance that we might be able to leave and visit the twins, and Joasia and Max. But as soon as I rounded the corner onto the corridor, I saw that something was wrong.

My father was in deep conversation with a soldier, a guard of some sort that I had never seen before. His black uniform marked him, and the others who stood behind him, as someone else, someone new.

'We are telling you that they would be relocated,' the man told Father. His Polish was laced with German, and he had made several mistakes with his tenses.

'Yes. I gave you the list, and I understand, but you also must understand that some of these patients cannot leave – they are too unwell.'

The man shrugged. 'Give them sleeping pill. We'll wait.'

Father was not going to give up without a fight, and I could see that he had drawn himself up to his full height and had inched his way forward as much he dared towards this man.

'I said they cannot—

Before Father could get any more words out, the man had struck him on the side of the head, so that he fell against the doorframe, his head making a sickening *thwack* as it connected with the wood.

The man did not seem interested in the fact that my father was now a crumpled heap, his hand against the side of his head, where blood trickled through his fingers. He turned to another guard, a man holding a gun and said something to him in German, the sound of it a *snip snip* as he spoke. The man with a gun screwed up his face in thought, and then said in Polish, 'Sedative.'

I ran to Father and knelt by his side.

'Go to the patients,' Father told me, his voice ragged. 'Do not be here right now, Helena.'

'I'm not leaving,' I said.

The man had noticed me now and pulled me up by my arm so roughly that I let out a yelp of pain as his fingers bruised into the soft parts of my upper arm.

'Get sedatives,' he said. 'You understand? Sedatives,' he said again, slower this time as if I were a patient.

I looked to Father who gave a nod.

'Just the mens,' the man said. 'Just mens.'

The fact that his Polish was so bad infuriated me. Here he was, a foreigner who had come to tell us what to do and yet he couldn't even be bothered to learn our language. It was in that moment that I realised we were nothing to them, nothing to the Germans who had marched in here. We were to be treated with as much disdain as possible.

I hurried off to collect the sedatives that would be needed, a hundred of them – and took them to the male wing, where one by one, a female nurse and I administered a dose that would keep each patient calm.

My last patient was Piotr. The same person I had met when I was eight and he was supposedly cured. Now, he was my age, and had come back here countless times as his condition had worsened – the obscenities he screamed turning into hallucinations and psychosis.

'Helena.' He grinned at me, happy that I had come to visit him. He wasn't supposed to call me by my Christian name, but I had always allowed it with him – in a way he had been my first friend.

'You have to take this.' I gave him the tablet and he took it quickly and without complaint.

'What's happening, Helena?'

I shook my head, trying to think of something to say that would comfort him, but nothing was forthcoming.

'It's bad, isn't it?' he asked.

'No. No, all will be well.' I placed a smile on my face and stood to leave. Piotr quickly reached out and took my hand, just as I had taken his, years before. 'Goodbye, Helena,' he said, smiling that lopsided grin of his.

I could feel the tears coming, my chest tightening and my eyes burning, so I did not say goodbye to him. Instead, I left him and the others and went back in search of Father.

He was where I had left him, only now, he was standing in his office doorway, leaning against it to hold himself up.

'Twenty-five,' the man in the black uniform said. 'Twenty-five each bus.' He pointed towards the window where I could see buses ready and waiting, their engines running.

Father managed to get himself together, and we both slowly but surely got each male patient into a bus. As the last one stepped inside, Father stood back by my side. 'You too,' the man said.

'Me?' I asked him.

'*Nein. You.*' He pointed at Father.

I held on to Father's arm, but he was already nearing the bus.

'Where are you going?' I half screamed. 'Why are you doing this?'

The man was smoking a thin cigarette now and did not care to answer me. Instead, Father turned. 'I'll be back,' he told me. 'I just have to go with them because I have to care for them until they are settled in their new hospitals. Don't worry, Helena. I'll come back very soon.'

Before I could say goodbye, before I could kiss him, or hug him, the doors to the buses were closed and I watched as Father took a seat next to the window at the front, not looking back at me, keeping his eyes focused straight ahead as the buses one by one disappeared down the driveway.

Inside, Zosia stood in the doorway with three nurses, her hands clenched, clasped, her eyes wide. 'Where are they going?' she asked.

'Father will be back soon,' I said, trying to keep my voice steady and calm. 'They're just going to new hospitals. He'll be back very soon.'

I could not stay long and talk more with them. I could not give them instructions about what to do. I could not bring them comfort. I needed Mother and went in search of her, hoping that although Father, her husband was gone, she would still be able to tell me what to do and hold me tight, letting me be a child in her arms.

EIGHTEEN

MAKSYMILIAN

Saturday, 28 October 1939
Żerków, Poland

Before the sun had properly risen, I sat at the kitchen table, Joasia with me, both of us drinking our coffee in silence. Poland had not only fallen but was a shell of itself. According to Antoni, the government was now in exile in England, Jews were being rounded up, shops closed, people shot, people simply disappearing. We heard it every day, yet I had not seen it with my own eyes. Here, at Joasia's, so far, we were relatively safe. Although the town was teeming with soldiers, they had little interest in us, or others – to them, we were Polish peasants, there to attend to their every whim. But it would not last; it could not.

As we both sat, lost in our own confused thoughts, the door swung open to reveal Olek and Antoni, both of them shouting for Joasia. Seeing us at the kitchen table, they hurried towards us.

'He's gone,' Antoni wheezed. 'We ran here,' he said by way of explanation.

'Who's gone?' Joasia had raised her head now.

'Michal.'

'He's upstairs,' and she looked upwards.

'No. No. Your *brother*, Michal. He and the male patients are the hospital are gone,' Olek said, placing a beefy hand on her shoulder.

'Helena managed to telephone. She had to be quick as they're watching her every move. She said she tried to telephone here, but there is no connection,' Olek continued.

'They've cut most of the lines,' Antoni explained. 'Thankfully, Olek's is still working.'

'Where have they gone?' I asked.

'That, we don't know, *yet*,' Antoni explained. 'Helena told Olek that they were being transferred, but as far as I have heard, the buses went towards Poznań, and that's all we know.'

'When, when was this?' Joasia stood, placing her palms flat on the table, directly challenging Antoni as if the whole thing were his fault.

'Two days ago.'

'And no one has heard a thing?' Joasia exclaimed. 'I don't believe it. My brother wouldn't simply disappear without getting in touch!'

'But maybe he can't,' Olek said calmly. 'It's only been two days. We may get a letter, a telephone call from him – but we need to wait, be patient.'

'You can take a shit on your patience,' Joasia spat. 'Antoni. Do something! What can we do?'

For a moment, Antoni shook his head, and then he realised something.

'Max,' he said. 'It has to be Max.'

Three faces turned to look at me.

'My papers are here?' I asked.

'No. Not yet. But it's a risk you're going to have to take. Come back to the inn tonight with me and Olek. You can start now. Talk to those officers, those soldiers. Get drunk with them, make them laugh, offer to help. See what you can find out. It has to be you, Max. You're ready.'

It was what I had been waiting for, wasn't it? To step up, to help, fight back. And yet, there was a twist of something in my stomach – fear?

'I'm ready,' I said. And only I noticed it.

A trace of a stutter as I spoke. A trace, nothing more, but it was there.

The rest of the day was a blur of rushed conversations with Antoni and packing to get to the inn.

'Befriend them,' Antoni suggested. 'They need translators, and have asked other locals to help. But do not register with them – do not go back inside officially as you'll be found out, of that I am certain. Keep it as though you are doing them a favour.'

I agreed to everything he said, noting that my new name was to be Maksymilian Wagner. I was a proper half-breed of Polish and German and would show the officers that I was on their side, not these Polish peasants.

As I packed, a jiggle of nerves made themselves a home in my stomach, making me feel sick. I sat on the edge of the bed and for a moment rested my head in my hands, thinking of the enormity of what was happening. Not only was Helena locked away in the hospital, which had worried us all, but now her father was gone. At least, one thing had kept me from worrying too much – her father was there, he would take care of her.

I had not spoken to her since the night she had left, when I had made a fool of myself. Now, I felt a wave of embarrassment and regret. I should have told her properly about my feelings for her, I should have asked her for a walk in the garden and made it plain that I wanted to see her more formally.

But that night, that last night, I had chosen to have a vodka or two with Olek before he returned to the inn, giving me a misplaced sense of confidence. As soon as he had left, I had sought out Helena, realising she was in her room, a sliver of candlelight apparent under the door.

I knocked gently, and she invited me in. At the time, I had not thought of the impropriety of the whole thing – it was only the next morning when I woke with a thumping head and furry tongue that I was doused with shame. How could I go into her room? How could I ask her about love?

Thankfully, she left to go to the hospital, and for a moment I was relieved, which was short-lived, and by the evening, I found I was missing her and have missed her every day since.

Would she be all right in the hospital? Where was her father? What could I find out? Could I get to her – to the hospital and bring her home? The questions swirled around in my brain so that I got up and started packing again. *Action, keep moving, don't think too much.*

'Max, can we play pirates again?' Agata's voice sang out.

I turned to see her standing in the doorway. 'You can hobble like you have a fake leg again and I will help you find treasure.'

'I can't,' I told her. 'I have to go with Olek and Antoni.'

'Where?'

'To Olek's inn.'

'Can I come?'

'No sweetheart, you can't.'

I could see that she was on the verge of tears, her hands pulling on the hem of her dress, her feet shifting from side to side as she bit on her bottom lip.

'But what will happen if you go? Michal says we can't go back to school in the city, because we'll be shot by the Germans. Is that true, Max? Will we be shot? Will they come here and shoot us? Who will stop them if you go?' She gave in to the tears now, letting them take over, screwing up her face and making her cheeks redden.

I crouched down to her level and took her in my arms. 'Nothing will happen to you. I promise... I promise,' I told her again. 'I won't let a thing happen to you.'

'And Helena?'

'And Helena. I won't let anything happen to any of you.'

I let her cry into my shoulder, feeling her small body shudder with all the emotions of fear, of missing her father and sister, of not knowing what was happening.

I wished I could cry too.

NOVEMBER 1939

NINETEEN

MAKSYMILIAN

**Wednesday, 1 November 1939
Żerków, Poland**

I had been in the town of Żerków for a few days, staying with Olek and Filip above the inn, all three of us sharing a bedroom. I had wanted to stay with Joasia and the twins in the evenings, but Olek had insisted that I should not. He clearly did not want me to put them in any danger and I didn't want to bring harm to their front door.

Yet, I missed the twins. I had enjoyed their company each day; Agata's incessant chatter, playing cards with Michal, noticing how he kept so much to himself – so unlike his sister – so that sometimes trying to get him to have a conversation was like pulling teeth. But his company, and that of Agata and even Joasia had brought me joy. They had taken me in, trusted me, and treated me as one of the family, and it was only now that I was away from them that I realised the warmth of simply eating and chatting with others at a kitchen table, or someone wishing me a good morning, or asking how I was.

Instead, I was stuck in one bedroom with Olek who passed

wind in his sleep, and Filip who would sleep soundly, then all of a sudden, scream some nonsense, waking me, then settle back down.

During the day, I had seen that Olek had not been honest about the situation in the town. Things had changed – not just soldiers enjoying themselves on leave, but every Jewish person had been rounded up and taken, and some who had resisted had been shot in the street; in broad daylight as people shopped and went about their business, a whole family had been gunned down, their bodies thrown into the back of a truck, leaving a stain of red on the pavement.

When pressed, Olek and Filip would say no more on the matter. They had witnessed the shootings and had no desire to add any more description than was absolutely necessary.

There was little to do in the town, so Jewish homes had been requisitioned for those soldiers enjoying some respite, and I could not bear to think of them sat on someone else's sofa, sleeping in their beds, enjoying their homes whilst the residents were either dead or had disappeared.

I did not venture far in the day, and stayed close to the inn, under the assumption that I was Olek's distant cousin from Germany, there to help out with the many guests that now flocked to the town.

'Max, another beer,' one SS Hauptmann demanded. His name was Leo Wagner, the same surname as the one I had adopted, and it had seemed to make us instant friends.

'You know, I was thinking, Max,' he belched out my name. 'We might be related. Somewhere along the line, you know, we're probably kin.'

His face was ruddy from drink, and he seemed to enjoy Olek's cellar that was beginning to run dry, yet Leo had said that he would be able to procure anything Olek needed, as long as he got first taste.

As I placed the glass in front of him, I saw that the whites of his eyes were now red, the blue-grey irises flickering, unable to stay still. I knew it would not be long before he fell off the stool, as he had done the previous night, and would have to be half carried back to the house on the corner he had all to himself, that used to house a family of four.

I wondered as he drank whether the house he was in was the one that had belonged to the family that had been killed, and I wondered, too, whether it had been by his hand.

'So, what do you think?' he slurred. 'Cousins... twice removed?'

He did not wait for my answer, but then he very rarely asked me anything, preferring to talk about himself. 'What does that even mean? Twice removed?' He sloshed his beer glass on the bar, and I wiped away the drops. 'Does it mean that we were removed by marriage? Well, we must have been, mustn't we? I mean, you're half Polish. But that doesn't matter, because you speak German, you are German, you want to help. You're a good man, Max.'

Suddenly, he leaned forward, his arms wide to take me in a clumsy embrace, then he sat back again. 'A good man. You know it's so pleasant to speak to you in our language. These people,' he waved his arm around the bar, 'they don't. And it's so irritating that I have to talk to them in their language, you know. So irritating.'

'You need a translator,' I said. But then I had said this the night before too, and he never remembered, never picked up on the hint that it could be me – that I could help him.

'I know, I know. I have one young man who speaks it, but he's not with me all the time. And now I've been transferred to the Fort, well, he won't be coming there. I don't know why. I suppose they think we don't need a translator there.'

'The Fort?' My ears pricked up. This was new. What was the Fort?

'*Ja, ja*. Fort Seven. This cold, ugly thing, all built underground. Been there for years – hundreds of them, maybe thousands – I don't know. Anyway, that's where I am now and it's not hard work, not really, but it's tiring, you know? And it's not fair, really it isn't. I mean, Lange, he's in charge, but he's never there and they leave it to me. I mean, I have done a good job with getting people there. That is true. And they said it was a promotion. But it doesn't always feel like one, you know, especially when Lange isn't there and it's just me.'

I nodded along sympathetically; the words slippery on my tongue – what work? What was tiring? What was happening in this underground place? But I did not let the words escape and just let him ramble on.

He soon turned to a comrade of his, and both of them enjoyed a shot of vodka – a cheap, homemade brew that I was sure would soon see the pair of them on the floor, but if anything, it gave Leo more energy, and he directed it at me.

'I saw this woman the other day,' he began, reminding me of Karl and his women. 'She was in this place, and we had to take people from there. And she was pretty, you know. But I wasn't sure whether she was, you know, *one of them...*'

Again, I nodded along, polishing a glass as he spoke. *One of them. A Jew.*

'I mean you should have seen them – drooling they were! Drooling!' He laughed. 'She wasn't one of them. I know that now. She worked there. But still. You never know, do you?'

I agreed, that no, you never did.

'But I'll see her again – just a matter of time – next week I think.' He nodded at me and then let out a belch that I was sure was going to produce vomit.

'Time to go... Bed.' He climbed off his bar stool and steadied himself with one hand on the bar, weaving himself away, and out the door, into the night and into someone else's bed.

It was only after he left that I thought of what he had said –

drooling? Who was drooling and why? That was such a strange thing to say that I wondered if I had misheard him.

I shook off the comment and concentrated on another customer who was not quite as drunk as Leo, and perhaps someone who might be able to give me the answers I needed as to where Helena's father had gone.

TWENTY

HELENA

Tuesday, 14 November 1939
Owińska Mental Hospital, Poznań, Poland

After Father had disappeared, the women were left at the hospital to care for the rest of the women and children. For days, the staff talked in hushed conversations, each one of them wondering where the men had been taken to.

I didn't dare express what I had heard from the gardener, who had managed to get word to Zosia that he had seen graves in the woods. Piles of dirt, not there one day, and the next, there they were. There was one way to find out, of course, and that was to walk into the darkened woods and search for piles of freshly dug earth. But it wasn't something I could do. I was stuck at the hospital now and was prevented from leaving, even to visit Joasia and the children, by soldiers with shining guns, and equally shining boots.

The soldiers did not seem to care where they were, or what was going on around them. Each of them seemed bored by the whole exercise of manning the exits and entrances, and I found a few of them asleep at their posts. It would have been an opportune moment to escape, perhaps, and the thought did flit through my mind from time to time. Yet, I could not leave Mother, the staff and the patients with these men. I had to stay, to try and protect them.

Małgorzata was hardest to deal with during these days. She could not understand why there were so many men about, and as the soldiers saw her distress each time she saw them, they would taunt her, try and lift up her nightgown and laugh at her. This, of course, made her terror worse, and she had to be restrained on multiple occasions, with tears streaming down her face, and there was nothing I could say to give her comfort.

I had not heard from Olek, from Max, from Joasia or anyone else. I was no longer allowed a telephone, and my every movement seemed to be monitored, so much so, that I was afraid that at some point a guard would stand over me and watch as I slept.

I tried not to think of my family – it was too much to bear. The thought of them, worrying about me, worrying about Father, made me want to scream with helplessness so I tried to shut my mind off from them. But now and again, snippets of each of them would filter through and take me by surprise. Now and again, Max's face would appear to me with his cheeky grin, and I would be taken back to that last evening together when he talked to me about love and I wished I go could back in time and tell him that I liked him, that I thought that maybe I was falling in love with him. Even if I wasn't sure, I should have said it as now, I wondered if I would ever get the chance to say anything to him ever again.

The buses returned on a Tuesday afternoon. I sat in the common room, Mother talking to Basia as she knitted the endless baby clothes, Hanna sitting close to the gramophone that had been switched off, yet she still heard the imaginary music and sang along.

'Hush,' I told her, more than once, fearful that the guards

would become irritated by her and seek some sort of sport with her.

As we all sat, I heard the pitter-patter of feet and turned around to see Agata and Michal running to me.

'What on earth are you doing here?' I asked, my eyes searching for Joasia who did not appear.

'We've been here for hours,' Agata said. 'Joasia brought us early and got us to the kitchens. She said she had to go into the city for something important.'

'Papers,' Michal whispered in my ear. 'We are to go to England, and she said we wouldn't be safe in the city.'

Before Michal could say any more, I heard the crunch of tyres on the driveway and went to the window to see those same buses appear that had arrived for Father and the male patients.

Suddenly, I was sweating and yet at the same time, a coldness came over me and there was a buzzing in my ears.

I felt Mother at my side, but she did not speak and I willed her to give some words of comfort, though none were forthcoming.

A soldier came into the room, the same one that had taken Father. He looked me up and down, and smiled. 'Twenty-five,' he said, as he had before. 'Get them to line up. Twenty-five at a time.'

'Where are they going?' I asked, my voice barely above a whisper.

He did not answer, his eyes now had shifted and were trained on the twins.

'I asked, where are they going?' I tried to inject as much authority into my voice as I could.

'You too,' he said by way of response, his eyes not moving from the twins. 'And the staff. Twenty-five at a time.'

His Polish was a little better than before, but for some reason I could tell that he had rehearsed what he had to say, and nothing else would be said.

I watched as he bent down to Agata and Michal, and produced a sweet from his pocket. He handed it to them, and I wanted to run over and stop them from taking it, but I was rooted to the spot.

'Take, take,' he said.

They took the sweet slowly and held it in their hands, staring at it.

He stood now and turned to another soldier, snapping in German. The second soldier then turned to me and said, his Polish a little better than the other man's: 'Patients?'

'No. My brother and sister,' I told him.

He relayed this information, then asked, 'Twins?'

I nodded.

This seemed to please his boss, who grinned at me, and I could see that his blue-grey eyes were bloodshot.

'Good. Good,' he said, then let out a little laugh.

Agata and Michal looked to me, confusion etched on their faces – what was this? Who was this?

The blue-grey-eyed man laughed some more, then clapped his black leather-gloved hands and bent down once more to them, pinching their cheeks, making them red and sore.

Suddenly, more soldiers had appeared, all of them dressed in black, and began to get the patients in file. First, they took the children, giving them a sweet, one by one, the shadow of my mother leading the way to the front door.

Michal and Agata were left with me, and I was ordered to give some sedatives to the rest of the patients. But as I did so, I realised we did not have enough, and by the time I reached Małgorzata and Hanna, I had none left.

I pretended instead to give them something and told them both to swallow; not that the soldiers noticed at this point. They had become bored once more, and leaned against the walls and smoked, whilst the first buses left and we had to wait for some more to arrive.

I looked about for Zosia and could not see her. Was she in the kitchens? Could I get the twins downstairs to her? I wondered.

'Excuse me,' I said, walking to the man with the blue-grey eyes. 'Would it be all right for the children to get some food? Just downstairs. They'll come back.'

He did not understand, and the soldier whose Polish was a little better did not properly understand either. It ended up that I had to act out what I meant, noting the ridiculousness of the situation.

Eventually, the blue-grey-eyed man made his decision. '*Nein.*'

No.

I sat back down and gathered Agata and Michal to me, trying not to think past this moment, trying not to think of the buses that would soon arrive to take us away, trying not to think of the graves in the woods that the gardener had spoken about.

After maybe an hour or so, more buses arrived and I led the sedated patients towards them – all of them sleepy, with dream-like smiles on their faces. Only Hanna and Małgorzata were fully aware and both of them held tightly onto my arms as we walked.

'There are... *men*,' Małgorzata whispered, suddenly stop-ping only a few steps away from the bus.

Under her breath, Hanna began to hum a tune, no doubt to calm herself, when one of the guards stepped forward and dragged her onto the bus.

Next, he went for Małgorzata, who began to scream at such a pitch that one of the soldiers actually placed his hands over his ears.

I could see the blue-grey-eyed man reaching for his rubber truncheon on his belt, and I held Małgorzata to me, letting her sob and wail onto my shoulder.

'It's all right, it's all right,' I told her, and soon she relaxed into me, and the blue-grey-eyed man let his hands drop to his sides, then gave me a strange smile.

Behind me, Agata and Michal stood, each of them holding onto my coat.

'*Schnell, schnell!*' a guard yelled, moving forward to take my arm and make me step forward to the bus.

I wanted to scream. I wanted to yell and demand to know where we were going, but I knew if I did, I was putting myself, the twins and especially Małgorzata in danger – the soldiers' fingers itched to get to the guns and batons that hung from their belts, and I did not want to give them a reason to use them.

Slowly, I managed to shuffle forward, getting Małgorzata to let go of me and to sit on the bus, then I stepped on, followed by the twins.

Before we even sat down, the driver started to edge down the driveway, so that I didn't even have chance to sit and look out of the window at the hospital and the few staff who were being lined up to get onto the last bus. I wanted to see if Zosia was there, I wanted to take a look at the hospital, just in case it was going to be my last.

I sat beside Michal and Agata, Hanna and Małgorzata on the seat in front of me. Hanna was still humming a tune, and the guard who sat behind the driver kept turning his head and looking at her, irritation marking his face.

'It calms her,' I said, bolder now that the blue-grey-eyed man was not here. I had seen him get into a black car as I had boarded the bus, and I hoped that would be the last I ever saw of him.

I began to hum along with Hanna, and placed my hand on Małgorzata's shoulder so she knew I was there. Neither of them looked out of the window and both sat rigid in their seats, whereas the others seemed happy, almost relaxed from the sedatives and I wished I had had enough for these two too.

'Where are we going?' Agata whispered.

I saw that she and Michal were holding hands, their fingers entwined, their knuckles white with the force of their grip.

'I don't know.' My mouth was dry, my stomach twisted in knots. I didn't want to even try and think about a possible answer to their question as the only image that came to mind was the fresh graves that Zosia had told me about.

I took my hand off Małgorzata's shoulder and wrapped it around the twins, drawing them close to me.

'I'm sorry,' I told them.

'We're all right,' Michal said, but he would not look at me when he said it, and kept his eyes trained on the windscreen.

'I should have hidden you, I should have done something,' I said, more to myself than them.

Agata leaned her head against my arm. 'Keep singing, Helena. Keep singing with Hanna. We'll be all right. Max said so. He said he wouldn't let anything bad happen to us. So keep singing, Helena.'

I did as my ten-year-old sister told me, and sang along with Hanna, now and then other patients joining in. It was ridiculous, given the circumstances, but there was a comfort in it – all we had to do at that moment was to sit on a bus, travelling to God knew where, and sing little songs, keeping our hope alive.

Soon, Michal piped up; 'Poznań,' he said, pointing towards the road in front of us. And of course he was right – we were heading home, heading towards the streets we had grown up on, to our apartment, past the children's school, past the green-domed cathedral, and then past the botanical gardens, turning onto a road I had never been down before.

'Alek lives here.' Michal pointed left where a few houses were hidden by a line of trees. 'Maybe we are going to live there?'

I hoped that would be the case – were we just going to be rehoused in a suburb of the city, perhaps where Michal's friend, Alek, lived?

Then the bus slowed. It did not turn left in the direction of the houses, but right, down a rutted, potholed track, thick trees on either side, soon stopping outside of sturdy iron gates that were opened by more men dressed in black.

Once inside the gates, the driver applied the brakes and switched off the engine. In front of me I could see a walkway that led to a cavernous doorway. Red bricks outlined a building of sorts, and atop was a mound of grass, almost hiding the building away altogether.

'It's the Fort,' Michal said. I saw then that he was right. It was Fort VII, one of the many sunken defence forts that had been built around the city a hundred or so more years before. I had a vague recollection of learning about them in school, and had visited one before – but not this one – not this one that had a moat surrounding it with only one way in, surrounded by men dressed in black uniforms, with shining silver buttons.

What were we doing here? Surely, we weren't going inside it?

Someone ordered us to stand and I tried, but my knees would not work properly. I sat, seeing my legs shake and knock against one another. Then I tried to stand again, this time managing to find some strength. I let Agata and Michal walk in front of me as we disembarked and kept my hands on their shoulders, seeing that my hands were shaking too. All at once I was cold and felt sick. I wanted to shout or scream or run, but I couldn't. My mind wasn't working, my body following its lead and becoming useless.

'It's all right, it's all right,' I told the twins over and over again.

We were led off the bus and ordered to line up. I kept Agata and Michal's hands in mine and followed the others as we were led over the concrete walkway, into the gloomy, sunken unknown.

As soon as we were inside, I could feel the dampness

coming off the walls and attaching itself to my skin. The smell of mould assaulted my nostrils, and the stale air was cold, and had a taste to it that caught at the back of my throat.

'Helena, Helena,' Agata was crying now, so I picked her up, letting her wrap her legs around my waist, taking some of her weight. Michal held onto my coat and did not speak; perhaps he could not – I certainly seemed to have lost my voice.

In front of me I could see Małgorzata and Hanna, who were now holding hands too, shuffling forward, both still humming the tune that Hanna had picked up on once more.

The tune that Hanna sang ricocheted off the curved, low ceilings, and as we walked, it seemed that the walls were closing in on us, as we went deeper and deeper into the blackness.

Soon we stopped outside a metal door and each person was led inside, one by one. I could see that the room was small, too small for all of us, and I wondered if Mother and the other patients were here too.

As Agata, Michal and I reached the entrance, Małgorzata suddenly turned to me, hugged me, and whispered, 'Run', into my ear. Then, before anyone knew what was happening, she began to fight the guards with a strength that I had never witnessed in a woman, nor a man, before.

The guards, one by one, piled upon her, hitting her with fists, with batons, but nothing was stopping her. She fought back, bit them, kicked, screamed with such ferocity that the whole fort echoed with the sound.

I had hesitated when she had told me to run, but now I saw my chance. The guards were dealing with her, and the three of us had been left somewhat unattended. I placed Agata on the ground, took their hands in mine, and began to run down the labyrinth of darkened, damp corridors, searching for some light, some way to know which way the outside world lay.

Just as we reached the light – that ball of freedom that announced itself with such joy – a shadow appeared in the doorway, and I stopped dead. It was the man with the blue-grey eyes.

'Going home?' he asked.

'I—'

'It is all right,' he said, slowly, measuring his words out so that I could understand him. He held his hands up in submission to show me not to be scared.

As he reached us, he stroked the side of my face and smiled. '*Die schöne*,' he said. 'Pretty,' he then said in Polish.

'*Und die zwillinge.*' He bent down to the twins. 'Very good. Twins.'

I did not like the way he had looked at me, I did not like his interest in the twins, but he led me away from the room where the patients had been taken, and took us down another corridor, this one a little lighter, with cells and doors opening off onto each side.

He stopped outside one door, and with the hoop of keys on his belt, found the right key, fitted it into the lock and swung the door open with a heavy squeak and creak. Before I entered, a scream, then a howl boomed towards us, and I looked about to see where it was coming from. It was pain. Someone, somewhere in this place was in pain.

'Please, please,' he said, nodding at the open door.

We stepped inside, us three, to reveal a room no bigger than my office. Strewn on the floor was straw and in the corner, two women were huddled, seemingly asleep.

As I took in the sight in front of me, I heard the door squeal shut behind us, leaving us in the dark, with only a small, barred window, up high, letting in a sliver of light.

TWENTY-ONE

MAKSYMILIAN

Tuesday, 14 November 1939
Żerków, Poland

Filip was gone. He had been gone now for eight days.

I had awoken on the morning of his disappearance, noting the lack of other bodies in the room. Had I overslept? I stood and opened a curtain, seeing that the weak autumnal light had yet to brighten the sky. It was early – 6 a.m. So, where were Olek and Filip?

I dressed quickly and made my way down the stairs, trying to be as quiet as possible, and not to wake the sleeping Germans in the other rooms.

I found Olek in the bar, smoking his pipe, a tumbler of whisky in front of him. Antoni was there, pale-faced and jittery, nibbling on the skin around his thumb, his eyes staring into nothing.

'What's wrong?' I asked.

Antoni still did not look at me, and it was Olek who turned and waved me over to join them at the table.

'It went wrong,' Antoni was muttering over and over again.

'We've been through this, Antoni, there was nothing you could have done,' Olek the bear-man said in hushed tones.

'I shouldn't have let him. I really shouldn't.' Antoni tore the skin away, making his thumb bleed, looked at it, then moved on to the fresh skin of his forefinger.

'Filip was arrested,' Olek said. 'He went into Poznań with Antoni. They were there to pick up some papers, fake mind you, to pass on to a few friends to help them get out of the country. Filip was taken – he had his own papers on him, but the real ones, not the fake.'

I tried to swallow, but my mouth was suddenly dry. Filip was an academic. And men such as he had been disappearing for weeks. Why hadn't he taken the false papers Antoni had given him?

'What does that mean for you?' I asked Olek, knowing that there was a possibility that Filip could be traced back to here, to him, to us.

Olek shrugged. 'We need to just take it one day at a time. One day at a time.'

Antoni quickly glanced up at me as if only just noting my presence. 'Here,' he said glumly, passing me an ID card. 'Your new papers. I managed to get them finally.'

My fingertips touched the blue card in front of me and gently slid them away from Antoni. As glad as I was to finally have a new identity, I felt deeply guilty at the way it had happened.

'It's not your fault,' Olek said to me, reading my mind. 'He was stupid. He shouldn't have had his old papers on him. What was he thinking?'

Antoni shook his head as if to say, *who knew?*

'Do we know where he was taken?' I asked, not really knowing what we would do with the information even if we did have it.

Neither answered, and Antoni scraped back his chair,

comprehending the danger that lay above him – the sleeping bodies of Germans – and bid his goodbyes, disappearing into the dawn, leaving Olek and me to stare at the tabletop, lost in our own thoughts.

We were unable to sit for long: soon the guests upstairs awoke and wanted feeding; then they began to drink by lunchtime, morphing the afternoon into the evening, singing songs and playing cards at tables.

I worked and tried not to think about Filip. But his pale face and wire-rimmed glasses kept appearing in my mind, then it would change into Helena's father's face, and then Helena herself.

As soon as her face appeared to me, I felt like I had when Karl had taken me out one evening, soon after we had first met, trying to introduce me to women and to find some confidence.

'You're not a fat little child any more,' he told me, as we reached the bar. 'I keep telling you, look in the mirror and tell yourself that that child has gone, never to return. You just need some self-confidence.'

'That's e-easy for you to say.' My stammer was almost gone but had raised its ugly head at finding itself in a new situation.

Karl nodded. He knew what he looked like – he was handsome in that way that charmed any woman. He had a natural manner of talking to anyone, making them feel at ease and made sure to make them laugh. 'I was nervous too, you know, the first time.'

I laughed because I couldn't imagine Karl being nervous about anything.

But his face was serious now. 'I was. I was in love with this woman – not a girl, a woman. I was eighteen, and she was twenty and she was incredible to look at – she had these eyes that I swear were purple – can you imagine that, purple eyes? Like lilacs. She always wore red lipstick and dressed herself in the latest fashions – clothes which most women would be scared to risk wearing. But she wasn't scared of anything.'

He stopped. 'So, what happened?' I pressed him.

'We met here, as a matter of fact. I would come in here and watch her with her friends, laughing and smoking, always keeping her friends at the table entertained. I could see that they looked at her the same way that I did – lovesick and almost envious of her.' He shook his head. 'Stupid, isn't it?'

He waved Horst over to refill his glass and asked for a more expensive whisky – he could afford it with the family money that he had, and I was always left with the slop. Yet, this time, he ordered Horst to give me the best too, and said he would pay.

'So, one evening, I was in here, watching her, and she caught my eye and smiled. That smile, Max, it did something to me. It was like my stomach twisted and knotted and my mouth went dry, and my heart started to beat really fast. Then she came over to me, and told me her name. "Liesel," she said, and kissed me on my cheek. "Join us, won't you?"'

'I didn't answer her – I couldn't; my mouth, you see, it was dry, and my tongue seemed to have swollen to twice its size. So I followed her like a dumb little puppy and sat at her table, listening to her talk, watching how she moved – it was like...' He stopped for a moment, trying to find the right word. 'Magic,' he concluded.

I had never heard Karl talk like this, and I had never thought he had it in him to do so – not the way he always carried on about women he had met, those he took to dinner and those he took home. Yet, here he was, a man who had been dumbstruck by love of a woman he barely knew.

Suddenly, Karl stood. 'Come on,' he said. 'Time to talk to some women.'

I followed him, much like he had followed Liesel that evening, trailing around in his wake, trying to talk to women, feeling the nerves overtake me.

I got better at it eventually. But I was never like Karl – I couldn't be so instantly charming; and at times I saw that the woman I spoke to would flick her eyes towards Karl, who had his arm slung over her friend, and I knew that she would have preferred Karl to me.

Now, standing behind Olek's bar, drying yet another glass, I knew I felt those same nerves from that evening when I thought of Helena, but also, I could now appreciate Karl's story about Liesel. I had never thought you could feel something so strongly for someone you barely knew, and had often questioned the veracity of Karl's story. And yet, here I was, wondering what Helena was doing, imagining her as she tucked a loose strand of hair behind her ear, or how she would suddenly go quiet, daydreaming, her eyes fixed on nothing in particular, but she would have a secret smile on her lips.

'Max!' Joasia's voice woke me from my own daydreaming, and I looked to see her standing in front of me, her cheeks flushed, her hair wild, and her eyes even wilder. 'Where's Olek?'

'In the cellar.' I nodded towards the floorboards.

'Come with me. Come now.' There was an edge in her voice that brooked no argument, and I left the bar unattended, telling the half-drunk crowd I had to get some more stock and would be back.

In the cellar, Olek was manhandling barrels around, grunting with effort.

As soon as Joasia saw him, she ran to him, and wrapped her arms around him and sobbed.

'They're gone! They're gone!' she cried over and over again.

'Filip?' Olek held her at arm's length for a moment. 'Yes, we know.'

'Oh God! Filip too? It can't be, it can't. What's happening, Olek, what's going on?' she screamed and wept, and we could not get her to make sense for at least five minutes until Olek made her sit on an upturned barrel, and kneeling in front of her with a hand on her cheek, he asked gently, 'Tell me. What has happened?'

Joasia told us she had taken the children to the hospital to see Helena as they had whined and moaned for days about how much they missed her. Plus, she saw it as an opportunity to go into the city alone, and see a friend of hers who would be able to get papers so that they could get to England.

'I didn't want to take the twins with me.' She sniffed. 'I didn't think it was safe. This friend of mine, he's not exactly the best of men, and I was worried about taking the children near him, and near his friends.'

Olek huffily told Joasia that she should have told him, and he would have gone instead of her. But she ignored him.

'When I got back to the hospital, they were all gone – all of them. Only Zosia was left. She was hiding in the pantry. She said they came, just like they had for Michal. Buses, soldiers and had taken them all.'

There was a moment where none of us could talk – none of us could really comprehend what had just been said. Helena and the twins were gone.

I thought I had felt fear before. Fear when I was bullied and punched at school, fear when I took my first flight, fear when my parents got sick and died. But that was nothing compared to the feeling I had now. This was fear that made my heart pound against my chest, as if it were trying to break through skin and bone. This was fear that made my legs go weak and my mind become fuzzy as if I were going to faint. This was fear that made me think the worst – soldiers shooting families in the streets, talks of new, random graveyards appearing in woods and fields.

'Where?' I finally asked, my voice barely above a whisper, dreading to hear the answer.

She shook her head. 'I don't know.'

'We'll find them,' I told her. 'We will,' I tried to sound confident, but my voice was weak and broken.

This set her off crying again. 'We haven't even found my brother and that was more than two weeks ago – how do you think we will find Helena and the twins?'

I wanted to offer her the words that she wanted to hear and tried a few sentences out in my mind, but none were sufficient.

A shout from upstairs alerted me to the soldiers who had been left alone with the bar, and I left Olek to take care of Joasia, my mind going over and over the news.

Helena and the twins were gone, and suddenly I felt utterly alone.

TWENTY-TWO

HELENA

Wednesday, 15 November 1939
Fort VII, Poznań, Poland

The day turned into night, and I watched the sky through that tiny, barred window change from blue to dark blue, and then inky blackness. The two other women huddled on the floor together did not move for those few hours of our arrival, and Agata and Michal and I sat in a corner of the room, our backs to the cold walls, the straw itchy underneath us.

I tried to talk to them during that time; reassuring words that we would not be here long, that soon someone would come and unlock the door and set us free, that this had all been some sort of mistake. Yet, even to me, the words did not hold the ring of truth that I wished them to; hope was missing from them.

Agata and Michal did not talk. They held on to me with both hands and stayed still. I thought at one point they had fallen asleep, but when I looked down, the pair of them were staring silently at each other, as if they were having one of their strange twin conversations that they had done since they were small – with one look, each of them could convey to the other what they felt or what they thought.

As darkness enveloped us, Michal shifted his weight. 'Helena,' he said. 'I need the toilet.'

I had remembered seeing a bucket in the room when we had first entered, but now in the darkness I could see nothing.

'You'll need this,' a voice came out of the dark. A soft voice. Soothing. Suddenly, a face appeared, lit by a tiny stub of a candle and approached us like the ghosts in Dickens' *Christmas Carol*.

'I'm Ola,' the ghostly head said. She handed Michal the candle. 'Be careful. Don't drop it. We'd go up in flames!' She was joking, of course she was, yet it didn't hit right, and I felt Agata move closer to me, squishing her body so close it was as though she were trying to get under my skin.

Michal took the candle and went to the bucket to relieve himself, then soon returned.

'They'll give you some sacks, maybe old blankets tomorrow. But you won't get anything tonight,' Ola said.

'Come, come with me. Sleep next to me and Sabina over there. We'll huddle for warmth and then tomorrow you can find your own spot if you want to.'

'They're not coming back?' I half asked Ola.

'Not tonight. Tomorrow, though. They'll bring breakfast – if you can call it that. After that, they'll make you work. And then you'll come back in here and sleep.'

'Why?' I asked. 'Why is this happening to us?'

Ola took the candle from Michal and raised her finger to her lips. 'Let's get the little ones warm, eh?' she said. 'Then we'll talk.'

I took Agata to the bucket, and after a minute or so she managed to go, embarrassed that Michal and two strangers were in the same room as her. Then we went to the corner where the other woman, Sabina, who looked to be in her forties with a large bruise over her right eye, smiled at us and indicated that the children should get into the little den they had made of the straw. She then covered them with thin blankets and three old potato sacks that stank of the rotting vegetable.

Whether it was the events of the day, the fear, or the warmth that the two now felt, Michal cuddling Agata to him, they quickly fell asleep.

'Lovely children you have,' Sabina said, lighting another candle, this one with a little more wax than the stub Ola had.

'They're my sister and brother,' I told her.

'And you are?' Sabina held out her hand and as it passed through the slice of light, I saw that the skin was engrained with dirt, the fingernails broken and ragged. She saw me look, and went to withdraw her hand. But I quickly took it in my own, holding it tight. 'Helena. And that's Michal and Agata.'

Introductions over, Sabina took her hand back, looked at it, then smiled at me. 'Sorry about this,' she said. 'I'd normally have beautiful hands. I had every cream you could think of that I'd smother them in at night, trying to keep them looking young. Because that's where age shows first, did you know that, in the hands?'

Ola let out a little chuckle. 'I couldn't be bothered with things like that. My hands before this were already a mess – I'd always chew my fingernails and it would drive my husband crazy.'

I couldn't help but be aware at the normalcy of the conversation. It was as though we were three friends, just sitting in someone's parlour, chatting about our lives.

'So... What brought you here? Is your husband a politician too?' Ola asked.

I shook my head, then told them about the hospital and the patients.

'That's new,' Ola said.

'What is?' I asked.

'Well. Sabina and I have been here for two weeks. Both our husbands were politicians, and we were arrested alongside them. There have been others here too – but again, most of them were politicians, or from rich families or academics. No one from a hospital.'

'I just don't understand why,' I said. 'Why us?'

'I wouldn't even try to answer that question,' Ola said. 'Because there is no rational answer, is there?'

'How long will they keep us here?'

'Again, best not to think about the answer to that question either,' Ola said. 'You just have to take it day by day, minute by minute. Don't think too much.'

'Where did the other women go – you said there had been others?' I pressed. Surely they could tell me something about this place, about what I should expect.

Neither answered for a moment and the silence seemed to drag in the cold room. 'Let's just say,' Sabina said quietly, 'you'll see for yourself. It's best you don't know. It's best you sleep tonight and try and forget where you are for now. We could warn you of what you might see, but then, they change the rules day by day, so who knows what you would have to live with. All I can tell you, Helena, is keep on the good side of our overseer – Leo Wagner. You met him, he brought you in here and I watched him out of the corner of my eyes. He likes you, and the children. Try your best to keep on his good side.'

'And what happens if I don't?' I asked.

Sabina pointed to the bruise on her eye and winced. 'Let's just say, it's easier if you don't resist. Just do what he asks. The others, they fought against him, and fought against the other guards, and you can see that they are no longer here. So don't fight, Helena. Trust us. It's not worth it.'

I didn't want to think about what I would have to agree to with the blue-grey-eyed man who now had a name – Leo Wagner. I didn't want to think about why he was so interested in me and the children, nor why he had not led us back to that cramped cellar room with the patients inside.

Ola yawned. It was time for sleep. Ola and Sabina let me sleep next to the twins, and the two of them then slept either side, almost like they were making a protective barrier for us, and despite myself I fell asleep.

I woke with Agata whispering in my ear that she needed the toilet. The room was lightening a little, and I could make out shadowy shapes as my eyes adjusted to the gloom. I took her to the bucket, then went myself. As I sat, I could feel underneath me that the bucket was almost full, and I wondered what I was to do with it. It wasn't like there was somewhere to pour it away.

'Can we go home now, Helena?' Agata asked me.

'Soon, my darling. Soon.'

She rubbed at her eyes and yawned, when suddenly the door was flung open and a guard came in with two metal trays that he slid across the floor, then closed the door behind him.

Ola and Sabina raced towards the trays, then looked at each other. 'They didn't bring much extra,' Ola said.

As morning was breaking, light was trying to fill the room as best it could, and I saw Ola hold up mouldy bread and indicated the three cups on the tray, each filled with coffee and two bowls that seemed full of hot water with a few vegetables floating on top.

'I thought they would have brought more – you know, for the twins,' Sabina said, shaking her head.

Between them, they broke up the bread, and told Michal, who was now awake, to come to them and eat.

'You too, Helena,' Ola said, dipping her meagre piece of bread in the warm water.

I shook my head. My stomach would not take it, I was sure

of it. I let them eat, telling Agata and Michal to eat too, even though they pulled faces at the taste.

Halfway through, Sabina told the children to stop eating.

'Why?' Michal asked. 'I'm hungry.'

'It has to last all day,' Ola said.

Michal placed the tiny bit of bread that he had left on the tray, and Agata followed suit.

My head was banging with pain, and my ears were ringing too. All of a sudden, the reality of the situation was too much. I wanted to cry out. *Where was Mother, where was Father! Why were we here! I want to go home!* I didn't, though. I counted my breaths instead, trying not to show the twins how scared I really was.

The door swung open again, and Leo Wagner himself stood in the doorway.

'Come, come,' he said gently to the twins, then looked at me and smiled. 'Come.'

I looked to Ola and Sabina, who both gave me a weak smile.

'Come,' he said, sterner now, and I walked to him, Agata and Michal following in my wake.

Wagner led us down the rabbit run of bricked, stale corridors, his booted footsteps echoing as we walked.

'*Helena*,' I heard a voice, no more than a whisper, and wondered whether I had imagined it. '*Helena*,' the voice said again, weaker now, and I looked to a barred cell on my left but could see no one inside the pitch black.

As we walked away, I realised how tired I was, how confused and upset I was, and had obviously imagined that voice. But why, my mind asked me, did it sound like Filip?

Wagner took us into a room, and I saw that we had obviously gone uphill now, away from the dungeons beneath, as the windows in this room looked out onto a few trees and I could finally see the morning sky.

It was a doctor's office, that much was clear. There was a

patient bed, on the right, a large lamp, and of course a doctor, dressed in a white coat, green glasses and a look in his eyes when he saw the twins that made me feel uncomfortable.

Leo Wagner spoke to the doctor, and I understood nothing. Then the doctor tried to ask me questions. Again, I could not answer – I did not speak German. Wagner tried to speak to me in Polish, but I couldn't understand it either.

The doctor shrugged, then made the twins sit in front of him. He made them open their mouths, looked into their eyes and ears with a torch and then made them stand to measure them.

There was something inside of me that was telling me that this was not normal practice. Of course, I didn't know this for sure – perhaps each new arrival did meet the doctor – but there was something so uneasy about the situation that it made my skin crawl.

Some more conversation ensued between Wagner and the doctor and then we were led out of the office and down back towards the cell we had only recently left. As we reached the door, a guard stood outside, a tray in his hands, food piled high.

Wagner took the tray and gave it to me, then bent down and patted the children on the top of their heads like obedient dogs. 'Good, good, very good,' he told them and smiled.

Agata and Michal smiled back – genuinely. They had done well at something, even though they didn't know what, and accepted a sweet that Wagner produced from his pocket. 'Very good,' he said again, letting the guard open the door and then seal us back inside once more.

I set the tray down, and Sabina and Ola rushed over to look at what we had been given.

There was a large bowl of steaming porridge, fresh bread, some cheese, thick black coffee in a steel urn and an apple. Their eyes widened as if seeing a Christmas feast.

'He gave you all this?' Ola asked. 'What did you do?'

'I don't know,' I replied, lifting a small cup that had been given with the coffee and taking a grateful gulp.

'Can we eat?' Michal asked. I nodded that they could.

Ola and Sabina watched the twins as they spooned the porridge into their mouths. 'You too,' I told them, gesturing at the tray.

'Really?' Ola asked.

'Of course. You shared what you had earlier, and we will share what we have.'

They did not have to be told twice, and delved in, and though the situation we found ourselves in had little joy in it, I did feel a twinge of happiness watching them eat and being so utterly grateful for it.

'I still want to know what you did for this,' Sabina said through mouthfuls of bread.

I told her about the doctor's office, how Wagner had not asked me for anything, and how we had simply been brought back here.

'A doctor?' Ola said.

'Have you seen him?' I asked.

She shook her head. 'I didn't even know there was a doctor here.'

TWENTY-THREE

MAKSYMILIAN

**Wednesday, 15 November 1939
Żerków, Poland**

Filip has returned. He came back, bloodied and barely standing. He had been left in the doorway at around 2 a.m., a pounding at the door alerting us to the fact that someone was outside.

It hadn't woken us as we were still awake, talking with Antoni in the kitchen about Helena and the twins, his face paling further when we told him what Joasia had said. Joasia herself was tucked up in Olek's bed upstairs, half-filled with brandy.

Olek went to the front door, and Antoni stood by the kitchen door, ready to run in case that ominous knock was meant for him. I understood his fear – he had been seen with Filip, the Gestapo were surely looking for him.

'Max, come!' Olek waved me over as he revealed Filip curled into a ball on the doorstep, the sound of a car engine rumbling away. Olek and I managed to get him inside and into the kitchen, where Antoni leapt into action and began to tend to the wounds that littered Filip's face. It was then that I noticed he was not wearing his glasses, and saw them peeking out from his jacket pocket.

I took them out, seeing that one arm was missing.

'Where am I?' Filip murmured, his eyes so swollen he could barely see. I put the glasses back in his pocket.

'It's me,' Antoni said. 'It's me, can you hear me?'

'They said I was an example,' his speech was almost slurred. 'They said I had to tell you, so you can tell others what will happen.'

Antoni glanced at the door, but he did not move away from Filip.

'Where did they take you?' I asked him.

'Underground,' he said. 'All the way to hell...'

'He's delusional,' Olek said.

'No. No. I'm not. It was underground. They put me in a cell. It was so small I could not even sit down. I had to stand. They beat me, constantly. Then they dragged me to this room – this room...' he cried, tears running down his red, bulbous face.

'Leave it,' Antoni told him. 'Don't say it. Let's get you cleaned up.'

Filip tried to shake his head. 'I *have* to tell you!' he cried, the energy seeping away as he spoke. 'It was a room. There was a hook in the ceiling. There was a man, I think it was a man. You know him, Antoni. He was that politician you worked with...'

'Timon?'

Filip nodded. 'He was hanging from the hook. Head towards the floor. They hit him and hit him. He cried out a bit, I think, but then he made no noise. The guard, he told me it was called the *Die Glocke, The Bell*, and I was to tell you this. I was to tell you what it is like in there, so you knew where you would end up if you carried on.'

None of us spoke. What could we say? I couldn't even

imagine what he had seen, what he had been forced to see. All so he could come back and spread fear – and it had worked. Antoni was already making towards the door, his instinct was to get away, and get away fast.

'I saw Helena,' Filip said, stopping Antoni in his tracks.

'Helena?'

'I think so. And the twins. They were with this guard, this man. They walked past me. I am sure it was them, but then I could have been dreaming. You should try to get to the hospital, check that she is all right, check that I am wrong.'

Filip had exhausted himself and slumped forward in his chair. Olek checked that he was still breathing, then went to fetch Joasia.

I couldn't believe it – Helena. He had seen her. She was alive! It wasn't until the thought of her being alive entered my head that I realised I had been expecting the worst news possible – I had been thinking she might be dead. All of a sudden, I felt a little lighter and the tense headache I had had was now abating, my thoughts becoming clearer.

Within minutes, Joasia was in the room and ready to take charge.

'Olek, Antoni, you'll help me to get him to my house. He'll stay with me.'

'It's not safe—' Olek began.

'They won't know. They won't come walking down, out of town to the one house in a middle of a damned field looking for a man they set free so he could tell his story. They want him alive, Olek. He'll come with me. And you,' she looked to Antoni, 'will help Max find Helena. Find out where this place is. Promise me, you will.'

Antoni nodded weakly, whereas I already knew what I was going to do – Leo Wagner would be back in a few days. He had told me so himself. And he had also told me where he worked – a fort, underground and suddenly the stars had aligned themselves. I had to befriend Leo, I had to work for him, help him, and in doing so, he would get me to Helena. My thoughts of how to get her free did not go that far; instead, I heard my father's voice in my head: '*One step at a time, Max, that's all it takes for change. One step at a time.*' And now, I knew what my first step *had* to be.

TWENTY-FOUR

HELENA

Wednesday, 15 November 1939
Fort VII, Poznań, Poland

The rest of that first day was spent inside the cell and both Sabina and Ola told me that this was unusual.

'Normally, there is roll call when we stand outside and they call all our names,' Sabina started.

'They do more than that,' Ola remarked, but Sabina shot her a look.

'Then they make us work – cleaning the sewage pits or moving things.'

'Moving what?' I asked her.

'Just things,' she repeated but would not look at me when she said it.

The day got more unusual for them, as soon a guard appeared with more blankets, handing them to the twins, a bowl of warm water so we could wash, and more food. Rather than being delighted with the extra comforts, Sabina and Ola distrusted them and spoke in hushed whispers about what might be going on.

The twins had oddly adapted to their surroundings and made the rest of the day into a game whereby they were searching for treasure in an exotic place. I had tried to stop them, but Ola had scolded me, saying, 'Leave them be. Let them distract themselves. God, I wish I could!'

At one point I saw them using a loose stone they found on the floor to carve their names into the wall – adding a smiling face that seemed so at odds with our surroundings.

The relative ease of that first day was not to last. And the following morning we were woken by yet another guard before the sun was in the sky. As we walked past him, I looked at his face, trying to see if I had seen him before, yet, to me they all looked the same – black uniforms, caps pulled low, eyes that never blinked, lips that never smiled.

As we walked the hallway, other cells were opened and more prisoners joined us, and the guards seemed to appear from nowhere – perhaps multiplying in the shadows, and began to shout and scream at us, hitting the backs of legs, backs, heads with their batons. They smiled then. Not proper smiles. Not ones of pure joy. But some form of sadistic joy that they took pleasure in.

No one touched me.

The guard who had let Sabina, Ola and me out, locking the children back inside with another tray piled high with food, stuck close to my side.

I heard Ola yell out behind me and the echo of a *thwack*, as something or someone had hit her. But she did not cry, did not fall, and continued to walk.

Soon, we were outside, made to line up, in a small court-yard, surrounded by trees that were almost on the same level as the grassy knolled roof of the Fort.

There were perhaps a hundred or more of us, and I scanned the downturned faces for ones I recognised – Mother? Basia? Hanna?

But there was no one that I knew.

As another guard called out names, the guard that was positioned by my side pulled me a way a little from the others, close to the trees.

As soon as we were out of sight, he placed his hand under my skirt and began to pull at my underwear. Stupidly, I did nothing for a moment, so incredulous was I that this was happening, it was as though I took leave from my body. I could see myself, outside of my own body, hovering above it as this man touched me where a man had never touched me before. His face was sweating and moving closer and closer to my own. It was then that I re-entered myself and slapped him so hard on his cheek that his cap fell off.

There was a moment where nothing happened. Then suddenly he grabbed hold of my arm and threw me to the ground, my face landing in damp soil that clogged up my nostrils with its earthy scent.

The noise had alerted the others and two more guards appeared. There was some conversation going on between them, harsh, brittle words, then a laugh. All of them laughing at me.

The sweating guard pulled me up to stand and spat in my face. Then he roughly shoved me back towards the lined-up souls who dared not look at what was transpiring in front of their very eyes.

The others began to move back towards a door that would lead them once more back inside the cavern. But I was held in place by the sweating man, his fingers digging into my arm, squeezing and pinching at the skin.

When we were alone, with just one other guard, I was led to a concrete staircase that rose up to the top of the Fort. I was pushed in the direction of the staircase, and realised I was to walk up it. As I did so, they screamed at me; then I felt it. They were behind me, smacking me on my spine with their rubber batons. '*Schnell! Schnell!*' they yelled, pushing at me to go faster.

When I finally reached the top, I stood for a moment, feeling the heat of the pain on my back begin to spread. The sweating guard was now next to me once more. He smiled at me, baring teeth that had a yellow tinge. Then he pushed me.

As I fell, I disappeared again, outside of my body. And I could see myself falling, falling, my body bouncing, smacking on the stairs. Then I saw her, Mother. She stood at the bottom of the steps, her arms wide open as if she were going to catch me. And then I knew. I saw it all. I saw my mother who was not there, who had not been alive for years, who had also fallen down a flight of stairs.

I had been here before. I had seen her die ten years ago, and now it was my turn.

DECEMBER 1995

TWENTY-FIVE

HELENA

Wednesday, 20 December 1995
Wallingford, Oxfordshire, UK

I forgot to remember.

I forgot to remember that my mother had died.

On that day when my body had fallen down a concrete staircase whilst two guards laughed at me, I had seen what I had wanted to see, I had seen something that would bring me comfort, and, it was then that I understood how I had been imagining her for weeks, months now, even. And the worst thing was that this had not been the first time I had done so.

My father had been the first to see this turn in me. He had seen that I was starting to fold inside myself and had written about me in his patient notes in his private journal, something which Joasia rescued from the hospital soon after it was emptied out, and before it was transformed into a barracks.

He saw it. The elusive patient he worried about constantly, even when the war was raging around him, even though he was consumed with his own fears and worries. That patient was *me*.

My mother had died less than a year after the twins were

born, on a Tuesday afternoon, when I had returned from school, my satchel full of new books that I had got from the library on my way home. I remember that day now. It's always there, etched in my mind, but, as I told you, I did forget. Twice.

As I opened the door to our two-floor apartment, I remember I was greeted with the sight of the nanny holding a screaming Agata, walking up and down the hallway, trying to calm her.

'Where's Mother?' I had asked, dropping my satchel on the floor, removing my coat and shoes, leaving me in grey-socked feet.

'Upstairs, resting,' she had said, rolling her eyes. No one could get any rest with the wail that came from Agata. She liked the sound of her own voice, and it was something that we did not know then, but it would continue her entire life.

I padded up the stairs and looked into the nursery where a baby Michal was lying in his crib, gurgling happily at the ceiling.

'Hello baby,' I said to him.

His eyes found mine, and he tried to roll over onto his side to get into his crawling stance – he wanted to move, and he wanted to move *now*.

I took him from his crib and held him to me, kissing the soft skin of his cheeks, his head and even the creases in his neck, smelling the milky sweetness of him.

He pulled on my hair, but I did not care and sat in the nursing chair so that I could bounce him up and down on my knee. He liked this game and laughed as my legs bobbed up and down, so I began to sing him a song about horses that I had made up, delighting as it made his eyes crease with his giggling, drool escaping his open mouth.

I heard Mother in the room opposite get out of bed; the floorboards creaking with her weight as she made her way to the door.

'Helena, you're home,' she said, almost surprised to see me. 'What time is it?' She yawned.

'Three,' I told her. 'I'm a little late because I went to the library and got some new books.'

'Good girl.' She came to me and patted me absentmindedly on my head before yawning once more. 'Come downstairs with me and let's see if we can hush that terror that is Agata!'

I loved that she included me with the twins – as if they were ours, and together we could joke about them, love them, coddle them and then talk to one another about them, drawing us close in our own little world.

I carried Michal on my hip. He had shoved one fist in his mouth and was gnawing on it as more spittle dripped from his mouth, onto his chin, and then onto my school uniform. His other hand was firmly embedded in my hair, his chubby fingers rooting around for something he thought was perhaps hidden between the strands.

As we reached the top of the stairs, Mother turned to take Michal from me, and I saw her arms outstretched, a smile on her face as she reached for her chubby son, then her eyes widened, her mouth opened, and a mask of fear took over her face.

Within a second, she was falling backwards down the stairs, her arms still outstretched, waiting to take hold of her baby, her head bumping crudely against the banister, the wooden steps, and then a final sickening thud as she hit the floor.

I cannot remember getting down the stairs. I just remember the fall and then, as if by magic, I was by her side, standing next to her crumpled body, her arm bent at an impossible angle, her neck seemingly twisted, leaving her face blank, mouth and eyes open, a pool of crimson seeping from underneath her.

Did I give Michal to the nanny? Did I scream? Did I try to wake her? I perhaps did all of these things, but nothing is clear in my mind. All I know is that time moved on from that point, much like a scene in a picture show, and now I was sitting in the parlour, my father crouched in front of me, my hands and uniform covered in blood.

He kept saying my name over and over again, but for some reason I couldn't respond. I could see well – there was a doctor, his stethoscope round his neck, talking to a policeman. There was Antoni, my father's friend and there was Joasia. *Why was Joasia here?* I wondered.

'Helena,' my father said again. 'Can you hear me, Helena?'

I nodded, concentrating on his face, seeing that his eyes were red. Why were they red? Was he sick?

'Helena, your mother...'

I do not know what he said next. I can assume that he told me that she was dead, that it wasn't my fault, that the body now covered in a sheet being taken away by two men, was in fact her, and not a piece of furniture, which I had decided it was in my muddled mind.

I had heard the words. Of course I had. But something in my mind did not let me listen to them, did not let me register the pain that they delivered.

Instead, my mind began to play tricks on me. In much the same way that a child invents stories in her mind, I reverted to this state and imagined that my mother was still alive.

I had always had made-up friends – invisible friends I would talk to as a child, as so many other children did too. But when Mother died, it was as though that childhood habit became something much more. I began, of course, talking to her as if she was there. I knew she wasn't; somewhere deep, deep down, *I knew*, and yet, it comforted me so much that it escalated to a point where I had shut out the reality of her death completely and instead, had created a world where she still existed.

Four months in hospital, my father's hospital, cured me of it. I was forced to see reality, which was devastating as I finally had to leave my warm dream-world of denial and deal with the feelings of loss and utter sadness.

Father had given me focusing strategies whereby if I ever felt like 'talking' to Mother again, reinventing her, I suppose, I had to write in a journal instead and this did work. I could still talk to her and derive some comfort from it without letting my mind wander away and create a new world for itself.

I remember now the night I had brought her back to life again, this summer, after drinks with Anna and Rolf. The conversations about the problems in Germany, the talk of impending war had left me anxious and unsteady. I knew, of course, that I could speak with Father about the fear I felt that war might happen, that people might die, perhaps my own family, and the fear I felt for the children. Yet I did not think he could assuage these fears, for he was obsessed with every news item, chatting to people about the likelihood of war each day, and it would end up compounding my own dread.

That night, I climbed into bed and realised I had left my journal at work. Sitting there, I felt utterly alone and desperate. I wanted Mother; no, I *needed* her. I needed her voice telling me things would be fine. I needed her to sing to me like she did when I had a nightmare, I needed her warmth. So just that once, I imagined her sat on the edge of my bed, and I told her about my evening, about the things people were saying, about the fear that if there was a war, something might happen to the children and that possibility made me feel utterly sick.

I let her talk back to me, imagining what she would say, and immediately felt calmer. As I turned out the light, I had a thought that perhaps I had been wrong to indulge in something that had once sent me to hospital; yet, it was just this once. There was no harm, surely?

Yet, somewhere in those hot summer days of 1939, I began to see her more and more, especially at moments of stress and worry. I resumed my childish habit of imagining her, letting it once more consume me. It took me away from reality for a little while, where no one was dead, nothing was wrong, my mother was here, and all was well.

But, reality came down hard on me this time. There was no Father helping me gently to deal with my delusions; there was no Joasia, no Antoni.

There was just me.

Falling down concrete stairs towards a figment of my imagination.

NOVEMBER 1939

TWENTY-SIX

MAKSYMILIAN

Friday, 17 November 1939
Żerków, Poland

Leo Wagner sat at the bar, a small measure of vodka in his glass that I had purposely watered down. He had already been here one day, and today he told me was his last and he would be leaving in an hour or so. He had to get back to work – *'so much to do, so little time,'* he had muttered, reminding me of my mother who had said the same thing when she was spring-cleaning the house.

'I like her,' he droned, a hint of melancholy in his tone.

'Who?'

He shrugged. 'Just some woman. She doesn't understand me, though, and I need her to.'

Sensing my chance, I pounced. 'I can help you. You wouldn't need to pay me, but I could help you.'

'What? Teach me Polish? I don't want that,' he spat.

I felt weariness in my brain as I repeated what I had said to him so many times over, but he had always been too drunk to remember.

'As your personal translator,' I said, emphasising the word *personal*. His ego required someone just for him – for no one else.

I could see him thinking, so I continued. 'I can tell them whatever you want me to tell them. I mean, someone in your position should have this kind of assistance, no? It would ease the heavy burden that I can see you are carrying – working so much, so little time for anything else.'

He nodded his head in agreement as I spoke – yes, he deserved it.

'That bastard Schneider thinks he runs the place, you know. He brings them in to interrogate them, to frighten them and sends them back out. But he's not really in charge, Greiser himself put me in charge – it's part of his bigger plan. He's just letting Schneider and his Gestapo comrades use it. But I'm the boss – *me*,' he pointed a finger at his chest. 'And I do deserve some respite. You have no idea, Max, what it's like, day in, day out, for me. I have to run this place with hundreds of people in it, and all the while, I am trying to look after my own career. I don't want to stay there, you see, I have aspirations too, you know, and I am almost there – I'm *this* close,' he emphasised, placing his thumb and forefinger just a millimetre or so apart.

'So, let me help you, Hauptmann Wagner,' I said. 'It would be my honour to serve you.'

'Please, Max, you call me Leo. We are friends, are we not? Go. Get packed. You will come with me today. You are right, I deserve this. I *need* it. You and I will change history together.' He laughed and slapped me on the back, nodding at the vodka, which I happily grabbed and heartily filled his glass.

Then I turned, ran up the stairs and packed a small bag before he could forget, or before he drank any more.

TWENTY-SEVEN

HELENA

Friday, 17 November 1939
Fort VII, Poznań, Poland

I woke to see Sabina and Ola looking down at me.

'Can you hear me, Helena?' Ola asked.

I blinked. I could not nod. I could not speak.

'I don't think you broke anything,' Sabina said, but her voice was wobbly – nervous. 'So I think you will be fine.'

I could hear a whimper from Agata and I tried to turn my head to find her, but a searing pain shot through my neck and into my head, and I cried out in pain.

This made Agata worse, who was now by my side, and next to her Michal, who cried silent tears. I tried to lift my arm and found that I could – it obeyed – and I reached up and held Agata's face in my palm.

'Please don't die, Helena,' she cried. 'Please, please don't die. Don't leave us like Mama did. Please, Helena...'

Mama. Mother. She was dead. Yes, I remembered that now. That staircase had brought back the memory of her death, and the realisation that I had been playing a game of make-believe for the past few months.

'I won't die.' I managed to get the words out and could taste metal on my lips. I licked the blood that had dried and motioned to Sabina and Ola that I wanted to sit up.

They managed to heave me to a sitting position, leaning me against the cold wall. The bruises on my spine welcomed the cool surface, and I looked down at my legs to assess the damage. My knees were scraped and bloodied, my skirt ripped. My hands too, were covered in blood from my torn fingernails. I reached up and with gentle strokes let myself feel my own face and the thick swollen skin, the cut on my right cheekbone and my split lip.

Slowly, I tested my legs, bringing each up into a bend and as painful as it was, I could do it. Perhaps Sabina was right – perhaps nothing was broken at all.

Agata and Michal came to my sides and rested lightly against me.

'I'm all right,' I told them. 'I'm still alive. Everything will be fine.'

For two days I did not leave the cell, and Agata and Michal were always by my side. Ola and Sabina had to leave intermittently to work, and always came back with a new bruise or blood on their skin, but neither one of them complained.

The extra 'gifts' still appeared – warm water, more food, and even some gauze and soap.

When the sweating guard who had pushed me down the steps appeared with the water, gauze and soap, he told Ola, who spoke some German, that she had to get me cleaned up, and be quick about it.

'Take her to the doctor,' she had told him.

But he had shaken his head and looked about nervously. 'Be quick. By tomorrow. Make her look... well.'

Ola did her best, cleaning me, tending to me like a child and letting me cry onto her shoulder when the pain got too much.

'You're so lucky,' she would remind me. 'You're so lucky to be alive. Most would have died with that fall. I know some who have...'

I wanted to tell her about Mother, how she had died from such a fall, how I had watched, helpless as she fell, but Agata and Michal were always within earshot and I could not, would not, torment them with this tale. As far as they knew, their mother died suddenly, the angels wanting to take her to God early because she was too good for this world. They still believed this story, and I knew that that would not last. Soon they would want to know how she died, but now was not the time to tell them.

That night, lying back on the straw, I thought about how delusional I had been in imaging Mother, and I realised that I could not give into it ever again. If I ever left here, I could not pretend that this reality, however harsh, had never happened. I had to be the twins' comfort. I had to face the reality and whatever it brought, so that I could remember those who died, those who lived, and perhaps tell their stories. I had to focus on the here and now, watching, looking at what was in front of me. My mother could not bring me comfort now – I had to find some through caring for Agata and Michal.

All night I analysed myself, as if I were my own patient and felt all at once foolish and vulnerable that as a grown woman, I had ignored everything I knew, everything I had learned, and given into a fantasy instead of facing my fears, my own thoughts and seeking Father's help.

I realised too, that my imagining Mother's presence had intensified after I had seen Max in the children's fort. I had sensed it then – a moment of déjà vu. There he lay, crumpled and bloody, just like Mother and that feeling I had that day, that *want* to help him despite anyone's protestations was because I hadn't saved Mother, but I could, perhaps save him. She had been there, through it all with me, by my side, in my thoughts.

I remembered now, those moments when I had had auditory and physical psychosis – hallucinations of my mother. That afternoon in Father's office when he suggested I go to Joasia's for the weekend. He had looked concerned because I was doing it again – the headaches, the drifting away and then I saw the scene as it was – it had been Father and I alone in that office – Father had not seen her, he had not spoken to her – she was not there.

Then there were the moments at Joasia's after Father came up suddenly on that Sunday when we had found Max – how I had seen Mother in the kitchen with Joasia, I had heard her voice.

Each time I refreshed a scene in my mind and focused on the reality, I saw clearly that Mother had never been there. One after the other after the other; the morning in the office with Father after the radio announced we were at war. Had he spoken to her? No. I could see the scene in front of me now, me and Father huddled around the radio. No Mother.

They had all known too – they had all seen this strangeness in me and now, finally I saw it in myself.

I would remember. I had to.

I could not forget anything again.

TWENTY-EIGHT

MAKSYMILIAN

**Friday 17 to Saturday 18 November, 1939
Fort VII, Poznań, Poland**

The drive from Olek's was not uncomfortable. Wagner had
fallen asleep as soon as we had got into his chauffeur-driven car,
the driver seemingly unbothered that his charge was passed out.

I watched the countryside give way to denser housing, all
the lights off as the day slipped into night. The quiet in the car
gave me time to think of all that had happened – of Helena's
father missing, of Filip, of Helena and the twins. I wished I had
had time to see Joasia before I left, but there was no time and all
I could do was to tell Olek to get word to Antoni where I was
going, and that we were going to need his help.

I knew that Antoni had joined a resistance group. I had
heard him tell Olek, thinking that I would not hear him. He still
hadn't trusted me completely, and I didn't blame him. I was a
man who, only a month or so before, had fallen out of the sky, in
a German uniform, and I was now making friends with them
once more. Although it had been Antoni's suggestion I do this, I
couldn't help but wonder if he feared that I would go back to

them properly – that all along this had been a part of a bigger plan.

But what Antoni and the others didn't realise completely, is that night that I jumped out of the plane, I had no plan other than to feel the Polish soil beneath my feet once more. I had no plan other than to escape that feeling that I was alone in the world – my father gone, my mother too, there was no one and nothing left for me in Germany, and I wanted no part of it any more.

The irony was not lost on me as the car chugged its way through the night that I was now back – back in the belly of the beast – but at least I was back now on my own terms, with my own objectives.

Relaxing into the leather seat, I tried not to think of Helena and the twins. I did not want my mind to go into a black hole of imagining the worst scenarios, and I had been doing this for days now, training my brain not to think of the danger, the fear, the 'what ifs'. I wasn't completely without feeling, however. There were moments, chunks of time in the day, where my armour ripped wide open and I felt everything. I felt the grief I needed to feel for my father, I felt the sickness in my stomach at seeing Filip's face and hearing what he had witnessed, I felt a clamminess over my skin as I thought of Helena and those children and where they might be. And, only now and then, I found myself missing Karl, my friend.

Karl, though, was my enemy. He was no longer a friend, and I had to keep telling myself that. But the feelings were so complicated. I had known him for years and we had been at times almost like brothers. We had laughed together, gone out to bars, talked late into the night about everything and nothing. But he believed in what he was doing – in Hitler, in the promises that were being made to the country. So he was the enemy, wasn't he?

I could not imagine that Karl would support what was

happening on the ground. Did he know? I supposed he didn't.
He was high up there, in the skies, looking down but seeing very
little. Would he have helped the guards with that poor man,
placed upside down on a hook from a ceiling like a carcass of
beef left to drain the blood away in a butcher's shop window?
Would he have taken out his gun and shot a family in the street
because they were Jewish?

I hoped to God that he would not have.

Leo woke as the car began to slow. It had started to rain, a light
pitter-patter on the roof. The headlights lit up wrought-iron
gates that were being slowly opened by two men, the rain
already soaking them through.

'I have to apologise in advance for my lodgings,' Leo said
with a yawn. 'I'm still waiting for an apartment in the city. I stay
in a hotel sometimes.'

I wanted to ask him why, if he could go into the city, he
came to Żerków when on leave, but he answered for me. 'I came
from a small town myself. Near Frankfurt. When the others
told me about Żerków, I felt it was right for me – it would feel
like home for me. And it is, isn't it?' He smiled. 'I met you. A
friend in a little inn, behind a bar. At that is what I like. Quiet
conversation with a friend in a bar. None of this city stuff for
me. I have thought about asking for a permanent house in
Żerków, but I haven't yet found one that takes my fancy.'

The car pulled to a stop and Leo waited for the driver to
open the door for him, leaving me to open my own.

The lodgings he led me to were a small, red-bricked house,
just off the main road but within the razor-topped wire fences
that ran round a perimeter, with floodlights illuminating the
rain as it fell and was sliced on that wire.

Inside, the house was fairly bare. A couch in the sitting

room and a blue armchair, a small table with two chairs and a kitchen that wasn't even half the size of Joasia's.

It was then I realised that perhaps Leo was not as far up the ranks as he had led me to believe. Whilst a captain, he had Lange and Neumann as his superiors, and then it became clear to me why he came to Żerków with the other soldiers and lower ranking officers – he had nowhere else to go. Perhaps he oversaw and ranked above the guards, but he wasn't the man he made himself out to be – he wasn't in charge.

'There's only one bedroom,' he said. 'You can take the couch. We'll find you lodgings tomorrow. But I want you close tonight. As soon as morning breaks, we have to get working.'

I sat on the couch and although Leo had drunk a fair bit already, he went to a decanter and poured us both brown liquor, which I found out with a sniff was brandy. He sat in the armchair and leaned back.

'I have so much I want to do, Max, so much I want to achieve.'

I nodded along with him and did not drink.

'It's hard to be me, with the ambition I have. It's hard to have friends because they don't understand, and are scared of what I might accomplish. But you, Max, I can see in you, you are like me. I mean, both of us Wagners – what are the chances?'

I forced a laugh, which he seemed to like.

'You see, Max' – he leaned forward in his chair, cupping the glass with both hands – 'my uncle, he's a doctor, back in Berlin. And he is working on experiments at this very moment which will give us a greater understanding of life.'

'What kind of experiments?' I asked.

'Well. On the Jews of course. Seeing what's inside them and such. But not just that. He's coming up with new drugs every day, but they have to be tested on someone, you understand...'

I could feel my skin begin to crawl. Small goosebumps appeared, making the hairs on my arms stand on end.

'Children. Twins. Hunchbacks. Disabled. Old, young – it doesn't matter.' He sat back and sighed, as if that explained everything.

Twins. Children. Michal. Agata.

I swallowed the brandy back in one go.

'That's what I need your help with. I can't talk to these people, but you can talk for me. Tell them we're giving them medicine. Keep them calm. It's easier that way, until some other way will be found. But I told my uncle about a few people I have seen and he's interested, very interested and wants me to bring them to Berlin. And I will, Max. I will take them and when I do, I will get a new rank and get out of this place and have a nice house, just like our illustrious Reichsstatthalter of the Wartheland has. And he, Greiser, will see that I am a key part of his and our Führer's plans. I mean, Oberführer Neumann and commandant Lange too, are of course, doing a good job, but it's my turn soon – mine.'

The jealousy he felt towards his immediate bosses radiated off him. He could not comprehend that he was here, in a small cottage, not quite being the celebrity he thought he would be.

'It's not too much to ask, is it? I mean, Lange has promised a promotion soon, as this place is going to fill up quickly in the next few weeks, so I'll be in charge of more and more things. I already have a secretary,' he said proudly. 'But soon, I'll need two, then perhaps even three.'

I don't know how I did it, but I talked along with him. I made sympathetic murmurings as he complained about his bosses, how he wanted more and was overlooked. I nodded as he told me that he was compelled to be in the Fort day in, day out, executing orders whilst Lange and Neumann could sit in their fancy apartments.

The more he drank, the more bitter he became about his

situation, and I grew worried that I had backed the wrong horse. Yes, he had access to the camp. Yes, I might be able to see Helena, but would I be able to convince him to set them free?

Then a thought occurred to me, and I almost let out a comical laugh. I didn't need to convince this fool of anything. I would get them out, right under his nose and with his help, whether he realised it or not. I had backed the right horse.

He believed in me, and that's all I needed.

TWENTY-NINE

HELENA

Saturday, 18 November 1939
Fort VII, Poznań, Poland

When roll call came, Agata and Michal had to help me stand properly, leading me to the door with Ola and Sabina. Once again, the children were exempted from this, and were locked back inside. Although they cried when I left, I was glad that they could not come, I was glad that they could not witness what I did.

The sun that morning seemed not to have risen and thick, angry grey clouds hung low in the sky and a cold wind blew, alerting us all to the fact that winter was almost upon us. There was little noise other than the crackle of branches as they bowed under the weight of the wind, then, now and again, an angry bark from one of the dogs that patrolled the top of the Fort's mound with their handlers.

As I stood, shivering, I saw that there were more prisoners in the courtyard than usual, and I scanned them again for Hanna, Basia and Małgorzata as I had done a few days before, this time not looking for Mother as she was not there and never had been.

The roll call lasted, to me at least, an hour or more. My legs were wobbly with pain and my stomach was still empty as I could not bear to eat. I tried to tell my legs to stay still, stay standing, and not to let me faint. The icy wind whipped at my body, finding its way through my clothes to my skin, puckering it with goosebumps.

Eventually, it came to an end and the women were ordered to go to a nearby bunker. I followed suit, of course, and we stood outside this red-bricked facade, waiting for the grey metal doors to open. When they did so, I almost vomited from the sight. Inside were bodies, naked, one on top of the other.

Ola looked at me. 'It's been like this for days,' she whispered. 'We have to move them. Bury them.'

I couldn't understand at first what I was seeing, nor what Ola was telling me. There were dead bodies, almost spilling out of the bunker, lying at grotesque angles, eyes and mouths open in shock, and Ola was saying we had to move them. We had to bury them. It was then that I realised that these were the 'things' that they had told me on the first night they sometimes had to move. These things – these bodies, these people.

Ola and Sabina bent down and lifted a naked, white corpse, a shock of red hair illuminated to an unnatural brightness against the pale skin. I gasped. Małgorzata.

I looked at her face. It was calm, free of those worry lines, and she seemed younger and yet all at once older too. Małgorzata, who had tried to save me and the twins – allowing the guards to beat her whilst I ran down those endless tunnels seeking daylight. I leaned down a little and placed my hand on her forehead, gently moving the hair away from her face.

'*You*,' the sweaty guard who had pushed me down the stairs was back. He grabbed my arm but with less force this time and led me away from the bodies.

At that moment, and it may sound ridiculous, and it was, I didn't care if he was going to take me back into the trees and rape me. I didn't care what he was going to do. I just wanted to be away from those bodies – my patients, whom I had cared for, loved and desperately tried to help, and yet here they were, and I had let them down.

'*No, you didn't.*' My mother's voice was there, and I ignored it. This was when I would normally seek her out – I hadn't saved her; I wanted to save others. But I knew that I could no longer let my mind play these tricks. I had to focus. I had to remember. I had to live in this disastrous reality that was not of my own making.

He did not take me to the trees but instead, took me back to my cell, where he beckoned for the twins to come with us.

We three were then led back down the labyrinth of corridors that were ripe with the smell of not just mould, but bodies, people, sweat and blood.

We came to the doctor's office once more, and the sweating guard opened it and gestured for us to go inside. As soon as we did so, he closed the door, and it was then that I saw him – Max.

He stood there wearing a white shirt and brown trousers, his arms already outstretched for the twins to come to him. I checked my brain. I was hallucinating – I had to be. But no – he was there. I wanted to cry with relief, I wanted to run to him and fall into his arms and let him take me away from this place. He was here – he had to be.

'Come, be quick,' he whispered to them.

They, too, could not believe their eyes and barely made a sound, walked to him and let him take them in a quick embrace.

'We have to play a game,' he said, his voice rushed, urgent. 'A man will be here in a moment, and you have to pretend you do not know me. Do not try to cuddle me, do not say much – he can understand some Polish. You have to do this. Do you understand?'

'But—' Agata started.

'Please. You have to.'

'We will,' Michal said, stepping backwards, edging closer to me.

'Why?' asked Agata, her voice edging on tears.

'Please, Agata. You do not know me.'

Before I could say anything, before I could ask the twins if he was in fact real, or was I imagining the whole scene, Wagner came into the room.

He smiled at me and gave a slight nod of the head, then bent down to the twins and pinched their cheeks. Crossing the room, he plopped himself down in the doctor's chair.

He spoke rapidly to Max, who turned to me and relayed what he said in Polish, speaking quickly so that Wagner would struggle to understand.

'Hauptmann Wagner would like to apologise, first of all. He says that the guard who did this to you, Möller, had no right to do so. He had been explicitly told that you and the children were not to be touched, and to be properly fed. He says that he will be punished.'

There was a pause when Wagner looked to me. Was I supposed to thank him? I gave a brief nod of my head. It would have to suffice. There was no way that words of thanks were going to leave my mouth.

Wagner started talking again, and Max translated.

'This here is Max. You can call him Max. He is my translator, and we can finally get to know one another better.' Max had said this with scorn in his voice as Wagner sat there smiling as he spoke.

'Max will help us get things sorted. First of all, I want to tell you that the children are very special, very special indeed. Twins. A boy and a girl, yet they look so alike. And I know people with certain interests in twins – how their brains work – are they any different to us, who do not have a mirror of ourselves. So I have hand-picked these children and will ensure they are well fed, well looked after, even in here, until I can take them away.'

'Away where?' I asked Max.

'Berlin,' he answered without even asking Wagner.

'But why?'

Max turned to Wagner and said something, then nodded and began.

'They are to be taken to see specialist doctors. He says they will become famous. He says that you, too, can go with them perhaps, if things go well in the next few days. He says the doctor will be back tomorrow and he wanted you to see that the children will be taken care of. He wants me to tell you that the doctor would like to measure them and if I am not here to trans-late tomorrow, then you are to do whatever the doctor says to do and to keep the children calm. Then he says that you might all be able to leave with him – the doctor and Herr Wagner. But don't worry. You won't be going.' Max looked at me. 'I won't let it happen,' Max added.

'How did you get here? What's going on?' I was so confused I asked more and more questions – why Berlin? What would happen there? What doctors?

Max made a downward motion with his hands that I should remain calm. There was more talk from Wagner and more talk from Max.

'You will be fine. I will take care of you,' Max said.

'Is that you or him talking?'

'Me.'

Wagner stood and clapped his hands, spoke to Max and then opened the door where a frightened Möller was waiting.

'He will take you back to your cell now. Then some more food will be brought and you, Helena, will be allowed to shower. Then later, Hauptmann Wagner would like to see you.' Max was behind me now, and I could feel the heat from his body and even smell the soap on his skin. For a second, his fingers brushed mine, so quickly that I wondered whether I had imagined something yet again.

As we left, Möller kept his distance from me and seemed happy when I was locked back away inside that cell again, the twins by my side. Both of them were as bewildered as I was.

But Max was here. My Max. I felt relief flood through me, and I fell onto the floor and broke down in tears.

THIRTY

MAKSYMILIAN

'I think that went well, very well,' Leo said, as soon as Helena and the twins were gone. 'She seemed calm, didn't she? Don't you think? And don't you think she looked at me once or twice with something in her eye? I think so. I think she quite likes me...'

I wanted to tell him what she thought of him – that clearly they were scared. Their whole bodies were rigid, their faces pale, smeared with dirt. When I had seen the bruises on Helena's face and her bloody knees, it took all my resolve not to fly at Wagner and beat him to death.

More than once my hands had formed into fists by my side, and I kept looking to Agata and Michal to remind me that I had to keep going with this charade if I had any hope of getting them out.

'Don't you think she likes me, Max?' Wagner asked me again.

He was sitting back in the doctor's chair, swivelling it around and around like a child.

'Maybe,' I said slowly.

'I *want* her to like me, Max. I do. From the moment I saw

her at the hospital, I wanted her. But I'm not like these brutes' – he waved his hand towards the corridor outside the room. 'Like Möller. There's not as much fun in it if you have to hold them down or if they start screaming. It's pointless. It's much better, much easier, if they like me – even a little.'

I clenched and unclenched my hands.

'I was thinking, you know. She's not Jewish, so really I could marry her, if I wanted to. I was thinking, I take her to Berlin with me and we hand over the twins to my uncle, so we won't have to worry about them any more or them getting in our way. Then I'd get promoted and we could start a life. I mean, I know she's Polish, but I can tell by just looking at her that there's some German there somewhere, and you can always beat the Polish out of them, I'm sure of it.'

He sat, twirling, in that chair, in his despicable daydream.

'It could work, couldn't it, Max?' he asked.

'It could,' I managed to say.

But it never would.

THIRTY-ONE

HELENA

Sabina and Ola were in the cell and made a protective circle around me as I wept. Agata and Michal held on to me, asking me not to cry.

'These are good tears,' I told them. 'They're good.'

Soon, I managed to stop myself and stood. 'There's more food.' Sabina nodded at the floor.

She was right. On the floor was bread, cheese, ham even. 'We didn't eat any of it,' Ola assured me, but she could not take her eyes away from it.

'Please, eat it,' I told them.

The children got to it first, followed by the two women, both of them now and again scratching at their arms. I too had felt itchy this morning and wondered whether lice had now found their way beneath the already scratchy straw.

'We were told to come back here, have to wait,' Ola said, her mouth almost full of cheese.

'For what?' I asked.

'Taking us later to dig. We moved what we could to the truck. You saw someone you knew, didn't you?' Sabina asked.

'Out there, the... bodies,' she whispered so that the twins could not hear her.

I nodded.

'Who did you see out there, Helena?' Agata turned to me. 'Was it Max?' she asked. 'Did you see him before us?'

'No, it wasn't Max.' I was glad she had said his name. It was true then. I wasn't delusional. He had been there, in that cold doctor's office with that man who looked at me the way Ola was now looking at the piece of ham, and I wanted to cry all over again.

'Eat, you need to eat,' Ola told me firmly.

I ignored her and took the coffee.

'I think that's the last of them,' Ola said, sitting next to me, keeping her voice low, her eyes on the children as they ate with Sabina.

'That's the third lot that you saw this morning. They've been doing them in batches.'

'Doing what?'

'Gas,' she whispered.

I shook my head – I didn't understand.

'They put them inside and I don't know what they use or how, but they fill it with gas. We saw it with our own eyes when we were cleaning the sewerage pits. There were SS guards all around, and Lange, he was there – you know who Lange is?'

'No.'

'He runs this place.'

'I thought it was Wagner?'

'He's just in charge of the guards. Has no real say. I mean he can decide if we are beaten, but I don't think he can decide if we have to go into that bunker.'

She said all this to me with ease. With no emotion. People were gassed in a bunker. Not just people, my patients. I thought then of Father and the male patients – was this where they had gone, was this the fate they had met?

'You said in... batches. Did you see any men?'

'No men. But a few of the women who had been here before us told us that they had to dig graves before. In some woods, and there were some men there. All of them shot in the back of the head.'

So what the gardener had told me was true. Father and the male patents were buried in the woods. Shot. Dead. All of them gone.

'I'm sorry,' Ola suddenly collected herself. 'Oh God, Helena, I'm so sorry. I'm talking to you as if this is all normal, as if you didn't know those people. Please, Helena, I'm sorry. It's this place, it's changing me.' She began to cry, and I let her lean into me and let the tears flow.

'Why are you crying, Ola?' Agata came to us and wrapped her arms around Ola. 'It's all right to cry, you know. My father says you have to let the bad things out and then the good things will come in. so just let it out. And don't worry' – Agata looked at me – 'Max will help us. He's here now. He will help.'

In that moment, I wanted to cry along with her too. I wanted to cry because of seeing Max, because I was proud of Agata – how in amongst all this, she still felt for others, would still try to help. I wanted to cry for Father, for Małgorzata, for Basia and Hanna. For everyone. But I didn't. I wouldn't let another tear fall, I had to be stronger than this, strong for the children.

Agata had mentioned Max again, and I still couldn't believe it. Max was here. Max was Wagner's translator. How had this happened? Then a voice deep within me asked if I could trust it. Max was, or had been German. I had heard his story and fully believed him at the time. But what if my trust had been completely misplaced?

'Don't be stupid, Helena.' My mother's voice was back. 'Of course you can trust him. Do you think he made sure to get a job, to return to the Germans, just to torture you? Or do you think it's *because he's here to help, like he said he would? Use your brain, my Helena.'*

I tried to ignore her voice, as I knew I should, but I let the words creep in. It was too much of a coincidence that Max was here – he had to have engineered this with Antoni. I had to trust not only my mother's voice, but that feeling in my gut that Max was someone special, someone who had awoken childish fantasies of love, and I knew that he was not like Wagner whom I had immediately hated. Max was here.

Max was here for me.

For the next few hours, I watched Agata and Michal closely. They had been very quiet since we arrived, then had moments of playing, of using their imaginations to escape their surroundings and at times, they even imagined that Father was there and spoke to him. Then they had seen me bloodied and bruised. And now they had seen Max and heard talk of doctors in Berlin.

If a patient had come to me months ago with this in their file, I wouldn't have known where to start. I would have said that the trauma ran deep, and that it would take time and support to get them ever to live a normal life again. Here I was though, faced with it now, in the twins, and it was not over yet.

'Helena.' Michal came to me with some bread in his hands as I watched him and Agata make straw dolls. 'Please eat. You have to.'

I opened my mouth to protest, but Michal was quick and put the bread inside, then he laughed.

Oh, that laughter! The joy of it. It spread to Agata and then to Ola and Sabina, finally to me. I took the bread out of my mouth, grabbed Michal and held him to me, not caring that his weight on my body pressed against my bruised skin.

That afternoon, in that stinking damp cell, the walls drip-

ping with condensation, the lice nibbling at us, the bucket
almost overflowing with our bodily waste, we found some joy,
some comfort and I knew that we had to survive – we had to. I
had to hear that laughter again. I lived for it.

That evening, as Michal and Agata snuggled against Ola and
Sabina, Möller came for me.

As we went out into the corridor, I saw that his face was a
patchwork of bruises. He had been punished, and for that I was
glad. I just wished that it had been my fists ploughing into that
doughy skin of his.

He led me down a different corridor this time and opened a
door that led into a crude toilet – a hole in the floor, with rough
wooden planks surrounding it. On a small table was a bowl of
water, soap, a towel and some fresh clothes. He closed the door
and left me alone.

At first, I did nothing. I stared at the hole in the ground, at
the warm water and thought how far removed from my previous
life this was. We had had inside plumbing, a bath, scented
creams, hairbrushes – all the things that had seemed completely
mundane before. Now, seeing the basic bar of soap in front of
me, I let the tears flow even though I had promised myself I
wouldn't cry again. In a matter of days, I had been reduced to
an animal – literally sleeping on the floor, on straw that was
filled with lice, and constant rustling which meant that not only
humans lived in that squalor – the rats and mice, too, were our
bed-mates.

The reality of where I was hit me then. That bar of soap,
that change of clothes, and look: there, a hairbrush. How had I
not fallen apart yet – how had I kept going, kept moving? How
did Ola and Sabina do it, day in day out?

Father had once had a patient, a young boy, who was
constantly beaten by his father, which had resulted in him

trying to kill his own parent. Yet, when I or others spoke to him, you would not have guessed it as he hid his fear, his trauma, so well that I often wondered if he should have been in the hospital at all. Father told me the boy had 'compartmentalised' his trauma. He had found a way to push the beatings and abuse into one part of his brain, allowing him to carry on as if nothing had happened to him. But then one day he had snapped and had attacked his father with a carving knife, stabbing him more than ten times before someone was able to stop him. He was one of the cases that Father had taken over from the police – he had understood that the boy's past had made his mind work differently, and that prison was no place for him.

That was what I was doing now, I supposed. Placing pieces of fear, of trauma in a locked part of my mind so that I could still walk, still talk, still try to care for the twins.

A thud at the door alerted me to the fact that Möller was outside, waiting. I did not want him to come inside to get me, so I stripped off my clothes as quickly as I could, each bend of the knee singing with pain. I stood, naked, and looked down at my stomach, which was a mess of purple and blue. My thighs, my forearms, everything was covered in bruises and cuts. There was a layer of dirt atop the bruises too – of sweat and filth that I was sure one small bowl of water would not shift.

I tried, though. I washed as best I could, the water quickly turning grey, then darker and darker until I was sure it would turn pitch black.

The clothes I had been given were simple enough: underwear, a brown skirt, and a lighter brown shirt. They were too big for me, but I didn't care – it was nice to feel the clean material against my skin. I tried to brush my hair, but it was matted and each drag of the bristles nicked at my scalp and the bruises that lay there, so that soon I gave up with it and simply tied it back.

Once done, I placed my feet in the same shoes I had been

brought here in and my bare, bruised legs ached for a pair of stockings to cover them.

I had seen that most of the prisoners wore their own clothes, and you could tell by the bloodstains, the dirt and grime how long each person had been here for. I supposed if someone had looked at me, they would have thought I might have been here for months, rather than days.

Another impatient rap at the door.

It was then that I remembered – why hadn't I pieced it together before? Max had said that Wagner had wanted to see me – was all this in preparation for him? A wave of dread drenched me, head to toe, making my stomach churn with empty sickness again.

I knew what this was for. And I had to do what Ola and Sabina had done – *do not resist*. I had tried that once and I had almost been killed.

'*It's all right, Helena.*' My mother was behind me, her hand on my shoulder as I took each step. '*I'm here.*'

THIRTY-TWO

MAKSYMILIAN

Saturday, 18 November 1939
Poznań, Poland

The afternoon after seeing Helena, I was dispatched to a small boarding house less than a mile from the camp. Leo wanted to sleep, he told me, he had things to do later that I would not be needed for.

Before I left, I was introduced to the guards and told that I was his personal translator, and that they would have to ask his permission if they wanted me to help them – I was *his* – he made it clear. He also handed me a new blue ID card, my name on it, a blank space for a photograph to be attached.

'We'll get one taken,' he said. 'That way you can come and go, and there will be no issues.'

As much as I did not want to leave Helena and the twins, there was little I could do, and as soon as I was out of the gates, I oddly began to run down the track that led to the main road, the camp at my back, getting further and further away. It was only when I was out of breath that I stopped, put my hands on my knees and took deep lungfuls of air.

There was a part of me, quite obviously, that couldn't wait to get away from that place and I could not comprehend how Helena and the twins must be feeling if I, after only a few hours in there, had had this primal reaction to flee.

The structure of the Fort itself was ominous to begin with – deep underground, with damp, stale air, no sunlight; and such a labyrinth of tunnels that you began to think if you took a wrong turn, you would be forever lost within those walls.

I had heard screams – torturous cries that seemed to be all around me, so that I could not discern exactly where they came from.

'Interrogation,' Leo had said, as we walked back to his cottage, picking at something in his teeth with a too long finger-nail on his little finger. 'Gestapo. Not for us to meddle in. We look after the others – the long-term prisoners. There's enough there for us to do.'

I did not like how he included me in the 'we' he spoke of. I was now a part of this in his twisted mind.

'You have to show them who's boss, you know. Sure, they're hurt, sure they don't like it, but they're not real people, are they? Like those patients from the hospital we gassed—'

'Gassed?'

'Ja, gassing. It's new. We're trying it here. Lange thinks we can use it elsewhere. It's quick, they don't know what's happening and it's over within a few minutes or so.'

I couldn't find words that didn't include me screaming at him, so I said nothing. My mind swam with the image of Helena and the twins, of the bruises on her face, the dirt smeared on their skin. I could not let myself imagine them being killed – gassed to death.

'It's a kindness we do, though. I mean, they have to be elimi-nated. Can't have them in the new Reich.'

He spoke as if the people he mentioned were mere rats and nothing more. 'I was asked by Lange to head the SS force that went to the hospital, you know,' he said smugly. '*Hand-picked*, Lange said so himself. Then when he saw how well it had gone, he told me to stay here so I could help with more if needed. I expect that soon that promotion will come through. Soon.'

It was as though he spoke to himself. His obsession with himself, with his role and his aspirations for promotion had no humanity in it, no realisation that his career came at a cost of how well he could manage to round people up, keep them locked up, and kill them.

I stood now, finally finding my breath again and walked down a road where cars still ran, where people walked to shops, where someone, somewhere yelled at a dog to stop barking. It did not seem right that life, just yards away, was carrying on as if that Fort did not exist. Did that man, there, who trimmed a hedge in his tiny garden realise what was happening? Did he know and just not want to think about it?

I wanted to scream at the top of my lungs and tell the world the truth, but then, I wondered, how many would actually listen?

As I walked, two tanks lumbered past me, their metal treads grinding on the road. I stopped walking for a moment to look at them – these enormous machines so alien in this city. No one else on the street looked at them, no one wanted to see them, so they simply didn't. I knew then that there was little hope for anyone imprisoned in the Fort. But I had seen, and I wouldn't pretend I hadn't.

I soon reached the boarding house that was wedged between two apartment blocks, looking as though it did not belong – almost as if someone had wedged the house between the two buildings and it had gotten stuck. The white paint was peeling unhappily from the walls and through the cracks in the pavement, weeds grew with wild abandon.

It was run by a harassed woman in her sixties, who told me her name, although I promptly forgot it. She showed me to a room with a narrow single bed and a wooden chair that only had three legs, then turned away from me to bustle about downstairs, shouting up at me not to be noisy and that the toilet was outside.

I sat on the narrow bed, feeling the springs in the mattress on my behind. There was nothing inviting about this room, no warmth, no cheer, and I wondered if the woman who had shown it to me had given lodgings to German soldiers on purpose; her house was grim and perhaps she felt it could be a form of punishment for them.

I stood up, went to the small window and looked out onto an unremarkable street where I could see little activity, then returned to the uncomfortable bed, wishing that I had someone to talk to – Olek, or Joasia, anyone. I needed to talk about what I had seen – to try and make sense of it all. How would I keep my mind busy between now and tomorrow morning? I wondered. How could I not think about what could be taking place inside the Fort? How could I free Helena and the twins?

The only way I knew how to silence my thoughts was to write them down. I made a brief journey to the kitchen in search of the landlady and begged her for some paper and a pen.

'Here.' She shoved the paper at me and a worn-down pencil. 'No pens,' she scoffed.

Back in the tiny room I thought of how many guards I had seen – four at the gate, two just inside after crossing the moat. Then there were others that seemed interchangeable and were everywhere all at once. Leo had keys on his belt – this I knew. On a giant ring that clanged against his thigh as he walked.

I wrote all of this down and more – anything I could think of that might prove useful.

Soon, my eyes became scratchy with sleep, and I lay down

on that thin mattress, listening to the birds sing outside and the rain that knocked against the window. I closed my eyes and tried to leave the world behind, my mind racing with a thousand possibilities of what could happen, not finding one scenario where it ended well.

THIRTY-THREE

MAKSYMILIAN

Sunday, 19 November 1939
Fort VII, Poznań, Poland

The following morning, I woke with a renewed sense of purpose. Looking over my notes as I ate a hurried breakfast of warm bread and butter and thick coffee in the landlady's parlour, I knew that I had to go back to Żerków. A plan was forming in my mind, and I needed Antoni's help to see it through – a plan so ludicrous that I realised it just might work.

I was at the Fort gates as the weak autumnal sunlight began to flit through the trees. The driveway was littered with leaves, damp and rotting already into the ground and for a second, I wondered where summer had gone, not remembering it leaving us so suddenly, giving way to these grey, dank days.

A guard at the gates nodded at me as I showed him the letter that Leo had given me, proving I was his translator and should be allowed entry.

The guard was young – too young, and he barely glanced at the letter, barely listened to me at all. His coat was speckled with the dew of the morning, and I could imagine that all he cared about at that moment was getting inside, somewhere warm and dry.

I went to Leo's cottage and knocked, once, then twice.

Eventually, he opened the door, still wrapped in his crimson dressing gown, yawing as he saw me.

He let me inside as he stumbled about in the kitchen, endeavouring to make coffee.

'How's the boarding house?' he asked me, as he banged cups on the counter. 'Shit, isn't it?'

'It's fine,' I told him.

'It isn't,' he said, carrying the mugs of coffee towards me, placing a steaming mug in my cold hands. 'It's awful. I stayed there one night, then demanded for better lodgings. I mean, I am a Hauptmann, after all.'

I watched Wagner as he sat back in his armchair, a relaxed smile on his face.

'She gave in,' he said, looking me over the top of his mug as he drank.

'Who?' I asked, my hands shaking, but I already knew the answer.

'Helena. She was beautiful. Beautiful. I mean there were the bruises and whatnot, but there was not much light in there, so it hardly bothered me at all.'

My jaw clenched, the teeth griding on top of each other and I thought that at any moment they would crumble into dust with the amount of pressure I was applying.

'I thought she may struggle a little, but she was quite calm, quite easy. I took her to the doctor's office, of course. Couldn't bring her here, and I'm not like those brutes who take them in the corridors or cells. I mean, I am a Hauptmann, after all.' He leaned forward, 'I think it shows she does like me, don't you think? The fact she was calm says it all, doesn't it?'

'I need to leave this evening,' I told him, trying to keep my voice level and calm.

He screwed up his face. 'Oh?' He was not happy that I was not engaging with him and his tales of his conquest.

I nodded. 'I need to see to something which I think will be beneficial for you.'

'You do?'

'Indeed, but I'll be back the following morning. It's just some information I have heard, and if it proves true, then it may help you in your career.'

He grinned now. 'What information?'

'I'd rather not say. Not until it's confirmed to be true.'

He nodded wisely. 'Good. Yes. Find out the truth.'

He began to talk again of Helena, of his flights of fancy to going to Berlin with her, but I tuned him out. My mind was racing, the idea forming so quickly that I wondered whether it had been there all that time, and yet only when he had spoken of what he was doing to Helena did it fully become apparent to me. I knew how to get Helena out. And I knew how to save the twins too.

But I needed help, and Antoni and Olek were the key to my plan's success.

THIRTY-FOUR
HELENA

Sunday, 19 November 1939
Fort VII, Poznań, Poland

I did not speak all morning apart from telling the twins to eat and answering my name at roll call. Both Sabina and Ola tried to get me to speak, knowing that something had changed, but I could not form the words, I could not even bear to remember what had happened last night in that doctor's office with my skirts pulled high above my hips, my shirt opened and my breasts revealed to a man who grunted over me.

I remembered how Anna, after she had married Rolf, had told me in giggly sentences about their wedding night, about how it hurt a little, but there was so much pleasure in the act that she couldn't wait to do it again.

Of course, it wasn't like that for me. I never wanted to remove my clothes again, I wanted to wear layers and layers of clothing so that I couldn't be unpeeled so easily. I wanted to crawl inside my own skin and hide forever.

When Möller came for me and the twins after breakfast, I followed him dumbly, not really taking in the new line of prisoners that were being marched the opposite way, each of them being hit and kicked as they moved. They were women. That I did notice.

We reached the doctor's office and Wagner, Max and the bespectacled doctor were waiting for us. Immediately, Wagner spoke and Max translated.

'The twins are to get undressed,' he said. 'Naked,' his voice struggled with the last word.

'No,' I told him, wrapping my arms around myself.

'It's for measurements and such,' he said, as gently as he could. 'The doctor wants to measure them, and he has asked that they undress.'

'It's all right, Helena.' Michal was already taking off his shirt. 'It's just a doctor.'

Agata looked to me, her eyes wide, uncomprehending – I knew how she felt.

I knelt down in front of her and took off her cardigan with trembling hands, hearing nothing in the room but my own breathing.

Soon, they were naked. Michal stood, arms by his side, eyeing the doctor with some form of defiance. Agata, on the other hand, shielded her body with her arms and then began to cry.

'They'll be quick,' Max said, as the doctor and Wagner spoke. 'And this won't last much longer,' he said, rapidly now. 'I'm going to get you out of here, tomorrow, or maybe the next day. It really won't be long, Helena, trust me.'

I heard the words, but they did not sink in and did not bring me hope nor comfort. I stood there and had to watch as the doctor measured the twins' skulls with a weird pronged device, then their height, the widths of their arms and thighs.

'*Gut*,' the doctor looked up at me.

'You can dress again now,' Max said. 'The doctor says you have done well.'

Wagner came close to us, and I flinched away from him. He bent down and gave the children a silver-wrapped sweet and before I knew what was happening, the doctor jabbed Michal in the arm with a large needle.

He yelped as it pierced his skin, then the doctor moved towards Agata who hid behind me.

'Come. Come,' Wagner was still at her level, grinning, holding another sweet out to her, trying to coax her like a belligerent animal.

'What are they giving them?' I screamed at Max, and suddenly my mind started to work again, my body releasing itself from the detachment I had felt all morning.

'I – I don't know,' he stammered.

Max spoke with the doctor and Wagner and then shook his head, not wanting to say what he had to. 'It's to help them. That's what he says.'

'Help them *how*? What is it?'

'They didn't say. They just said it was a test.'

It wasn't long before the doctor became impatient and stood, took Agata roughly by the arm and injected her too.

'Tomorrow, Helena. I promise. It will be tomorrow,' Max said urgently, as the door was opened and Möller led us away from that room which I hoped I would never see again in my life.

THIRTY-FIVE

MAKSYMILIAN

Sunday, 19 November 1939
Fort VII, Poznań, Poland

Helena was pale, drawn, her voice barely audible as she stood in that doctor's office. She kept wrapping her arms around herself and would repeat and repeat the action as if eventually her arms would sit right on her body.

When Wagner had made the twins undress, the distress in Helena's face made me want to cry. My stammer reappeared a few times – the shy weak child inside me – but I could not let my fears get the better of me.

Wagner would not tell me what they injected into the twins, but I knew of course that it was not good, whatever it was. His uncle in Berlin had sent the vials, he told me, and twins were a good subject to test on. I resolved in that moment that no matter what, Helena and the twins would be leaving tomorrow. Not the next day, nor the next. Tomorrow.

'I have to leave a little earlier than planned,' I told Wagner, as we left the doctor's office.

'You said this evening?'

'I did, yes. But I misspoke. I meant that I would be back here this evening – I have to leave now.'

Wagner shrugged. 'Where are you going? Will you tell me that at least?'

'I have to go back to Żerków,' I told him. 'I have to speak to someone I met there. Someone who can certainly help us perhaps find a few high-ranking politicians and such who, with their capture, by you, would get you that promotion within days.'

Wagner was animated now. 'Days? Really?'

I nodded. 'Of course. I mean, if the information is correct, then this could mean you getting perhaps two promotions.'

'Two.' His eyes seemed to glaze over as he entered into his dream world of ranks, big houses, accolades.

'Then take my car,' he said, turning to me. 'Take it. You will get there quicker and get back quicker, which means that we can move forward with whatever you have found out.'

He was so excited that I imagined that at any second he would start jumping up and down like Michal did when Joasia told him she had made chocolate cake.

I did not hesitate, accepted his gift of the car and let the driver take me to Żerków. And as I sat in the back seat, I planned the escape of Helena and the twins.

It took just over an hour to reach Żerków, and as we drove, I thought more and more about my ludicrous plan, honing it, and finally seeing that it was the only possible way to get Helena and the twins free. On arrival, I asked the driver to park outside of Olek's inn, where I raced inside – to Olek's surprise – and told him to find Antoni, and then meet me at Joasia's'. I would leave the driver here, and Olek's new barman, a young boy from the village was to give him food and drink and even offer a room for a small sleep if he so wished.

When I relayed this to the driver, his eyes lit up. 'Free food and drink?' he asked.

'Indeed.'

He didn't need to be told twice and quickly got out of the car, rubbing his hands together at the thought of a relaxing afternoon.

I ran to Joasia's house, my leg groaning with pain, but I did not let it slow me down – I would not stop.

Bursting through the front door, I found Joasia and Filip at the kitchen table, his face still a smattering of bruises, his glasses now mended with white tape in such a way that they sat lopsided on his nose.

'Max!' Joasia rushed to me and held me close. It was a strange moment as I suddenly felt as though I had come home, that she, Joasia, Filip, Olek even, were my family. And all I needed now was Helena and the twins, and I would no longer be alone, none of us would.

'I need your help, Joasia. I need those pills of yours, the ones I took that knocked me out. Do you still have some? Please say you do.'

'Where's Helena? Where are the twins?' She looked over my shoulder, expecting them to appear. Instead, she was greeted with a red-faced Olek and a dishevelled Antoni, whom Olek said he had found staying in a friend's house – not giving any more information away.

'I need them, Joasia,' I tried to focus her; her eyes would not settle. 'Please.'

'I have them. I do,' she finally snapped back. 'But why?'

'I know how to get them out, and I need your help – all of you.'

Within a minute I had them corralled around the kitchen table and I spread out the crumpled bits of paper I had written my ideas on.

'I need the tablets to drug Wagner,' I told their expectant faces.

'Drug him?' Olek asked.

'Yes. It's the only way. And I need you, Antoni, to call in some favours from your friends who can meet me at the Jeżycki cemetery at ten p.m. tonight.'

'What for?' Filip squeaked.

Slowly, trying to grasp at my own thoughts, I laid the plan out for them.

'I will return to the Fort this afternoon and tell Wagner that I know that Witold, head of the Polish resistance, will be alone in the cemetery at ten p.m. where he goes each night to lay flowers on his wife's grave. I will tell him that between the two of us, we will be able to take him on, arrest him, and Wagner, naturally, will get all the glory of arresting the most wanted man in the city. I will offer him a drink, and in the drink, I will put some of those pills of yours, Joasia, to knock him out.'

'But what if he won't drink beforehand?' Joasia asked. 'How will you get the pills in him?'

I laughed. 'He will drink. I can promise you that.'

'All right,' Olek said. 'So you go back, with his driver and tell Wagner and get him to drink. Then you drive out to the cemetery, where hopefully, by then, Wagner is out cold. Then what?'

'You will be there, Olek, with Antoni and his friends. Antoni will take the driver out of the car, by force if necessary, but I doubt that will be needed. From what I have seen of him, he doesn't look like the type to fight back. Then you, Olek will get in the car and drive me and Wagner back to the Fort.'

'And where will I be in all of this? I want to help!' Joasia was almost hysterical and thumped her fists on the table.

'You will be helping. I need you to drive Olek's car to the Morasko woods. There's a small dirt track that turns off from the main road. That's where we'll be waiting.'

'We who?' Joasia demanded.

'Me, Helena, the twins and Wagner.'

'And I'll take Wagner,' Antoni was cottoning on now. 'I'll take Wagner,' his voice was confident, strong. 'I'll deal with him.'

'So you'll just go back into the Fort, will you, and simply walk out with Helena and the twins? What if they won't let you back in?' Joasia was frantic.

'They will. Wagner will be in the car. They won't notice the driver. The guards at the gate know me, they all do, and have been told that I am his personal translator. I will take his keys, go into the cells and find Helena and simply walk her out.'

'Simply!' Joasia raised her hands in the air. 'Simply! Like they will just let you do that.'

'I have a gun,' I told her. 'I will use it if I need to. But you need to trust me. That time at night, the guards are cold and tired. There are fewer of them. If stopped, I will tell them that I am to take Helena and the twins to Wagner's car where he is waiting. If they look inside, they'll see him—'

'Yes, but he'll be asleep,' Joasia interrupted. 'Wouldn't that seem strange to them?'

'Maybe. Maybe not. I think they all know how much he drinks. Maybe they'll think he's simply passed out from that.'

Joasia went quiet for a moment, and I was sure she was going to tell me that it was too dangerous and it could not be done. But then she turned to me and smiled. 'Give him three tablets. Take a few extra if needed, but three will make him half-asleep. He will be able to talk but won't really know what's happening around him.'

'How do you know this?' Olek asked.

Joasia blushed, then shrugged. 'He'll be suggestible. That way, if you tell him you're getting Helena for him, in his state, he'll believe it and then possibly repeat it back if he's asked by anyone.'

'What will you do with Wagner?' Joasia asked Antoni.

'He'll disappear,' he said.

'They'll come looking for him,' Joasia warned. 'For you, Max.'

I nodded. 'I will disappear too. Antoni, I need your help. Do you have any friends in Warsaw? Or anywhere? Somewhere I can go but still help others too.'

He nodded, stood and said he needed to get to Poznań as soon as possible and would meet at the prearranged time.

'Are you sure you can do this?' I asked him, grasping his arm to make him turn away from the door to look at me. 'It's a lot to ask – can it be done?'

'You know,' he began, his voice low, 'I have loved Helena for years. I love the twins. I have loved their father, their mother too. It will be done. It has to be done. Just make sure you get them out, Max, make sure you can get them out and I will get them to England, to Oxford. You get them out, and I promise you they will be safe.'

'I'll get them out.'

Antoni nodded and began to walk to the door, then he suddenly turned to me. 'And Max,' he called out. 'Make sure you find them again, won't you. Take care of yourself so that one day you can always be with them, taking care of them.'

I nodded my agreement and watched him walk out of Joasia's house, realising suddenly that I was not the only one who thought of Helena, the twins, and the others as my family. They were Antoni's family too.

I reached the Fort with a half-drunk driver by eight o'clock, my hands sweating with nerves. I was aware of the bottle of pills in my pocket and could not stop thinking about all the things that could go wrong.

What if the tablets didn't work? What if Antoni could not

restrain the driver, or find friends to help him? What if he couldn't get me away? What if I were arrested? What if the guards stopped me when I went to get Helena? What if, what if, what if...

With these thoughts I got out of the car and made my way to Wagner's small house.

He greeted me with a grin. 'How did it go? Will I get that promotion?' he asked.

Drawing upon every ounce of courage I had, I played along. 'We can get Witold,' I told him. 'If you can get him, I expect that you would get more than one promotion. Imagine it – the head of the Polish resistance taken in by none other than Leo Wagner.'

The more I spoke, the wider his grin became.

'But maybe we should take a few others, you know, just in case,' he casually mentioned after I had told him what was to happen at the cemetery. I could see that he was nervous – I doubted he had ever really been in a situation where he could not rely on some form of backup, but it had to be him, just him and he could not tell anyone about it.

'It has to be *you*. Let everyone see how great Leo Wagner is, how he can take the most dangerous man in Poland down on his own,' I insisted. 'You can do this. And I will be there, of course. But I doubt you would need me – you could do this blindfolded!' I joked.

He soon came round to the idea, realising that more glory would be heaped upon him if he did this alone.

'A drink, to celebrate?' I asked him.

There was the briefest of pauses and I thought he was going to decline the offer, but he licked his lips, then said, 'I think one would be wise.'

I offered to pour the drinks and let him settle himself in his chair, talking over and over about the promotion he would get, the money, the houses. As he spoke, I felt around in my pocket for the bottle of pills, managing to open the cap and tip a few into my pocket. Then, taking three between my fingers, I crushed them and placed them in his drink, giving it a quick stir, then adding more brandy on top.

'A big measure!' he exclaimed, as I handed him the glass. 'I don't want to get drunk beforehand!'

I sat and sipped at my own drink, willing him to stop talking and knock back the drink like I had seen him do so many times before at Olek's. The minutes ticked by slowly, and I was sure it wasn't going to happen – he wasn't going to drink it. Sweat was gathering under my armpits, and I wanted to scream in frustration. But just as I thought the whole thing would have to be called off, at 9 p.m., he knocked the drink back and announced: 'Let's go. Let's go make my career!'

I let out a huge breath, relief that he had finally drunk it soothing me. I just hoped that the tablets would work in time and that everything else was in place.

That's all I had at this point. Hope.

By the time we reached the cemetery, Wagner was out cold. His driver barely noticed and when Antoni and another man wrenched the car door open, the driver immediately put his hands up in surrender and allowed himself to be led away. To where? I didn't ask – I didn't want to know.

Olek was soon behind the wheel, and I could smell his body odour – sickly and musty. He looked at me in the rear-view mirror and grinned, sweat on his brow, dripping down into his beard.

He gunned the engine, and we were soon making our way back to the Fort.

'Has it all gone to plan?' I asked him, keeping one eye on Wagner who now and again muttered something inaudible, opened and then closed his eyes again.

'Yes. Joasia has my car. She's a terrible driver. I thought I was going to die if I'm honest!' His attempt at lightening the atmosphere was welcome. This had been the easiest part. The next part would determine all our fates.

We soon reached the Fort, and the gates were opened without hindrance. The headlights lit up the entrance – that walkway into a gloomy hole.

'This is it?' Olek whispered.

'It is.'

'It looks like a nightmare...'

'It's worse than anything you can imagine,' I told him.

I got out of the car and instructed him to keep the engine going, and if Wagner woke up and tried to get out of the car for some reason, he was to punch him square in the face.

Two guards stood on the walkway, trying to shield themselves a little from the deluge under the lip of a roof.

There would normally have been more – I was sure of it – but the weather had made them act like small children. How ironic, I suddenly thought, they could mete out violence without compunction, but when it rained, they huddled together or crept away to stay dry.

I showed them my blue ID card, neither one of them that interested when I told them I was to bring a woman to Wagner who was waiting in his car.

Their eyes clocked his car for a second, then they both took another glance at my ID and let me through.

Suddenly, once inside, my mind went blank. The place was a warren of tunnels and I completely forgot where the doctor's office was, which way Möller had gone when he had taken them back to their cell.

Swallowing deeply, I tried to tell myself to remain calm. I could do this. I just had to think.

It was left, wasn't it? No, it was right. No, straight on.

'Herr Wagner,' suddenly Möller was beside me. 'Can I help you?'

His left eye was partially closed from where another guard had hit him, as per Leo Wagner's instructions – he couldn't even administer his own punishments.

'Yes, yes, you can,' I injected calmness into my voice and tried to keep my eyes on his face. 'The Hauptmann has asked me to come inside and collect a prisoner – Helena. He's waiting in the car. He wants the twins too.'

'What would he want the twins for?' Möller asked, looking beyond me to the outside where the bright headlights shone, reflecting in the raindrops that fell.

'To send them away to his uncle, the doctor,' I said authoritatively.

Möller was half-convinced, I could see it. He didn't like Wagner, it was literally all over his face in the form of bruises and tiny cuts.

'He wanted a moment with Helena too,' I continued, letting the unsaid imply more than I could ever say.

'He does, does he? Well, he is the boss, I suppose.'

'Tell me, is it left?' I pointed down one of the rabbit warrens.

He sighed, seemingly bored of me already. 'It is. You have a key?'

'I do,' I held up the ring of keys that I had taken from Wagner when he had passed out in the car.

He eyed the keys, then picked the one I would need. 'Down there, keep going until you can't go any further. Last cell on the left.'

I started to walk, then heard Möller call out my name again.

I turned, expecting to see a gun, expecting that he hadn't bought what I had to say, but he was simply standing there, eyeing the car. 'Say, how long do you think he'll be gone for? Me and a few others have a bottle of vodka and some cards, and the weather is shit so we were thinking of having a little break.'

'He'll be gone for a few hours, at least,' I half laughed.

'Good. Good. Don't tell him, though. Our secret.' He tapped the side of his nose, then walked away, disappearing into the gloom.

I went quickly, my footsteps echoing on the concrete floor. In just over a minute, I was outside Helena's cell. My fingers fumbling with the key, I pushed it into the lock, but nothing happened. Shit. Was this the wrong key?

I tried again, then again, then finally, there was the turning of the tiny mechanisms inside and the door opened.

THIRTY-SIX

HELENA

Sunday, 19 November 1939
Fort VII, Poznań, Poland

When we reached our cell, there were new faces – ten of them. Ola and Sabina talked to them, and tried to reassure them as they had done when I had arrived, but I could see that they struggled to find the right words and were no longer sure that there was any hope left.

The women looked up at us as we entered, especially when Michal vomited on the ground, soon followed by Agata. Ola came to us and asked what had happened, but I couldn't put it into any proper words, and I could see from her face that I wasn't making much sense.

'Let's get you settled,' she told Michal and Agata, leading them to a patch of straw that was still relatively clean, and not as damp.

The twins were pale, paler than they had been before. It was as though all the colour had been sucked out from under the skin and I could see blue veins in their faces, spider-like, patterning their cheeks.

Agata began to shiver and shake so I lay down next to her and held her close, but the shaking got worse, more violent and no matter how hard I pressed myself against her, she rocked and bucked in my arms.

Michal was the opposite. He lay rigid and I had to ask Ola to check if he was breathing as his chest didn't seem to be rising and falling. The other women soon crowded around, scared at the sight before them, and yet, they began to speak, full of concern for the twins, wondering what could be done to help them.

One woman knelt down beside Agata and lifted her eyelids, then checked inside her mouth. She did the same for Michal and said that we had to make sure that they did not choke on their vomit as they had gone into some form of strange sleep, where they looked awake, eyes open, and yet were no longer there.

'My husband,' she said, sitting next to us, 'was, no, *is* a doctor. I learned a few things from him over the years.'

She was around fifty, I guessed, maybe younger. I wasn't sure whether the wrinkles in her skin were caused by age or by the trauma of finding herself in this place.

I was glad of her help. I knew I should have checked on the twins as she had just done, but it was like I was in one of those dreams when every time you tried to move, to do something, your arms and legs felt weighted down and refused to comply. My brain just wouldn't work as it should have done – it was as though I had forgotten all my medical training, all my knowledge – it had all simply disappeared.

I liked her. She didn't ask questions, didn't force me to speak, and I was glad of not having to try and think of words to string into a sentence. Now and then, she would check on the twins breathing, their eyes, in their mouths and made the other women cover them with the blankets and potato sacks.

Whether I slept during that day, I do not know. I was in

some form of state where nothing seemed real and my brain was muddled with the distress of the twins, with what had happened with Wagner the night before and with everything, *everything* that had happened so quickly these past couple of months.

Could it really only have been a couple of months? I thought back slowly – yes. In August I was in my office with Małgorzata, I was in Joasia's garden, with the sun on my face, the tickle of grass underneath me. And then there was Max. Then the war. Then Father. And now, here.

It seemed that it was impossible that so much had happened in such a short time frame. How could I go from being me, bathing, working, eating, talking, laughing, to this?

How could it have happened to any of us?

By evening, the twins had started to come round from their comatose state, each of them confused by what was happening.

'My head hurts,' Agata cried, holding it between her hands and rocking back and forth.

Michal sat, hugging his knees to his chest and stared at nothing, and when I spoke to him, it took him time to turn his head and register where the voice was coming from and that it was directed at him.

There was extra food once more for the twins, obviously sent by Wagner, but neither wanted to eat, so I told the new arrivals to share it amongst themselves as they would not be fed until the following morning. I didn't dare warn them of the bitter coffee, stale bread and watery soup that would be their food for an entire day.

I sat for hours, watching as the cell darkened bit by bit, my back against the bricks, my arms around the twins as they leaned into me, the three of us unable to move, unable to do anything but sit. A piece of stone dug into my buttocks as we sat. I pulled it out and looked at it, then looked to the damp walls where the twins had carved their names and a smiling face. Moving only a little, I turned to the wall and began to etch my name too, finally realising that perhaps we would never be free, and this may be the only thing that I could leave behind – my name.

Soon, the room went from dark blue to black, and as my eyes adjusted to the darkness, all I could make out were hazy shapes of the women as they finally found some rest. I heard the door open with its heavy creak, and a thud of dread fell into my stomach – Möller again to take me to Wagner. I managed to stand and make myself walk to the door and almost didn't register that it was not Möller who stood in front of me, but it was Max, illuminated by the faint light of a torch.

'Helena, where are the twins?' he whispered urgently.

I nodded at where they sat, but I wasn't sure he could see my gesture. 'Over there,' I said, my voice unsteady.

'Get them. Get them quickly.'

I went to the twins and got them to stand, but Agata fell against me. I picked her up and with my other hand tried to half drag Michal out of the cell.

'Helena,' I heard Ola's voice in the darkness. 'Don't resist,' she said.

She obviously thought that I was going to Wagner again, and I was still unsure what was happening – did Wagner want me and the twins and had he sent Max to get us?

Max picked Michal up and began to walk quickly down the tunnels. We passed only two guards – one smoked as he leaned against a cell with bars floor to ceiling, the other talked to him. Neither seemed to look at Max, the twins and me, and it was within minutes that we were in the outdoors, walking across the concrete walkway of the moat and to a waiting car, its head-lights trained on us.

Max opened the car door and placed Michal gently inside,

then he took Agata from my arms and did the same, finally, he helped me inside and climbed in beside me. It was then I saw that Wagner sat in the front seat. He turned to look at me and gave me a weird smile, but did not speak.

'Are we going to Berlin?' I asked Max in a whisper.

'Berlin!' Wagner said, with a loud laugh.

The car began to move, steadily at first, negotiating the potholes of the track until it reached the main road and the driver gunned the engine so that soon the outside world was a blur through the window.

'You're not going to Berlin,' Max said, looking intently at me. He held my face in his hands, looking directly into my eyes.

'Did he give you something too, after I left the room?'

'No,' I said, but my words were coming out slowly. Did he? I didn't think so...

'When did you last eat, Helena?' Max asked me gently.

'Days ago, I think. My stomach wants to be empty,' I said. He would not take his hands from my face, then he placed his lips on my forehead, gently, ever so gently, then let me droop down, leaning into his shoulder.

To say that I was not completely aware of what was going on was an understatement, and I felt as though I was in a strange dream. I kept trying to hold on to one fact, one part of reality and then it would slip away from me and Wagner would slur, 'Berlin,' and Michal would stare at me, and Agata would cry out, and Max would try and ask me a question, but it was all too much.

Soon the car slowed and the door opened – were we in Berlin already?

But no, Olek's face was at the door, and Max got out, then Olek lifted Michal from the car and Max took Agata.

Finally, Max helped me out too.

'Helena,' Wagner slurred. 'I love you,' then Max slammed the car door shut.

Antoni was here too – had he been in the car? He came to me and wrapped me in his arms, then kissed the top of my head. He exchanged hurried words with Olek and Max, then he, and another man I did not know, climbed into the car and sped away into the night.

'Helena,' Joasia was here now.

I touched her face. 'Are you real?' I asked her.

She was crying. Joasia never cried. 'Oh, Helena!'

The twins were gone, and I saw another car, the doors open. This one old, not like the black car we had arrived in. I squinted through the darkness to see it, but my eyes would not work properly either.

'They're inside the car,' Max said gently. He took my arm and led me to it. 'Get in, Helena.'

I did. I did what he said. I got in the car and Joasia and Olek got into the front. I moved over as far as I could, waiting for Max to get in too. Instead, he leaned in, kissed the twins, then placed his hand on top of my head, the warmth of his palm radiating through my skull.

'I have to go now,' he said softly.

'Where?' I asked.

'I have to go back. Back inside—'

'The belly of the beast,' I finished for him.

He nodded and smiled. 'But I'll find you again, Helena.' Then he closed the door and Olek drove us away, into the night.

DECEMBER 1995

THIRTY-SEVEN

HELENA

Sunday, 24 December 1995
Wallingford, Oxfordshire, UK

It is Christmas Eve. My favourite day of the year. It's the one day when I truly feel full of joy and hope. In Poland, we would normally celebrate Christmas on this day, but here in England they do it the next, so what I do is celebrate both days – one Polish, one English.

Today, it will just be my husband and me, and tomorrow morning, the children and grandchildren will arrive, and we will celebrate the English way with a turkey and all those trimmings they love so much. The children have always felt themselves to be English and although they don't mind my Polish Christmas, they prefer the one that everybody else does.

I have been fasting all day and soon I will sit down at the table with twelve dishes, to reflect the number of Apostles, some beetroot soup, fish, pickled cabbage, *pierogi*, and much more. I cannot wait. There will be another plate set at the table, this one for the stranger – we did this when I was a child, leaving a place setting for anyone who may turn up at the last moment, someone who might not have any family or friends to celebrate with. I have never had a stranger appear at my door on Christmas Eve, but I don't want to not do it and this be the one year where there is a gentle knock and some lonely soul asks to come in. So I'll set the place, and wait and see.

I wonder now, who that stranger was that night with Antoni as they climbed into Wagner's car and drove away? I remember asking about it, but no one remembered him either. But I was sure there was someone else there, someone else who drove away with Antoni and Wagner.

Although, at the time, my mind could not completely be trusted. The trauma of everything had broken me and I barely remember what happened after Max left. I know we went to a house, somewhere. It was small, tucked away in a part of the countryside that I had never been to. There was a doctor there and at first, when he touched me, I began to cry – I remember that. Joasia was by my side and told me it was all right.

How long we were in that house, I do not know. I know I slept, and I had strange dreams, and sometimes I was awake and thought I was dreaming – reality had blurred itself into something else and like snowflakes in winter, I could not seem to grasp at it before it melted away in my hand.

I ate. I know this because I recall Joasia feeding me like a child. Even when I refused, she was patient, yet stern, and would eventually get a spoon into my mouth.

Perhaps days or weeks later, we moved again, but this time without Joasia and Olek, who said that they had to stay. Filip was still very unwell and was living at Joasia's.

'I want to come with you,' I told them.

But they shook their heads – I couldn't – it was too dangerous.

The twins and I were still traumatised by everything, so the goodbyes with Olek and Joasia were not as emotional as they should have been. If I had been completely lucid, I would have cried, I would have held Joasia to me and never let go. But all I did was let her hug me, kiss me, and place me in another car with the twins.

We drove, it seemed for days on end. Stopping only for fuel or toilet breaks until we reached a port, which I now know was in France, and we were ushered onto a boat and told we were going to England.

It may seem strange to you that I cannot detail that long trip in a car from Poland to France. It may seem strange that I noticed nothing, thought of nothing. But I cannot adequately describe to you how muddled my brain was – not just mine – the twins too. It was like we were shells of ourselves – yes! – like an oyster shell, with the oyster inside all scooped out, leaving this open, useless mollusc. Imagine, try now, to imagine what that is like, having your insides all gone and you look human, you're breathing, you're eating, but you are no longer you. That's what it was like for us.

The escape – how it happened, I had to have repeated to me at least once a year. So daring was the plan, so dangerous, that even now, sitting here, evidence that it happened, I still cannot believe they pulled it off.

DECEMBER 1939

THIRTY-EIGHT

HELENA

Saturday, 2 December 1939
Oxford, UK

Oxford was damp and cold when we arrived, and it stuck to our skin, under our coats and wouldn't allow us to get warm, reminding us all of the Fort and the constant dankness. The chill that came from the rivers, which I soon learned were called the Thames and the Cherwell, seemed to permeate everything in the little flat that was allocated to us on the Banbury Road, the black mould stark against the whitewashed walls.

William and Valerie Gould were friends of Joasia's; William had worked with her on the publication of one of her books, and Joasia had visited them a few times over the years. They met us off the boat at Southampton, the salty wind whipping into my face, stinging my cheeks. Perhaps it was that cold that snapped me out of myself a little, or maybe it was fully realising that I was no longer in Poland, no longer anywhere near the Fort and the dangers it held, but my brain began to wake up a little.

They welcomed us with literal open arms; William tried to

speak in the little Polish he knew, saying that he had been lazy and let Joasia always speak English so that he had never really tried as much as he should have. I told him that Joasia liked to flaunt her knowledge of languages and would have been glad to speak English to him, but I could see as I spoke that he did not know what I was saying.

We drove to Oxford, and this time I noted our surroundings that reminded me so much of Poland – the large green fields, open spaces and patches of woodland. The biggest difference, however, was the busyness of the country. Car and trucks were everywhere, people on the pavements, people in the shops. The war had not reached these shores and so far, people were living as they normally would.

I wasn't sure how I could go back to being 'normal'. How could I go to the shops now, or work? How could I sit, like one woman I saw, in a café, drinking tea and talking to a companion? It all seemed so alien to me.

I thought of Max as we drove, trying to remember that evening when he got us free from our cell. But my memories were like cotton wool, and I could not pin down anything concrete. All I could know was how I felt – and that was bereft. I was free, but my aunt, Max and the others were still there, and in a way, it felt as though I had left them to die. Yes. There was guilt there too. And relief. And something else. Something like love, like gratitude. I wanted to hug Max to me, to tell him how thankful I was that he had done this for us, and perhaps I wanted to tell him more.

Brushing the thoughts aside, I tried to concentrate on my immediate surroundings and reality. I spoke to the twins, and as we drove, I pointed out things to them to get them to engage. But neither of them did. They sat next to each other, holding hands, now and then looking at each other, but saying nothing.

We soon arrived in Oxford, on a bustling street that William told me was called Banbury Road. Large houses, three, four storeys high bordered each side of the road, reminding me of home a little.

They were kind to us, and patient as we went inside and immediately apologised profusely for our meagre lodgings – a one-bedroom basement flat beneath their own modest home.

'It can be better,' William told me in his rudimentary Polish, then waved his hands about pointing at the walls, the damp and the lilac wallpaper that curled in the corners.

I tried to respond in the little English that I knew, 'It's good,' I said, and gave a smile so big it was obvious that I was trying too hard.

Valerie switched on a small three-bar heater in the corner of the living room, and then showed us to the one bedroom which Agata and Michal would share, and I, it turned out, would sleep on the couch. I didn't mind this arrangement and was glad that the twins would have their own space, and I could not wait to curl up tight next to the orange glow of the heater that spat out the scent of burning dust as it warmed.

A small kitchenette offered a tiny stove-top, a fridge and some plates and cutlery and Valerie had taken time to stock the small cupboard over the stove with tins of peaches, soups and some sort of meat. She had also made sure we had bread, tea and coffee, and I wondered if the war had affected them at all, as from the food available, it didn't seem to.

'You'll raise up for dinner,' William said, then seeing the confusion on my face, pointed upwards – he meant that we were to come *up* to their home for dinner.

I nodded my thanks as Michal and Agata stood like ghost children in the doorway to the bedroom, neither one sure of what to do or what to say.

Our hosts left with quick, warm hugs and more pointing to the upstairs and a finger at the clock to say that 7 p.m. would be the time we were to go up. As soon as they left, I felt as confused as the children did. It had been a week or more of getting here, and now we were away from the Fort, I was finally feeling the effects of our captivity. Someone would normally be telling us when to eat, when to sleep, and now we were free, yet those few months of being dictated to had obviously left a mark, as I felt unsure of what to do next.

Oddly, it was Michal that took charge. Michal who had barely spoken since the day he had been given that injection, but I saw him look to his sister who was whiter than the walls in this flat, her eyes almost bulging out of her thin face, and then he stepped forward.

'We should wash,' he said simply. 'Then we should change. Then we should eat.'

I nodded at him. He was right. That's what we normally would have done if we were at home – wash, change, eat. It sounded so simple and yet I had needed for someone, anyone, even a child, to tell me what was normal now.

I smiled at him and took his face in my hands and kissed the top of his head, and he did not pull away from me as the old Michal from the summer would have done. Instead, he relaxed into my touch. Agata still hadn't moved from her spot in the doorway and Michal gently took her hand and led her to the couch, and showed her how to warm her hands in front of the heater.

I watched her as she copied him. It was as though she was learning once more all the things a child should know how to do. As I watched, I hoped that one day the Agata who chatted and sang would come back to us again.

THIRTY-NINE

MAKSYMILIAN

Sunday, 10 December 1939
Warsaw, Poland

Warsaw was only a fraction of what it used to be. Bombed-out buildings were everywhere, rubble littering the streets and the people who walked around seemingly did not notice.

I stood each day in awe at the sight of it – I had never seen the capital when I was a child, but I had seen pictures, and this was not the city I had always thought of.

Antoni and his friends in the resistance had been as good as their word. After the exchange in the woods, Antoni and his friend had driven away with Wagner and within fifteen minutes an old delivery van pulled up, a man at the wheel, a cigarette clamped between his lips as he spoke.

'Max?'

'Yes.'

'Get in,' he said with a growl.

This man called himself Kaminski and gave me no Christian name. He was a large man and reminded me of Olek, a little furry, gruff and yet gentle at the same time.

He drove like a madman, as if the devil himself were hot on our heels, and constantly smoked and looked in his mirrors, then smoked some more. It was only when we were a good way away from Poznań that he relaxed and opened up a little.

'A translator, eh?' he asked. 'We need one of those. You should see what's happening – Gestapo everywhere. If you get in good with them, then you can give us information when there'll be an arrest, a round-up and we might be able to save a few more.'

'How bad is it?' I asked him.

He looked at me for a moment. 'It's bad. But it's going to get worse.'

Kaminski was right. When we arrived in Warsaw, not only Jews, but anyone who was considered an enemy of the Reich were starting to be rounded up, arrested and sent to forced labour. Only a few weeks later, more restrictions came in, targeting Jewish homes, bank accounts and businesses, and soon Jewish stars marked out their homes and workplaces, and they themselves had to wear a white armband so that it was clear just who was who in that rubble of a city.

I roomed with Kaminski and one other man, Jan, a wiry, nervous man whose legs jittered and jumped when he sat and smoked in the evenings, and whose hands never seemed able to rest, constantly tapping his fingers on a table.

At first, he irritated me. I couldn't bear the constant move-ment, but Kaminski told me I would get used to it and probably develop strange tics of my own. I didn't tell him that I already possessed one – a stammer that appeared when I was afraid or nervous, and one which I had thus far managed to control most of the time. I was sure he didn't need to know this detail; other-wise, my work as a translator might be questioned – how could they send a possibly stuttering man out to gain information?

Yet, it worried me that maybe it would come back. Seeing Jan made me understand just how dangerous a job we were in, and indeed I had already been in, and perhaps the stammer would come back and affect me once more.

In those early days in Warsaw my job was simple: I was to visit bars, cafés and restaurants that German soldiers, Gestapo and SS frequented, and I was to do as I had done with Leo Wagner – offer my assistance and see if they took it.

At first, nothing happened. No one seemed to want to talk to me – a half Pole, half German? I could not be trusted in their eyes, so I spent a lot of time wandering the city, with nothing much to do but be left with my thoughts.

Seeing the wasteland of the city made me think of Karl and how, if I had stayed in Germany, I would have perhaps been responsible for this. I would have sat in the cockpit alongside him, indicating areas to be bombed, allowing the gunner in the rear to shoot, to drop our loads on unsuspecting people in their homes, perhaps asleep as a rain of fire fell from the skies.

Did Karl look down and see what he had done and feel proud? Or did he feel guilty? I hoped the latter – I hoped that the goodness I had known in Karl would raise itself up and overcome all the propaganda he had been taught.

I thought, of course of Helena, of the twins, and of that daring escape. My heart had broken on seeing them so broken themselves – the children like small ghosts, Helena too, who could barely speak, barely comprehend what was happening. When they had sat in the car with me, I could smell them – urine, sweat and something more that I had never smelt before. In that moment, I wanted to kill Wagner who was half-asleep on the front seat. I wanted to beat him with my own fists, I wanted to see the fear, the terror in his eyes as he realised he was dying, and then finally feel the life slip out of him.

Antoni, I knew, and his friends would have this pleasure. This gruesome revenge. And I could not, would not, do anything whilst Helena and the twins were in the car. Instead, I had held them to me, ignoring the smell that emanated from them and trying to control the anger, the hurt, the relief all of which were fighting for my attention.

Each day I would imagine where they were and what they were doing. On those days when I ventured out around the city and found a park that still had green grass in amongst all the grey debris, I would imagine the twins playing on it, imagine Helena by my side, her hand in mine.

I did think about what might have happened to Wagner, and I worried a lot about the days following my leaving and Helena's escape. What had happened? Had Möller told the authorities that Wagner had absconded to Berlin with Helena and the twins? Perhaps he told them that Wagner had taken the twins to his uncle? There was no way of knowing, but I was sure of one thing, my name would surely have been mentioned.

And so it was that in Warsaw I became someone else once again. Max would still be my Christian name, it was decided, as it was common enough and it would prevent me from making a mistake, but my surname became Becker. Max Becker. I didn't like it, but then I suppose I hadn't liked Wagner either. When, I wondered, would I be able to become Max Nowicki once again?

At night, when I could not sleep, I went through each step of that escape, seeing now how horribly wrong it could have gone. If Wagner had not drunk the brandy, or had not believed me, or if the driver had not so willingly been led away by Antoni with a gun trained at his back, or if the guards that night had been more vigilant – there were so many ways it could have gone wrong and so many ways in which so many of us could have died.

When those thoughts plagued me, I turned my attention to thinking of Helena and the twins. I worried desperately for them. I knew that they had got to England; a message had come through from Antoni, and I was glad that they were safe. But my concern for them was deeper than that.

Helena that night was broken, not just physically, but she

seemed to have disappeared in some way. Her speech was incoherent at times, and her eyes either stared, unblinking, or moved around wildly, as if trying to find something to focus on – there was no in-between. The twins, too, were dazed. I hoped it was from the drug that they had been given by the doctor and that soon it would wear off; however, I also knew that from being in that Fort, from their pale faces, they had lost something of themselves too.

I just hoped they would find it again.

'Max.' Kaminski stood over me at the beginning of December as I sat on a stool next to a small fire in our half-shelled apartment, trying to read a book I had found on the street. Some of the pages were missing, but I didn't care – I needed to keep my mind busy and away from memories or the constant worry I felt.

'We've got one,' he told me.

'Got what?'

'Gestapo. A youngish lad. Jan's been working on him for a while now – bribing him with cigarettes and such. He wasn't really forthcoming, but then there was mention that they were in need of a translator. Jan will tell you where he drinks, and you need to get this one – make him need you.'

I was never sure what role Jan had exactly. He seemed to scurry about in the dead of night like a rat, in and out of the apartment, and then during the day he slept. He spoke German too, so why wasn't Jan putting himself forward? I asked Kaminski who replied, 'Too skittish,' and I had to agree that, yes, he was.

The following night I found myself in a bar to the west of the city that was heaving with soldiers. Inside, bodies pressed against each other, whilst from a gramophone a female singer sang about love and loss. Cigarette smoke hung in thick swathes so that I could barely see the faces of those bodies packed inside, and there was a sickly sweet stench of alcohol along with sweat that mingled in my nostrils.

I wanted to leave the bar – unnerved by the crush of bodies, by the lack of clean air, but I pushed my way through and finally saw Jan, sat in a corner with a pretty blonde woman who smoked her cigarette from an ivory holder.

Jan nodded at the woman, who then stood and came to me, the other men in the room parting like the Red Sea before her, each of them eyeing her from head to toe.

'Max, darling,' she purred in my ear, her German perfect. 'So glad you could make it. Come, come sit with me.'

She led me to the table, her body swishing under the silk dress she wore that was too fancy for this bar, and it was then that I realised Jan was gone – seemingly disappearing amongst the crowd.

'Sit, Max darling.' She looked about her for a waiter and ordered us both a drink, then turned to a man who stood nearby. 'Harald, darling,' she half shouted above the clamour of voices and music, and he swung around quickly at the mention of his name. 'Come sit with me, and meet my cousin, Max.'

Harald did not have to be asked twice and scooted around to the empty chair, scraping it closer to the woman.

'Max, this is Harald. Harald, Max. And I'm Margot,' she added, and laughed. 'But we all know that, don't we? Everyone knows me.' She gave me a slow wink.

Harald barely looked at me. His eyes were for Margot only, and she knew it too. Her hair was shiny and golden, pinned into some elaborate hairstyle that I had only seen on a few women before, her lips slicked red, her eyes smoky. 'Now, Harald, you were telling me, and you told my friend Jan that you needed a translator because things were getting a bit tricky at work, didn't you?'

'They don't understand when we question them,' he said. To me, he sounded stupid, but then perhaps it was the effect

Margot was having on him as I, too, had sounded stupid in front of pretty women at times.

'And when you go to people's houses, they don't understand you then, do they?' She played along, dragging a fingernail over his forearm. 'It's so hard, isn't it, not to be understood.'

Harald nodded. 'We're getting some, officially, soon. *Translators,* that is.' He laughed nervously.

'But in the meantime, how about we let Max help you? He can tell you what he hears too – he hears a lot, don't you, Max?'

Harald looked at me now, finally sizing me up. 'What do you hear?' he asked.

'Well,' I said, trying to think quickly, 'I hear lots of things. Things like where people are hiding money, or things like what people are planning.'

He didn't seem impressed with my answer, and I couldn't blame him. I just couldn't think of what to say.

'Oh now, Max is being modest!' Margot protested. 'He's so modest, is our Max. But he knows so many people in Warsaw, so many, that he hears things all the time, all day. Like where some of those politicians you are looking for might be hiding – isn't that right, Max?'

She raised her eyebrows at me, encouraging me to play along.

'Of course,' I said. 'I know everyone.'

'I can't pay you, not yet. I'll test you out and see. If you're any good, then we'll make it official in some way.' Harald then looked to Margot to gauge her response to the offer.

'Ah, Harald! How generous you are!' She leaned in and kissed him on the cheek, sending his blood vessels into a frenzy, creating a pink plume over his skin. 'Max just wants to do his part, and here you are, my darling Harald, making that happen for him.'

Margot dominated the conversation for some time after that, and I realised that I was no longer needed and should leave. Before I did, Harald gave me the address to his lodgings and told me to go to him with any information I found over the coming days, and if it was good, then he would take me with him on some of his 'errands' as he called them.

I kissed Margot goodbye on both cheeks, and promised my 'cousin' I would see her again.

'Darling Max,' she said, as I made to leave, 'I do hope so.' Then she tinkled with laughter once again.

FORTY

HELENA

Sunday, 10 December 1939
Oxford, UK

On the tenth of December, William and Valerie suggested we all go together to buy a Christmas tree. We had been in Oxford a week and, so far, had not left the apartment. All three of us seemed consumed by sleep, and we would wake in a daze, eat, wash and then sleep some more.

I wasn't sure about leaving the apartment and looked at Michal and Agata who stared at a comic book that William had bought them, not understanding the words, but following the pictures.

'A Christmas tree,' I said to the pair, who looked at me expressionless. 'It might be nice. We can decorate it, can't we? We can go outside and get some air. What do you think?'

'Will there be lots of people?' Agata asked.

'I suppose so.'

'Will there be soldiers too?'

'No. There are just English people here. No Germans, no soldiers.'

'Are you sure?' Michal scrutinised me.

'I am sure. I promise.'

'And you will be there, won't you, Helena?' Agata asked.

'Yes, of course I'll be there too.'

With that, the pair seemed to relax a little and agreed to the outing. Indeed, since we had arrived, I had been by their side, never sleeping in the living room away from them; instead, all three of us slept tightly bound together each night, and if one of us needed the toilet, we all went.

I saw now that this could not carry on. We had needed that comfort, that feeling of safety, but we couldn't always sleep together, we couldn't always go to the toilet together.

'Come on,' I said, injecting some enthusiasm into my voice and giving them a wide grin. 'It'll be fun.'

If the twins were going to start to feel better, then it had to start with me. They had to see that I was healing, and maybe, bit by bit, they would begin to mend themselves too.

The outside world hit me like a brick. The noise of the cars as their tyres whooshed on the wet road, the rain as it hit my umbrella with incessant pitter-pats, the bells in the church towers that rang out the hour. And then there were the people. So many of them, like those bees that sometimes invaded my brain, they seemed to lurch into each other, bumping, knocking each other off course. I held Michal's hand with my free one, and he held on to Agata. I kept looking at them, to see if they were as discombobulated as I was, but something had happened to them, their faces had relaxed and they were chattering away to each other, pointing at the university colleges, William trying to tell them what each building was.

The city centre was a mass of old stone buildings, spires reaching up to the sky and disappearing among the icy clouds. Bicycles whizzed past every few seconds, the riders of them young, faces pink with cold and eyes bright.

'Students,' William told me, as one young man almost

careened into us. 'They are no good. Not good.' He shook his head.

I could see why they bothered William – there seemed to be hundreds of them all bustling about, laughing, throwing their caps at each other as they rode and shouting out to passers-by whom they thought they knew. And yet, there was something so joyful, so youthful about them that I wished I was one of them.

Soon, we came to the Ashmolean Museum that stood proud like a miniature Parthenon, which I had seen in books. Agata and Michal wanted to go in, but I insisted that we do it another day. I could not bear the thought of being stuck inside with people, with no way out. At least outside, I had fresh air, I could breathe.

Valerie led the way to an undercover market; butchers, florists, bakers all touting their wares, each shouting over each other, clamouring for custom. As I walked, the smell of cabbages and carrots mingled with the sweet scent of cold meat that hung in the butcher's windows and the fish that looked up glassy-eyed and open-mouthed from their beds of ice. I wanted to tell Valerie that I needed air – that this was too much, but I couldn't say anything – my mind seemed to have grown thick and thoughtless, and all I could do was follow mutely.

Finally, she found the stall she wanted that sold trees of all different shapes and sizes and let the children pick one and I hoped that we would now be able to leave and I could gulp in heavy lungfuls of cold air.

But Valerie and William were insistent that we go to a café, where the windows were steamed up with condensation from the bodies inside. Agata and Michal happily led the way, feeling more at home in this environment than me.

I sat on a hard wooden chair and did not remove my coat, watching the other customers as they talked, smoked and drank tea. The smell of frying oil caught at my nostrils and I sneezed, thankfully taking a handkerchief from Valerie who looked at me with some concern on her face.

William brought over tea and sticky buns, the icing slithering off the bun and dripping onto the plate. The sight of it, for some reason, disgusted me and I could not manage a bite. The twins were eager, though, and delighted in having a glazed cherry each that sat atop the buns.

I hated the café. The warm, damp bodies all pressed against each other, the tobacco smoke hovering beneath the ceiling, the crash and bang of cutlery and teacups from behind the counter. Every sound, smell and sight was heightened, and it was making me nauseous.

Valerie watched me with a close eye but said nothing, and let the children chatter, let William teach them words like 'bun', 'cherry' and 'tea'.

When we returned home to the flat, I let Michal and Agata stay with William and Valerie for a while. Their mood was one of joy, and from the way I was feeling, I did not want to ruin it, clouding the room with this fear, this indescribable fear. I left them decorating the tree and went downstairs and lay down on the bed.

As I lay there, I thought of Max. I wondered where he was and what he was doing. Was he safe?

As soon as I thought of any danger that he might be in, my stomach twisted and turned, and I wanted to cry out with the helplessness I felt at not knowing. It was torture. Not knowing for certain what had happened to Father, not knowing if Max was safe, not knowing how Joasia and Olek were doing. It was so bad that I rarely let myself think of any of them. Each time my mind slipped and wondered about them, I would wrestle it back and make it look at the twins, make it think about what William was trying to say in his broken Polish.

A knock on the door interrupted my thoughts – it was Valerie.

'Helena,' she said, and sat on the bed next to me. She held a book in her hands – a Polish-English dictionary. Then, in broken Polish, she spoke.

'Are you babies?' she asked.

Was I a baby? No. I shook my head.

'No?' She then found the word she wanted in the dictionary and showed it to me.

She didn't mean babies. The word was pregnant.

All of a sudden, a wave of nausea hit me. I couldn't be, could I? It wasn't possible.

She asked me again, then again. I couldn't answer. It couldn't be.

Without realising it, I was crying, and Valerie held me to her, shushing me like she would a child.

'Doctor,' she said again and again. 'We go to a doctor.'

The following day, Valerie and I ventured out without the twins to a doctor close by. The doctor, however, seemed to be retired. The crop of white hair on his head and his runny eyes said it all. But, he spoke Polish.

He led us into a cluttered living room, where books dominated the walls, slipped off coffee tables and became piles on the floor.

I sat down and he offered me tea, but I did not want any more tea.

'So,' he said. 'Valerie tells me you might be pregnant.' He got straight to the matter and for that I was glad. 'You're a refugee, yes?'

I nodded.

'My wife was Polish. Did Valerie tell you that? I had to learn to please her family. It was very unusual at the time for an Englishman to marry a Polish woman – perhaps it still is?'

'I was raped,' I said quickly. I didn't want to hear about him and his wife. I didn't care about his story, I just wanted to say what I needed to and hear what he had to say.

He didn't react much, then stood. 'Come this way.'

He led me into a room with a hospital bed and a pale blue curtain, told me to take off my underwear, lie on the bed and tell him when I was ready, closing the curtain around me.

I didn't want to undress. I didn't want a man in that area of my body ever again. But I had to know. Was I pregnant? Was I carrying Wagner's child? All night I had been awake thinking of it, wanting to tear it out of my body and away from me. I couldn't have his baby. I couldn't.

Once I was ready, I told him and he opened the curtain, made me place my legs in some stirrups and told me to be breathe out. Painfully, he found his way inside me, and I felt a tear trickle from my eye. *Don't think about it. Ignore it. You are not here*, I told myself. But this time, I could not leave my body, could not disassociate from the pain and I had to wait until he was done.

'Did you know you're bleeding?' he asked.

Was I? Yes. I had a little that morning, I remembered now, a streak of dark red – so dark that I hadn't been completely sure what I was looking at.

'Have you been in pain this morning?'

'A little,' I told him.

He told me to dress, then to come back into the room where Valerie was waiting. I sat by her side, and she took my hand.

'You are pregnant,' he said. 'Or rather you were. But you're having a miscarriage.'

'It's dead?' I asked.

He nodded. 'I wouldn't like to say *died*. It was very new. I would think it started this morning. Have you had any cramping?'

I had had a stomachache, but I had had such an ache for a while now and had dismissed it. But now he said it, I realised that the pain I felt in my abdomen was much worse than normal.

'Your body will get rid of it,' he said matter-of-factly. 'I'd like you to stay here, with me, until it happens, because if your body does not release it soon, we'll have to take you to hospital.'

He related this to Valerie who told him to tell me that she was going to stay with me and would not leave my side. She was as good as her word, and within the hour the cramps got worse, the bleeding intensified and the foetus inside me let go and was caught by the doctor in a steel bowl that he quickly whipped away.

Valerie took me home, and tucked me into her own bed, bringing me tea, cake, and a hot-water bottle that she placed on my stomach. All that while I cried. I wept so much that my eyes became swollen, and I could barely see. I felt a loss; even though I hadn't wanted the child, I felt it was my fault. It had known, last night as I lay there wedged between Michal and Agata, that I had wanted to tear it out of my own body – it had felt unwanted, and it had died.

'It's not your fault,' Valerie kept saying over and over, learning the sentence from the doctor who had told her to say it to me. 'It's not your fault.'

Her words meant nothing. I knew it was my fault.

FORTY-ONE

MAKSYMILIAN

Monday, 11 December 1939
Warsaw, Poland

Harald had found me out quicker than I had thought possible. At that bar, that night with Margot, I had seen a stupid, young, lovesick puppy dog, but I had underestimated him.

Badly.

After leaving the bar, I had spoken with Kaminski about what false information I could pass onto him, and we stayed up to the early hours, waiting for Jan to come home to see what he would suggest.

At 4 a.m., there was a knock at the door.

'He's forgotten his key,' Kaminski lamented and heaved himself up to answer it.

But it wasn't Jan. Instead, in walked Harald, two other officers behind him.

'Max,' he said and smiled. It was sickly sweet as though he were mimicking how Margot had greeted me.

I was still sitting at the kitchen table, and he scraped back a chair to join me.

'How convenient, don't you think? I tell Margot I need a translator, and her friend Jan is there, and then suddenly, poof, like magic, you appear. A cousin, no less. But here's the thing,' he leaned towards me, his blue eyes on mine, 'I am not stupid. I've been following Jan, Margot too and then I had you followed home this evening. I wanted to know what was going on, and then, there, I see it. You and Jan living together with that man. Margot always in that bar, always flirting with me. And then we find Jan, this evening, with a bunch of his friends listening in to our radios in a basement. So, what am I to think, Max? What am I to do?'

He placed his hand under his chin, pretending to consider his options for me.

I knew, of course, there was one option. My heart was thundering in my chest, a headache had appeared from nowhere. I was going to be arrested and he liked making me wait, liked this game.

The two officers came into the room and roughly pulled me to my feet. Then Harald stood too. 'Let's see what you know, Max,' he said. 'I'll take you to my office. Let's find out together what you know.'

FORTY-TWO

HELENA

Wednesday, 20 December 1939
Oxford, UK

I was uneasy about venturing out without William and Valerie, but William insisted that I should go to see Pawel alone, an academic in psychiatry that he and Valerie had met a few times over the years and one who had been recommended by the doctor who had helped me when I found out I was pregnant.

'You must trust yourself now,' William had told me in broken Polish that he read out of a Polish-English dictionary. 'You know the streets. I take care of the childrens. You must learn and then when you know, you teach the child.' He had handed me a note that I was to give to a porter at something he called a lodge and had drawn me a simple map of how I was to reach it.

Although William was trying so hard to communicate with me, I felt a wave of irritation each time he got tenses wrong, and then I realised that perhaps he felt the same about me with my pointing at things and random words I had learned.

I wanted Valerie to go with me and gave her a look, but she

just smiled and gently shook her head. It was time for me to try and go out alone, to try and live my life again.

For the past ten days I had stayed in bed, Valerie waiting on me. Around day five, she and William and even Agata and Michal had tried to convince me to leave the apartment and go with them to the park, but I refused.

In that time, I locked myself away in my mind and let my thoughts tumble about. I did not try and shunt away the thoughts that made me afraid, or angry, or sad. I let them all come, sometimes one by one, sometimes all at once, so that I was in such a rage I would scream into my pillow.

I let myself imagine Max dead. I let myself cry over the image of his body. I imagined Joasia dead too. I thought of Father being led away, and then I filled in the gaps that I did not know. I imagined him standing in the woods, a gun at the back of his head, and I tried to think, tried to feel what he would have felt – the fear, the indescribable fear that this was his last moment on earth. Then, when that wasn't enough, I imagined him in that cold ground, reeking of dampness, of rotting leaves and debris, perhaps even other bodies with him.

Why I wanted to think this way, I don't know. I just wanted to feel it all, in one go, in one moment and I wanted to punish myself, I think. Maybe a little. I hadn't wanted Wagner's child, of course I hadn't. But the grief I felt and knowing it had died made me feel relief and then more guilt piled on top of it for having felt relieved. It was all so confusing that I needed that time to rage, to cry, to imagine the worst. And to finally feel the pain and loss of the past few months in a place where I knew I was safe and where the twins were being taken care of.

I noted, and not without a hint of jealousy, that the children were beginning to come around. William and Valerie spent hours with them, as I was unable or unwilling, and they taught them English words and phrases, played games with them and even took them out to London for the day, and the pair of them came back telling me tales of a big clock and a palace where the King lived.

I wanted to be like them, to somehow shake off all that had happened, but I couldn't and I didn't know how to be. So I was to see Pawel. Maybe he could fix me.

Stepping out into the freezing fog, I wrapped my coat tighter around me and tried to ignore the flutter of nerves that plagued my stomach.

Girding myself, I walked determinedly down Banbury Road. This was the first step of many that I would have to take to overcome the fear, to break out of this prison I was in. First, I would learn English, then I would teach the twins. I would find a job, we would find a home and in spring, just like William had said, we would picnic on Port Meadow among the buttercups and daisies.

This, for me, was a memory that had not yet happened – not a dream, nor a hope, it was, I decided, something that would happen no matter what, and Pawel, I had suddenly decided, was the one to help me do this.

Soon I reached the stone monument that I had seen before on our first trip into the city, the stone spire reaching high, steps surrounding it, and small statues hidden within alcoves at the top. There were inscriptions in the stone, and I resolved that as soon as I had mastered English, I would read them to find out why this strange, gothic monument sat proudly on the pavement.

A woman bumped into me and, in doing so, dropped her shopping bag – a few potatoes scuttling over the damp, grey slabs. I bent down to help her, and she spoke to me, and of course, I had no idea what she was saying. I nodded at her, then she crunched her face up into an annoyed grimace, grabbed the potato I was holding from my hand and stalked away.

I stood for a brief moment, feeling utterly embarrassed. I wanted to tell her I was sorry. I wanted to tell her that I wasn't from here, that I was still learning like a child. I wanted to tell her that whilst she had gone about shopping, seeing friends and living her life, less than a month before I had been in a cold brick cell with other women whilst just metres away, people were led into a room where gas would fill their lungs, leaving them gasping for breath and letting out howls of anguish as they realised that this was the end. I wanted to tell her so much. And yet here I was, standing in a city that I did not know, whose people spoke a language I didn't understand, with heavy fog blurring any beauty that it might possess.

Suddenly, I heard my mother's voice: 'You are intelligent and capable, Helena. Keep moving.'

Her voice was so real to me that I scanned passers-by to see if she was actually there. A woman with her black hat pulled low could be her, and yet, there, another woman with a red scarf wrapped tightly around her neck to ward off the cold could also be her. For a minute I felt frantic and anxious, and I wasn't sure what to do. Then, just as suddenly as the voice had come and set me off into some sort of panic, it left me, and I felt calm and clear-headed.

Pawel. I needed to see Pawel. *Keep moving, Helena, keep going.*

I checked the crudely drawn map penned by William and found the porter's lodge of Christ Church college. It was a huge building, reminding me of a cathedral or a palace even and despite my reasons for being here, I felt a little nugget of excitement at going inside such a regal building. Inside, a portly man with a black bowler sat reading a newspaper, a steaming mug of tea in front of him. As soon as he saw me, he leapt up as if he should not have been relaxing at all and greeted me, tipping the brow of his hat.

I handed him the note and watched as his piggy eyes read it, then he looked at me and smiled, offering me his arm. I took it and together we walked under the archway into a quad of sorts where the brightness of the green grass could not be diminished by the wintry haze.

We ascended stone steps that led to a corridor, once more arched, then through a heavy wooden door into a passageway that seemed to go on forever. Soon we stopped outside a door, where from inside I could hear the scratch of Vivaldi coming from a poorly placed gramophone needle.

'Pawel,' the porter said, and nodded at the door.

He knocked heavily with his white gloved hand, three hard raps that suddenly brought the music to a close and Pawel to appear in the doorway.

After a brief few words, the porter nodded at me and went back down the corridor, leaving me with Pawel, whose shock of white hair almost stood to attention, a green bowtie askew at his neck.

'Helena, no doubt!' he greeted me with a grin, showing yellow stained teeth, and I was glad to see how happy he was to see me, even though he didn't know me; it felt so strangely like coming home that I almost cried.

'Come, come, my dear. It is the weather of the devil out there. Come inside, warm yourself.'

His rooms were tiny: a sitting room with two tattered leather armchairs, both with plaid woollen blankets resting on the arms. A fire bristled away in a tiny grate, and on each wall were books, books and more books, just like the doctor's house I had seen ten days before. I doubted there was actually any wall to be seen, as every available space had been taken with the green, brown and red leather bindings. Even piles of books were placed on the floor, almost concealing a richly patterned red and gold rug and I wondered if all doctors' rooms were like this.

Pawel motioned for me to take a seat in the armchair closest the fire whilst he busied himself over a tiny heating ring, adding a kettle to it and finding two cups.

'Tea? Or coffee? I'm sure that by now you may be sick of tea, but I myself find it comforting.'

'Tea is fine,' I said, and once more wanted to cry on hearing myself answer in my own language to someone who was not the twins or that doctor who had said I was pregnant, and to answer a question as if nothing had happened. *Tea, yes, I'll drink tea.* That was what I would have said just four months ago, and yet, since everything that had happened, it felt utterly absurd to be able to act normally once more.

'Now,' –Pawel handed me the tea and sat opposite, drawing the blanket onto his lap and indicted that I might do the same with a nod of his head– 'tell me everything.'

It was then that I cried. I let it all out. I cried for my father, still not knowing for sure what had happened to him; I cried for Małgorzata as she was beaten, and then her body after her death; I cried for the women still inside Fort VII – Ola and Sabina and the new prisoners. I cried for the twins, for what they had seen and felt. Then I cried for myself. For the beatings, the rape, the baby that fell out of me, and for Max whom I had tried not to think about at all. I cried for him too. For the man who rescued me and then disappeared into the night.

Pawel did not move. He did not try to hug me or give me words of comfort and for that I was grateful. He let me cry, and sob until I had no breath or energy left to do any more. He simply handed me his handkerchief, then stood and added two lumps of sugar into my tea. 'Drink it. You need it.'

I did as he said and somehow between the hot sweet tea, the warmth from the fire and the closeness of Pawel, I was able to compose myself.

'Forgive me,' he finally said, when I expect he thought he was able. 'I should not have said what I did.'

I shook my head. 'It was bound to happen. I'm just sorry that it has happened here with you. You must think badly of me.'

Pawel gave a gravelly laugh. '*Badly* of you? I doubt that very much. I knew that this may happen and indeed both William and Valerie have been waiting for it too and have worried about you. I'm glad that it has happened now. It tells me everything you have been through, so you have no need to put it into words.'

'I will, one day,' I said. 'I want to tell someone what happened to us.'

'Just not yet,' he said kindly.

I nodded. 'Not yet.' Then I told him about the woman I had bumped into in the city, how she had stared at me with some form of disgust and how I had thought then how I wished I could verbalise what I had been through.

'And you will. It is an important story to tell, my dear. A very important one and one which, when you are ready, I think needs to be told to the authorities here.'

I raised my eyebrows at him in question.

'I do not think that the government here quite knows the extent of what is happening overseas. Your story, your account could help. They need to know. But only when you are ready. I have friends in various high places, and soon, I hope you would be able to recount your experience.'

He was right, of course. Saying nothing was not going to help. I remembered that day with Anna and Rolf in a bar where I had said nothing to their appreciation and joy of Hitler's work in Germany. I should have spoken up. I should have done more. It was too late to change the past, but maybe my story could change others' lives. There were others, too, who could tell their stories – Filip, who had to endure days of torture and witness others' torture just so that he could relay the brutality and fear of the place. Max who had fallen out of a plane, just to return home, and had saved me and the twins. Perhaps Ola and Sabina if they survived – *if*.

I sat in that room with Pawel for hours, until he had to turn on another lamp as the day morphed into night. Everything came out – what I felt, the fear, the strange headaches. How in the past I had suffered from psychosis and how I was afraid it would happen again. How I wanted comfort but did not know where to find it. All the while, Pawel listened, now and again taking notes.

It was only when the bells of Christ Church rang out the hour of seven – calling out *ding, dong* into the still night, that I stopped talking and began to cry again.

MAY 1940

FORTY-THREE

HELENA

Wednesday, 1 May 1940
Oxford, UK

The first of May began very early. We rose just before 5 a.m., and William, Valerie, the twins and I walked the length on Banbury Road, up through Oxford High Street and towards Magdalen College and its famous bridge.

It was as though, that day, I were seeing the city for the first time. Gone was the cold winter fog and sullen clouds, and gone was my muddled head where one building had simply blurred into the next. Now, the sun rose, lightening white soft clouds and illuminated the city in front of me.

There, a cobbled tiny street that ran down between a thatch-roofed pub and a sweet shop, leading to goodness knows where. Grand university colleges with their thick brown doors which led into gardens brushed up against tiny shops that looked lopsided; stone-built museums jostled for places next to bookshops and tea rooms, and all the while students raced about on their bicycles, whooping and hollering to each other.

We soon found ourselves in amongst a throng that all

pushed forward as one in the direction of Magdalen Bridge, everyone chatting, happy, their eyes bright and cheeks stung cold from the nip of the early morning air.

Scores of people stood on the bridge and beyond, and I felt grateful that Pawel, with his connections at the university, had secured us a place on the riverbank, giving us some much-needed space.

We settled on a picnic blanket, and Agata and Michal ran straight down to the edge of the river where punting boats were moored, each of them knocking against one another with the slap, slap of the water's flow. Slowly, a boat appeared, a man standing on the edge of it, the long pole pushing against the river, whilst a young couple sat up front and waved to the twins who delighted in waving back.

Magdalen bell tower rose above us into the lightening sky, its turrets sharp as though it needed to pierce the clouds that hung low over them and Pawel explained that soon we would hear the bells chime and voices sing out from that very tower.

At 6 a.m., the bells around Oxford chorused their song, ringing in the May Day morning: *ding dong, ding dong,* they sang, calling us all to wake up and revel in this strange ritual of calling out to the spring time. Then the bells stopped and an eerie silence took over before the ghostlike voices of a choir atop the bell tower began to sing a Latin hymn.

Although I did not know what the words meant, I found the sound of voices rising up soothing, and I noted that everyone looked to the sky as if angels themselves were sat there singing to us mere mortals.

When the hymns ended, more tunes, folk tunes began on the bridge and there was the jingle of tiny bells.

'Morris dancers,' Pawel said. 'Come on, let's take a look.'

'I'll wait a moment,' I said, not yet wanting to leave this peaceful spot on the river. I just wanted to be still for a moment.

Michal, Agata, William and Valerie, headed for the bridge and I told them I would find them soon.

'You're not going?' I asked Pawel.

'I've seen it before,' he said.

These past months, Pawel had been like a father to me. He listened and never pushed counsel upon me until he knew I was ready, and seemed available to me at any point in the day – he never once turned me away.

I had, as yet, told no one else of my experiences inside the Fort and all it involved, but Pawel assured me that I would know when it was the right time – I would feel it deep down and would be unable to stop the words from pouring out once I got started. He had helped me too, in instructing me how to talk to the twins about their experiences and bit by bit, they opened up.

'Is Father dead?' That was the first thing that Michal asked me when I sat them down one evening to talk about everything that had happened. It was the second of January and although Christmas was over, the paper decorations we had made were still strung around the room, flapping when the warm air from the small heater reached them.

'I don't know,' I said truthfully. 'I think so. But I don't know for sure.'

'We spoke to Joasia about it, when you were stuck at the hospital and we didn't see you for ages,' Agata said. 'She said maybe.'

I nodded. 'He is. Maybe. Probably.'

Neither cried at that moment, but I knew that they would – I knew that at some point we would cry together, but because we had not seen him die, had not buried him, it didn't feel real. I suppose each of us held a tiny ounce of hope that he was still alive and would one day find us.

'Will we have to go back?' That was Michal's second question.

'No. We won't go back.'

'But if the Germans come here—' Agata started. I did not want her to go down this rabbit hole.

'They won't get here. It won't happen here.'

'Will we ever go home again?' Third question.

'I don't know,' I told Michal honestly.

Suddenly, he stood, thumped his fist on the table and stormed from the room into the bedroom, screaming at me, 'You know *nothing*!'

His sudden anger was to be expected – Pawel had warned me of it. *Let him speak, let him feel.*

In the days and weeks that followed, our conversations grew longer, Michal's temper calmed and Agata was beginning to talk like she used to – how when she was excited her sentences ran on and on, a never-ending babble of joy.

There were still moments, of course, when it was too much for them and for me too. Anger and frustration would raise their heads, especially as we tried to learn English. I was worse than Michal in those moments. I would shout and curse when I got my verbs wrong, or when my accent was too thick on a word.

It was then that Agata would hug me, or Michal would make me laugh, and it was then that I realised I had found my comfort – that elusive comfort I had sought since Mother's death and which I so dearly needed – it was them.

'Have you heard from Joasia again?' Pawel asked me, putting a stop to my rememberings.

I was going to answer him, but suddenly three students jumped off the bridge, into the river, whooping and laughing. As they hit the water, there was a second where the water had consumed their bodies and then they bobbed up, laughing again, splashing each other.

'They've been told, time and time again to stop doing it.

Two years ago, someone broke their leg doing that silly trick. But, boys will be boys,' Pawel said.

'I haven't heard any more from Joasia,' I answered him now that the whooping had stopped and the soggy boys climbed out onto the bank.

'News will arrive soon,' he reassured me.

The postcard I had received from Joasia had a picture of a rose that she had painted herself. The message was simple and plain: 'Sweetheart, I hope you are well. We are all fine. Do not worry. Give kisses to the children. I love you. I have sent you a package. It will be with you soon. Love, J.'

That had been over a month ago, and so far, no package had arrived. I hoped that she was perhaps sending a few of our things – maybe Agata's bear that she so loved, or Michal's board game that he was obsessed with playing, *Grzybobranie*, where you had to go around a board and collect good mushrooms, avoiding the bad. Perhaps she would send me some clothes as, so far, I had worn mostly Valerie's, and had acquired a few things through friends of hers.

I needed to begin to earn money, I knew this. But William and Valerie never pushed for anything and told me that there was no rush. But I wanted to keep moving forward now that I had found some peace, some way of coping. I didn't want the pace of my recovery to stall.

'I've been speaking with a few colleagues,' Pawel said. 'They say you will need to take the exam for certification here before you can work in a hospital, perhaps. But it is doable.'

'Is it? I'm not sure, Pawel. My English is coming along a lot slower than I thought it would, and I have to learn medical terminology, not just "Where is the post office? Excuse me, can you please pass the butter",' I said to him in my mock, posh English accent.

Pawel laughed. 'You're better than you think!'

Soon, the early morning wake-up was tiring the children,

who wanted food. We all trooped back to William and Valerie's house, William and Pawel dragging behind, deep in conversation about the war and how much of an impact it would have on English shores.

The children ran in front to open the gate and raced up the steps to the front door, Valerie behind them. I was not paying attention and found myself walking straight into Valerie's back. She stood still, the children in front of her also not moving.

What was it?

Slowly a new figure emerged, who had obviously been sitting on the steps. His head appeared over the twins and his eyes locked onto mine.

'Max!' the children screamed.

I opened my mouth, but no sound came out.

'Max!' the children were in his arms now and all I could do was stare.

FORTY-FOUR

MAKSYMILIAN

**Wednesday, 1 May 1940
Oxford, UK**

She walked to me, opening and closing her mouth. When she reached me, the twins let go of the grip they had around my waist. Then she found the word she needed.

'Max,' she said.

It was like warm honey, hearing her say my name. I grinned at her, then promptly stopped. I was missing two teeth on the right upper jaw, and when I smiled, it left a gaping hole in my mouth.

She didn't notice, or perhaps she didn't care, and she let me hold her to me, let me bury my face in her neck and let me shed a few tears.

The minutes after our reunion were something of a blur. We were bustled into the house by a woman called Valerie, a man called William, and another, older man called Pawel who trailed in their wake. He introduced himself to me the same way as Filip had always done, clicking his heels together and giving a tiny bow.

Inside the house I was made to sit, given tea and biscuits, and all of them sat around me, waiting for me to speak, and perhaps looking at the puckered scar that ran the length of the left side of my face, from jaw to ear.

I self-consciously touched it, then made myself stop.

'Where have you been, Max?' Agata climbed onto my lap. She had grown bigger, and my legs shook as she sat on them, so weak and battered were they that they could not bear her weight. I was glad that no one could see the mess that my legs were underneath these trousers – the whip-lashes, the bruises that would not go away.

She shifted herself so that she was wedged next to me on the sofa.

'I was in Warsaw,' I told her. 'And then a friend of mine helped me to come here, to see you.'

'Was it Joasia?' Agata asked.

'No. But she knew,' I said. 'She said that she told you all I was coming. Did she?'

'A package,' Helena said, a smile appearing on her face. 'She said to expect a package.'

'I think I might be it. I hope I'm not a disappointment?'

'Oh Max! I'm so glad you're here. Come. Come with me and Michal, and we'll show you our rooms.'

The children took over for the next few hours, taking me to their tiny basement flat, showing me their bedroom, the Christmas decorations they had made and still hadn't taken down. They told me about their morning at the river, how they had heard all the bells chime out and people sing from a tower. So excited were they to tell me of their new lives, I barely had a chance to talk, to savour the moment of finally being here.

It was not until late at night, when the twins finally tired and Helena made them go to bed, that I sat with Helena in her tiny sitting room, a heater next to me, turned on to one bar, whilst she made tea in her little kitchen.

Although small, I liked these rooms. They were warm and comforting. Blankets were folded over the arms of the sofa, little drawings Agata and Michal had done were pinned to the walls and books were stacked neatly on side tables.

'You like to read,' I said, as Helena handed me the cup of tea. It was a stupid thing to say, and I wondered why on earth I had said it.

'We're learning English, so we all read a lot,' she said.

There was a moment of awkward silence as we both looked at each other, smiled and then sipped at the hot tea. I noticed that Helena scrunched up her face a little as she drank.

'You don't like it?' I asked.

'No, it's not that. It's just that I feel I am always drinking tea. Everywhere you go, whenever you go to someone's house, or come home, or have dinner, it's *tea*!'

I laughed, then she joined in, and suddenly the nerves disappeared.

'I had to come and see you,' I said. 'I hope that's all right.'

'More than all right,' she answered. Then she reached up and traced the scar on my cheek with her fingers. 'Tell me, what happened?'

I took her hand in mine and she let me hold it, let me look at her fingers in mine for a few seconds, then she took her hand away and I began.

'I was arrested in Warsaw by a man named Harald. Not for anything I had done in Poznań, but I had simply underestimated him – perhaps I thought he was as stupid, as foolish as Wagner, but he wasn't.

Where I was taken to, I don't really know. Perhaps it was a prison, but it did not seem like it. Really, it seemed like a normal office building: doors with brass nameplates on either side of a long corridor, all of them closed. It was not until we reached the end of the corridor that I was then led down concrete steps to another floor.

An official-looking man sat at a desk, an open door behind him. He seemed uninterested when we entered, and stubbed out a cigarette in a glass ashtray whilst Harald told him that he needed the room.

"It's ready," the official said, tilting his head towards the open door.

It was only then that I became afraid. I don't know why it took me so long to realise the danger I was in, but during the car journey and even the walk to the basement, I had felt oddly calm.

Now though, that open door and the way that it was lit up from inside with a bright bulb made me want to run for my life. I must have turned a little with my reaction to being led to it, when I felt a hard smack on the back of my legs that sent me falling to my knees.

I was not allowed to stay in that position and was soon lifted by each arm and dragged forward into that strange, silent room.

Inside sat a table and two chairs and that was all. I could see bloodstains on the walls, on the table and even on the ceiling.

No one had followed me into the room, they had deposited me inside, then clanged the door shut, a click as they locked it from the outside. I didn't want to sit on either of the chairs – a bloodstain was evident on both of them and instead I sat down on the floor, leaned against the wall and drew my legs to me, rubbing the skin under my thighs where I had been hit.

My mind raced during the time they kept me in there. Was it an hour? Less than that? I had no way of knowing. All I did know was that whatever was going to happen in this room could be the last thing that ever happened to me.

Harald eventually came back into the room. He approached the desk and sat down on a blood-spattered chair, seemingly not caring about it or perhaps not noticing. In his hand he held a manila file which he placed on the desk in front of him; he opened it, then began to thrum his fingers on the table as he read, now and then murmuring to himself.

"Now then," he started. "Would it be wise, do you think, for you to get off the floor and come and sit and talk to me? There's nothing to be afraid of."

He smiled at me, and I felt my stomach drop to the soles of my feet.

I stood, my legs shaking and sat across from him.

"Who are you?" he asked.

"Max," I told him. 'Maksymilian Becker.'

"Try again." He narrowed his eyes at me and leaned forward.

I told him my name again, a small stammer appearing that I could not swallow away.

"Try again," he repeated.

I opened my mouth, but no words would come out.

"If that's the way you want to be about it, then who am I to argue?" Harald stood, opened the door and beckoned for someone else to come into the room.

The man that entered was huge. His jacket had been removed, leaving him with his white shirt tucked untidily into the waistband of his trousers. He rolled up his sleeves to reveal two thick forearms, and before I could even begin to understand what was happening, he moved forward so quickly for such a large man and his fist ploughed into my face.

"Who is Margot?" Harald yelled at me.

"I – I—"

Another punch, this time in my stomach, sending me flying off the chair.

"Who is she?" Harald stood over me whilst this brute kicked me over and over again.

"Who are you?" *Thwack* on the back of my head. "Who is Kaminski?" No answer. *Thwack* between the shoulder blades.

I cannot say how long this continued for, but it stopped as suddenly as it had started, leaving me in a bloodied heap on the floor, my eyes bursting with pain, seeing nothing but the crimson of my own blood that dripped steadily onto my face.

They let me rest a while or perhaps they wanted a rest – to smoke a cigarette and to drink coffee whilst I lay half-dead in that bright room. But they soon returned, this time with more vigour and a length of leather that slashed at my legs until the skin broke.

I gave in. I could not stand the pain any longer, I could not even think correctly. So I told them everything. My name, my real name. I told them I had lived in Germany, and in my delirium told them about Father dying and how he had been my best friend, then told them about the paper planes that hung from my bedroom ceiling. I don't know why I told them those things – I just kept talking, hoping that maybe if I did, then they would not hurt me again.

The words tumbled out, one after the other. I told them about Karl. How he was my friend, how he liked women and he had been kind to me.

"Karl Neumann, he was my friend," I slurred, sitting now with my back propped up against the wall, my lip swollen and bloodied, drops of it falling out of my mouth as I spoke. "He had everything. Money, women. But he liked me. I was his friend."

"What did you say?" Harald's voice cut across my ramblings. I raised my head to try and see him, but it was as though my eyes were sewn shut and only a sliver of light came through.

"Say it again. Your friend. The pilot. What is his name?"

"Karl," I mumbled.

"Yes, yes, his surname. You said Neumann, didn't you?"

I nodded.

"You mean Karl Neumann whose father is SS-Oberst-Gruppenführer Neumann?"

"Yes." I spat out blood onto the floor.

"You know him – really?" Harald's voice changed a little. It was softer, his words coming out nervously.

"I know him. He's a friend."

The silence that permeated the room after I had mentioned Karl went on for too long, making me fear that someone, or something else was going to be brought into the room. Then there was the quiet chatter amongst the two men, the opening and closing of the door and silence once more.

Days passed and the beatings stopped. I was taken from that bloodied room into another that had a small mattress on the floor, a bucket for waste and was given a piece of bread, porridge and coffee each day.

At first, I could not think straight. I could not think of why they had left me alone, and whether it was because of the mention of Karl and his father. All I could think about was the pain.

It was everywhere. It radiated through my legs, and felt like stones and knots had buried themselves deep within the skin on my back. My arms ached with every movement; my head thudded with such force that I was sure that a gush of blood would soon spill forth. My eyes remained sealed, but for a strip between the lashes where I could just make out where the floor was and see enough of the food to try and get to it and manhandle some of it into my mouth.

To try and escape the pain, I thought often of that sunny yellow room at Joasia's. I imagined the twins running in to tell me what they had found outside, and I talked to them. I imagined conversations between me and them, deluding myself that I was not here, I was not in pain, I was at home with the twins and we were talking about pirates and make-believe. And Helena, I spoke to you.'

· · ·

At this point, Helena grabbed my hand in hers and squeezed it tight.

'You must think I am crazy?' I asked her. 'Talking to people who are not there.'

'Not in the slightest,' she replied.

I laughed a little. 'You have to say that because you're a doctor.'

'No. I shouldn't say it *because* I'm a doctor. I just know what it's like to feel so much pain, whether physically or emotionally that sometimes it's easier to pretend that it isn't happening.'

I watched her as she spoke, her eyes darting to the corner of the room as she talked of pretending and imaginary things. There was nothing in the corner of the room, that I was sure of, and yet her eyes seemed trained on it.

Suddenly, her eyes returned to my face, and she gave a sad smile. 'I just understand,' she simply said, then squeezed my hand again.

I leaned my head towards hers and she followed suit, and for a moment, we rested our foreheads against each other's, just sitting there, our skin touching, not talking, and it was the most comforted and understood I had ever felt.

'You don't have to tell me any more,' she whispered, breaking that magical moment.

I leaned away from her and sighed. 'I'd rather tell you the rest and be done with it. That way, the past is the past and I don't have to talk about it again.'

She nodded and did not let go of my hand as I continued, feeling a tiredness wave over me as I spoke.

'Karl came. To say I was surprised, elated even, was an understatement. When he walked into the room, I thought I was imagining him and began to laugh.'

"Max," he came to me and bent down. "What's happened to you?"

"I'm dying," I told him, then laughed again. "Are you real?"

Karl didn't answer. He stood, then yelled for a guard and began a heated discussion with him. I could hear Harald's voice, almost whiny as he spoke to Karl.

"I didn't know," Harald cried. "I stopped as soon as he said your name and your father's. When he said he knew you, I thought I'd better check and see if it was right."

"So you kept him in here, like this, whilst you waited for me?" Karl shouted.

"You have to understand," Harald moaned. "So many people say so many things and they are not true at all. But I did stop – when he said he knew you, when he said about being your navigator, I remembered how on seeing your father a few weeks ago, right here in this building, he had said something about your friend jumping out of a plane. So you see, I did the right thing. Tell your father I did stop. I did contact you."

There was a second of deadly silence before I heard a thump, then a howl of pain. It was Harald.

"I'll tell him you almost killed someone he thinks of as his own son,' Karl spat.

Before long, arms were underneath me, gentler this time, pulling me up and helping me to the back seat of a car.

It was then that I fell into a deep sleep, my mind and body suddenly disappearing into nothingness.

When I woke, I managed to open my right eye more than the left and could see that I was in a bedroom, and Karl was sitting on a chair next to my bed.

"Not dead yet," he joked.

"Where am I?"

"A hotel. I couldn't risk taking you to a hospital. They think you died, you know. That night you launched yourself out of the plane. I thought you were dead too – I thought you'd done it on purpose because of your father."

"Not dead," I croaked.

Karl got me a glass of water and lifted my head to help me drink, then gently laid me back down.

"Tell me what to do, Max. Tell me. I don't know what to do."

I didn't know the answer either. If he made it known I was alive, I would be arrested for desertion. He couldn't let me go in this state. What was he to do?

"Helena," I told him.

Karl gave me a funny look.

"She's in England, in Oxford. Get me there. Tell Harald I died. Tell everyone I am definitely dead. Or tell them anything you like – they'll believe you."

Karl shook his head.

"Please, Karl, please. Don't send me back to Germany. Please. Don't send me away," I began to cry and still begged him to show me mercy, my stammer coming back. "Please. Find Joasia Rodzynska, she will help you. She will tell you where to send me. Please, Karl, please," I begged and all the while Karl watched me, gently shaking his head.

Exhausted, I could not hold the argument, the pleading any longer, and my head fell back against the pillows. "Please," I muttered to him, as I fell away into the blackness of sleep.

When I woke, I was no longer in the hotel but in the back of a car once more. I sat halfway up to see if Karl was there, but he wasn't. There was a driver and one other man, and neither turned to look back at me. My body was so broken, my mind too, that I could not stay awake for long. Each time I tried to shout, to say something to the men in the front seats of the car, my voice came out barely above a whisper and then I would black out once more.

The next time I woke properly, I managed to sit up somewhat and take in where I was. I looked to the driver and the passenger in the front seat and was sure that they were different people.

"Ah good. You're awake!" The passenger turned and grinned at me. He was Polish; his name was Leon, he told me. "You were given to us on the border," he said. "Not far to go now."

"The border?" I managed to ask, my mouth dry and lips cracked and sore.

"Between Germany and Belgium. You're in Belgium now. France soon. Then the boat. This is the easy bit, for us, anyway."

He did not speak much more – did not elaborate on what had transpired, nor where Karl was. But I did not care – Karl was setting me free. I was in Belgium. I was going to France. And then soon I would be in England.

The next time I was fully awake, and lucid, I was in a hospital bed with a nurse looking over at me. The pain was dulled, and my eyes now opened fully. She spoke to me, and I did not understand what she said.

She tried again and I shook my head at her. What was she saying?

Finally, she said one word, "London."

I understood that word. London. I had made it and I knew that soon, when I was well enough, I would find you too.'

'And you did,' Helena spoke softly. 'You found us.'

'How could I not find you?' I half laughed. 'I had to find you. You and the twins. I had to finally find my way home.'

NEW YEAR'S EVE

1995

FORTY-FIVE

HELENA

New Year's Eve, 1995
Wallingford, Oxfordshire, UK

So you see, how I forgot to remember. I forgot to remember my mother had died, and then when I re-remembered, I knew that I had to focus my brain. – I had to be able to bear witness to those traumatic days and nights, I had to keep going.

Max and I spoke a lot over the years, about fragments of memories and I always jotted them down, afraid to completely let them leave my mind, and yet it took me much longer than I ever thought it would to finally tell my story.

I think of those days spent with Pawel, in his office at Christ Church and how he told me that I would know the right time to say what I needed to – to be honest, though, I really didn't think it would take me this long.

I suppose it did take so much time, as life began anew when Max turned up, sitting on William and Valerie's front steps as though he had always been there, always belonged.

We moved forward in our lives, carefully, slowly, almost scared that the scars that we both carried would somehow prevent us from ever recovering that strange bond that we had both found in one another right from the start.

To say that it was a perfect romance would be disingenuous. We had something that tied us together – a shared trauma – and often I wondered when we argued, or got cross with each other, whether it was that that glued us together and whether we were in fact right for each other. Although who is to say what is right for a person?

Max and I built a life for ourselves, brick by brick, literally and figuratively. He learned English and found work with the government, dealing with Polish affairs, whilst I continued to get certified as a psychiatrist and helped all those who came to me.

In the years during, and for quite a few after the war, I dealt with many who had experienced a similar trauma to my own, and each time I heard their stories, it opened up the old wounds, taking away the blunt stitches one by one, leaving a bloody, sore gash, which would send me into a depression of my own, for days and weeks at a time. Not that I let it show. I kept it to myself until I could finally stitch myself back up again.

We married in 1946, and moved to a small cottage south of Oxford, which we renovated bit by bit and as money allowed. We were careful with the twins too – always making sure that they dealt with their traumas the best way they could, but who knows what wounds they still carry.

Our children came soon after we were married, a boy then a girl, and we named them Adam after Max's father, and Aleksandra after my mother.

And of course, there was Joasia – sweet, caring Joasia who had given us the gift of escape, staying behind to be with Olek, staying by his side through thick and thin. Once the war had ended, she visited once or twice, and never spoke of what she went through – keeping it to herself until the day she died, at just sixty years old, Olek dying a few weeks later, of what I assume was heartbreak.

I did return to Poland once, in the summer of 1991. I went with my daughter, son and their children, to show them the Poland I had once known. And we found ourselves back at Fort VII, they wanting to see it for themselves, and if I'm honest, I, too, wanted to see it again – I wanted to make sure that it was all real, that those things had actually happened.

To return to that place, after all those years, was not as traumatic as I thought it would be. The gates and guards were gone, replaced by a simple ticket booth – it was now a museum, a museum, as a testament to those who had died, who suffered here, and we were to pay a few zlotys to see it, which we did, the irony not lost on me.

Walking over that concrete walkway, the moat underneath me, did not take me back to 1939, when I had entered that cavernous place. Instead, it was as though I were a foreigner here now, seeing it for the first time, through my children's eyes.

There on the left, in a cell so small you could barely fit a cow, would stand twenty men and women, naked, huddled together for warmth. There on the right, that's where they hung people from a hook, feet first, head down, and beat at the person as they swung around.

Even when we reached the actual cell that Agata, Michal and I had lived in, I still felt nothing, and I ran my hands over the deep engravings in the bricks, finding my name, then the twins', then Ola and Sabina's, trying to summon some kind of recollection – some feeling, and yet none was forthcoming.

It was only as we left, following the signs to the exit, that something happened to me. On the right was a mock-up of two hospital beds, and posters on the walls told the tale of the experiments that were done on disabled people from the mental hospital – the very one I had worked at.

I turned away from it, remarking to my son that as horrible

as the place was, it had done well in preserving the memories of what had happened – it was a good museum. When I said this, I was near the exit. All I had to do was go through an arch, turn right, and then I would see the exit and the walkway and I would be free. Yet, for some reason, as I spoke to my son, as I told him how proud I was of the museum, I felt the fear of God enter me. I cannot describe the fear. I cannot tell you who, or what it was. But behind me there was something, someone, and I could feel my insides turn to jelly, my mind began to buzz, and my whole body went cold, and yet I was sweating.

I tried to talk, but no words came from my mouth. So, I did what Małgorzata had told me years before, and I ran.

I ran out of that cellar, down the arched corridor, into the light, past the ticket booth, through the trees and eventually found the main road.

I sat on the kerb for some time, letting myself hear the ragged breaths I took. I was still here, still alive. Yet, there had been something in there, something not of this world that had frightened me so.

I am not a sentimental woman. I never have been, apart from my mental disorder, that is. I do not believe in ghosts. I do not think that the dead haunt us, or try to reach out.

And yet. That moment of fear I felt, was it a traumatic memory? Was it nothing more than that? I cannot help but think it was more. It felt more. It felt as though the devil himself was behind me, waiting for me, angry that I had not been taken the first time around.

Afterwards, I tried to describe the feeling to my children, but the words seemed useless.

I do not believe in ghosts. I do not believe we still walk the earth after we die. Yet, I have found that I do believe that when such horror, such trauma has occurred, the earth itself does not forget and within it, the ghosts of the past, good or bad, reside. That is what I felt that day. The blood, the tears, the screams, the death had poured into the earth and had come back to remind me of those days.

I visited the woods too – those woods where I found out my father had been shot, as well as his male patients, the same day that he had been taken from the hospital. I sat on the cold earth and placed my hands onto the ground, digging them into the soil. I think my children thought I had gone mad – and perhaps I had, a little. But it felt to me as though it was a way to say goodbye – in feeling that soil in my hands, I was almost touching him, letting him be a part of me again. I took some soil home with me, keeping it in a tiny jar that sits atop the mantlepiece. My son tells me I am morbid. But I don't care what he thinks – I just wanted to take some of my father home with me.

There is a knock at the door, and I know who it is – Agata and Michal, with their spouses. I had asked my children to come this evening, to celebrate as a family and to bring the grandchildren and had told Agata and Michal to bring their children and grandchildren too. But, as is the way with the young, they have their own plans, their own friends and their own lives to lead and that is the way it should be – although I admit, it does make me sad.

'Helena!' Michal is shouting to me, finding his way up to the attic. 'You should use something for an office on the lower floors,' he says, his face red from climbing all the way up. 'There are too many stairs.'

The clomp of Agata is not far behind him, and she grins when she sees me. 'I've two bottles and so has Michal!' She holds up the champagne and I know what this night will bring – we will get too tipsy, borderline drunk and reminisce, cry, and then find something silly to talk about so that the laughter we bring forth will cancel out the rest.

'That's four bottles!' Max, my husband, excitedly says. I

look to him, sitting on the leather sofa, with Charlie our spaniel on his lap. He has been here the past few hours as I neared the end of the story, now and again leaning over my shoulder to check I had got his parts right.

I had pointed at my notebooks: 'I had it all in here,' I told him.

He had nodded at me, but still seen fit to remind me about conversations he had had when I was not present – filling in small blanks that I had never known and finding those puzzle pieces that were always hidden from me.

'We went through more last year!' I laugh at him now. Four bottles will soon disappear with us lot.

'True. Too true,' he says, nodding. 'Good job there's a few in the cellar for emergencies. I mean you never know!' He winks at me, his wink just for me, to say that we will laugh tonight, we will have fun and the bottles in the cellar will more than likely make an appearance; and they will startle us in the morning, when we wake with bad heads and begin to count the dark green bottles that loll on the carpet, spilling drops of their contents that we forgot to drink.

'Who are you talking to?' Michal asks me.

I nod at the sofa, and he scrunches up his face like Father used to when he was worried about me.

The pair have turned to descend to the lower floors, both of them good-naturedly arguing as to which of them deserves the guest room with the en-suite. They may be in their sixties, but when they are together, it is as though they revert to their childhood, and I know that their spouses will soon roll their eyes at them and perhaps even scold them for acting like children.

'Time to go now,' Max says.

I look to him and see only Charlie staring at me.

'I know,' I tell Charlie. 'I know he's not really here. I know he's dead. I'm not mad. But I can let him be here now, you see.

I've finished remembering. I don't have to do that any more. I can let him be here, do you understand?'

Charlie jumps down from the couch and does a long stretch, coupled with a yawn, his pink tongue sticking out, walks to me and places a wet snout on my leg. He understands. I talk to him, don't I, and he is a dog, so what's wrong with talking to my dead husband.

'Are you ready?' Max asks.

I can hear him, but I cannot see him now. I'll see him again later, sat in his armchair, a glass of champagne in his hand. And I'll see him again tomorrow, and the next day and the next.

It's such a shame that no one else will.

A LETTER FROM CARLY

Thank you so much for reading *The Airman's Girl*. If you'd like to keep up to date with all my latest releases, you can sign up at the following link. Your email address will never be shared, and you can unsubscribe at any time.

www.bookouture.com/carly-schabowski

There are so many little-known stories surrounding the Second World War and this novel, I believe is one such a story. Fort VII is one of many forts surrounding Poznań, built underground, cavernous and cold. On a research trip a few years ago, I visited the museum that is now held in Fort VII and could not believe that I had never heard about it in any history books. This Fort was essentially one of the first places where experiments with gassing prisoners were carried out, which happened with such speed it felt almost unbelievable that it occurred. Germany marched onto Polish soil on 1 September 1939, and by mid-October the first gassings at Fort VII began with the mentally ill from the nearby Owińska Mental Hospital and included staff members. Only one prisoner is known to have escaped; he was Marian Szlegel, who identified a time when the camp was less well guarded, and took the opportunity to abscond.

I remember when I visited the Fort, there were so many engravings of names, and even lines of poems scratched into the brick walls of the cells. I had run my fingers over them, thinking of the people that had lived within these walls, facing terror each day, and ultimately death. As I left the cells, I returned to the entrance. As I stood there, I thought of how good the museum was and that more people should visit. In that moment, just like Helena, I felt the fear of God run through me. To this day, I cannot describe the fear I felt adequately and I raced from the museum, not stopping until I reached the road. I do not believe in ghosts, just as Helena does not, and yet, and yet...

Another little-known story that I wanted to tell in this book was that of Leonard Bartlakowski, on whom the character of Max is based. Leonard, a Polish man who had been in the Luftwaffe, defected by parachuting from his plane to return home to Poland. He assumed the identity of Robert Krysinski and was posted to nearby Rawa Ruska as a German-Polish interpreter for the local Gestapo.

Through this deception, he was able to feed the Gestapo false information, and warn others when raids and roundups may occur.

On 4 September 1979, Yad Vashem recognised Leonard Bartlakowski as Righteous Among the Nations.

I hope that I have done justice to these historical facts; providing a reimagined past to allow us to feel, see and understand what it must have been like in those first few months of WWII.

 twitter.com/@carlyschab11

REFERENCES

Eds: Andrew Moskowitz, Ingo Schäfer, Martin J. Dorahy, *Psychosis, Trauma and Dissociation, Evolving Perspectives on Severe Psychopathology.* Wiley, 2019

Fort VII: https://www.poznan.pl/

Friedländer, Saul, *Memory, History, and the Extermination of the Jews of Europe.* Indiana University Press, 1993

Hargreaves, Richard, *Blitzkrieg Unleashed: The German Invasion of Poland, 1939.* Stackpole Books, 2010

Holocaust Historical Society: Posen Fort VII: https://www.holocausthistorical society.org.uk/contents/naziseasternempire/posenfortvii.html

Kujawski, Ryszard, 'Józef Bednarz (1879–1939) – psychiatrist, forensic expert and manager of psychiatric treatment in the interwar period': Psychiatr. Pol. 2019; 53(6): 1379–1395, PL ISSN 0033-2674 (PRINT), ISSN 2391-5854

Nasierowski, Tadeusz (2006) 'In the Abyss of Death: The Extermination of the Mentally Ill in Poland During World War II', International Journal of Mental Health, 35:3, 50–61, DOI:10.2753/IMH0020-7411350305

Owińska Mental Home and Poznan Fort VII: http://www.deathcamps.org/euthanasia/owinska.html

Paul, Marla, 'How Your Memory Rewrites the Past', Northwestern University, (2014) https://news.northwestern.edu/stories/2014/02/how-your-memory-rewrites-the-past.

Reviewed Work(s): *W.G. Sebald. History, Memory, Trauma* by Scott Denham and Mark McCulloh, Review by: Lynn Wolff, Source: Monatshefte, Vol. 100, No. 2 (Summer, 2008), pp. 313–316, Published by: University of Wisconsin Press, Stable URL: http://www.jstor.org/stable/30154495

The Polish Institute and Sikorski Museum Sikorski: <http://www.sikorskimu seum.co.uk/>

The Righteous Among the Nations Database: https://righteous.yadvashem. org/?searchType=righteous_only&language=en&itemId=4013818& ind=0

Vitti, Emiliano: 'Propaganda in Poland 1938–1945. The Conditioning of the masses between the Reich and the Generalgouvernement, *Il Politico*, Nuova Series, Vol. 79, No. 2 (236) (Maggio-Agosto 2014), pp. 216–233 (18 pages). Published by Rubbettino Editore

ACKNOWLEDGEMENTS

They say it takes a village to raise a child, but to write a book, I'm pretty sure it takes a small to large-ish town! My heartfelt thanks go to Dan Allen and Terry Lintin, whose knowledge of planes, the mechanics of them, and various other pieces of information proved exceedingly useful! Apologies there is not more about the planes in the book – I am sure you were hoping for more!

Big thanks as always to Michal Rodzynski, who helps with Polish translations in all my books, and I have thanked you in the best way I know how by naming a character after you! Sorry it wasn't an action superhero that you suggested it be, or a cool villain like some fella from *Die Hard*, but it's still a pretty good character!

A thank you to my agent Jo Bell and my editor Jess Whitlum-Cooper who still think I'm a good author and convince me to keep going despite me thinking I should jack it all in!

A huge thank you to my family who put up with my moods, tiredness and general grumpiness that comes when a deadline is looming. And last, but not least, thank you to all my readers. You all make it worthwhile!

Printed in Great Britain
by Amazon

21964492R00179